"To her, from him."

EPOCH DAWN

TRILOGY
Justin Daw

Published by Advanced Computer Interface Designs Ltd

http://www.epoch-dawn.com

ISBN 0-9552134-3-6

Printed in England by Matrix Response Technologies Ltd

This edition in one volume with author's updates.

The Epoch Dawn Trilogy comprises:

Epoch Dawn (2005)
ISBN 0-9552134-0-1

Écoute et Répète: Polymath Renaissance (2006)
ISBN 0-9552134-1-X

Equational Equivalence (2007)
ISBN 0-9552134-2-8

Contents

EPOCH DAWN

Justin Daw

Chapter One – Ignition sequence started

He was going to take the national transporter to Brightown, England. Travelling light was always the preferred option. Anything that was too much to carry could be bought or borrowed at the next location. Choosing to journey out of hours while things were quiet, he walked his way along the boulevard to the transporter interchange. Pretty much an average afternoon, bit of sunshine, bit of white cloud, occasional gust of cooling breeze.

His wrist tingled. He cuffed his sleeve briefly, and moved his arm up and back in a swift motion, ending up with his hand on the side and back of his head.

"Hello," he spoke into the microphone embedded in his sleeve. "Yes, that's correct," he said. "Confirmation booking 3:16 Brightown. One-way."

"We have confirmed your reservation. Please proceed to the boarding area."

Shaking his sleeve downward, he eyed the impending sensor of the autodoor. The engineers of the sensors had got it just right. You always had that instant of uncertainty of whether or not the doors would open in time.

He boldly dipped through the sliding doors and glanced briefly left and right and tried to guess which direction it would set off in, so as to gain his preferred forward facing. It wasn't always easy to determine, often the only ones who knew where they were going were the transports themselves. The transport was packed with outers mumbling macro phrases behind their shade displays.

Nestling back into his seat, he was pleased he had guessed correctly. He was journeying to his next waypoint, Brightown Cybertechnic. It was the next stage of his career progression, or education, depending on what the current viewpoint was. The apprentices sometimes wondered if it was all just a buffering queue. He hadn't so much navigated in this direction, as floated gently down the stream, sort of caught up in the flow of things. At least it felt like a natural progression to him, even if one he hadn't steered.

The transport hummed into action with a distinct clicking noise. It was like going forwards in an elevator. There seemed only a gradual change in position, and a disproportionate shift at each end of the thrust. The high pitching of the engines dampened into a hardly noticeable ringing, the chatter and busyness of the passengers would mask the sound completely for most of the distance.

He glanced over at the family sat on the other side of the transport. The children were on one side of the table, guardians the other. From the angle he was viewing, the table shone the unmistakable static mist of coalesced imagery that was a group projection rig. Laid out on the table in front of them was the silver slim case of the unit. The multiphased viewing panel was set at the optimum for their four viewers, his range wasn't in the setup. They smiled and laughed together, the earsets relaying sonics whilst they pointed out fascinations to each other.

He wondered whether those references beloved of filmmakers, where they would cameo a line or two from another film, were totally deliberate or whether occasionally they just didn't remember that it was just a memory of a previous observation rather than a new thought. Maybe they were like him, constantly reminded of their own childhood dreams in the communications of others. Maybe they had the notion first, and were determined to see it out.

He reached in his backage, rummaged a little, and pulled out the Isotech manual. The manual read a bit like heavyweight Russian literature. Dostoyevsky or someone, where sometimes you had to stop for a while to think about what the last sentence actually meant. Sometimes he wondered whether he was reading the correct language translation, always best in the original he thought.

He had to laugh at the contributed notes, the ubiquitous 555 timer further had its place confirmed in the hardware hacks of history. The sequential timing and pulse/burst generator modes were able to be utilised in grids to perform the functions of even the most pimped up Son-yan Corp ics, although they tended to fry much quicker. Still, at a cost ratio of several thousand to one it wasn't too much of a problem for most users.

He knew he wouldn't be able to get any true sleep on the journey. His overwatch senses were never going to relax enough whilst he was in motion. It was still possible to gain physical rest though, and he eased back into the seat and began the downward breathing regulation.

As he blink opened and closed his eyes, the retinal burn of the window view remained longer under the lengthening covers until their undulations rested shut. The placement of his tongue on the roof of his mouth aided the circle of breathing into its more sedated state. He heard his breathing and heartbeat grow louder as his scattered conscious thoughts lapped into a lucid calm dreaming whilst awake. A couple of full nerve fire jolts stirred him momentarily, but after a short period he settled more.

The hours passed sooner and the transport had arrived. He composed himself, and waited until the minute adjustments to full awakeness were effected. He raised his arms from the side position, and slowly stretched them forward to extension, flexing but never reaching full straightness. After all the momentum sways had finished, he allowed the most eager passengers to leave before standing and heading for the now fixed wide open doors, stepping out levelled while visually confirming the signposts to the exit.

Leaving through one of his precalculated routes, he passed this week's sanctioned busker near the interchange exit. The bard's old leather hands were strumming victoriously against his steel strung instrument. At the 'tuning end', they spiralled about into a collection of bopping dreadlocks which danced merrily along with his impassioned recital. His pursed lips sang out his husking tune.

My mind is full of the real me,
But is that the one that you can see.
My mind is full of the real me,
But is that who I want to be.
Am I who you think I am,
Or am I just playing my life's hand.

The real air outside of the interchange was cooler than the processed mix of air conditioning and heating that he had been used to for the past hours. He tucked up his collar slightly as protection against the coming night. A brief wander into the central buildings, allowing a few memories to run through and focus his senses on the new environment and the missions in hand.

Reality suppressant. That was first on his mind's list.

He flashed the credit strip across the local communications terminal. He didn't want to flag any of his own devices unnecessarily. There was a wait before anything picked up the connection, he clicked through a couple of levels of the on hold game, but it wasn't really enough to hold his attention, especially given the importance of the call.

"Hello, it's me. I'm back in town," he greeted.

"Oh, yeah, hi, how's it going?" said the human connectant.

"Yes, good, I've got a feeling it's going to be my year," he continued.

"Could well be. Listen, I kind of know why you're

calling."

It wasn't too hard a bet to hedge.

"The problem is, I sort of don't do that anymore," said the stockist.

Shit, not exactly a great start. Especially troublesome as he hadn't arranged anywhere to sleep. The groove would have been to stock up on the reality suppressant, catch up on new times, and hopefully borrow some floor space for a decent sleep.

"Ok, no problem, I know how it is," he covered well, but the act wouldn't last long, so he got out of the connection pretty soon after.

A major blow to the big plan. Danny had often said he was his best customer, and rightly so. He knew where he was on to a good thing. Danny always had the best equipment going, and at just the right price. Actually, thinking about it, he was probably everybody's best customer. Danny's batches of suppressant were always top notch, always ensured to be industrial strength, not like the watered quarts available down on the street. Suitable for some, who liked the more steady lager like consumption pattern to maintain a gentle long firing, but no good for his purposes.

'Last time I make a plan,' he thought. In actual fact, that was as far as the plan went. He had learnt long ago that even the best laid plans were always irrelevant after point two or three, so he figured there wasn't much point pinning things down any further than that. Combinations were the key. No preconfigured order or arrangement, just enough to have overlapping redundancy for any situation. Make things up as you go along.

Thus, although not exhausted, his options were lessened. There would be no virtual reality today without the suppressants, but he knew there were bound to be plenty around at the first meet tomorrow. It was just the way of the scene. Not that everyone was that way, it was the usual fifty-fifty. Horses for courses. One type suited one type, another yet another. You either used suppressants or you were totally clean, like no caffeine, alcohol or anything. Easy choice for most, but some were the meditative type, aiming to pass the corruptibility tests for failsafe and critical applications development.

The first sleep space was at least warm and dry, safe from the coming winter chill, and the knowledge of at least being amongst friends was reassuring. The spoiler was the refrigerator in the corner of the room. It was a comfortable spot despite the hardness of the floor, and body relaxation was easy enough. The pain in the ass thing was the noise. The humming and the occasional burp like metallic clatter. It just couldn't last, and nights three and four were spent readying in the digs with the smallest minimum let period.

He awoke to the sound of the window rattling against it's wooden frame. The four-inch masonry nails, that had been hastily hammered in at an awkward angle through the wood surrounding the misted glass, were not enough to stop the bass hum of the transporter being amplified by his window dolby system.

It was carrying used tyres for storage in the old mill warehouse for later recycling. He wondered how they were recycled, or if they were just redistributed to hold down some blue polythene sheeting. Most of the kid's playgrounds already had the safety rubber fallout zones around the swings and stuff, although making shoe soles from it made sense. The tyre-burning electricity generators were only moderately popular, despite their calorific value being comparable with that of oil and higher than that of coal. It was probably due to the 'dark matter' residue that the process left, as the contractors called it.

It was a brave Elected who initiated the energy transmigration progressions, the fuel corporations had been forced into investing considerably in electricity conversion efficiency by the harshness of the economic conditions artificially imposed on those not doing so. The benefits were quickly reaped in the clean higher population density centres, with hydrocars and 'park & drive' transport exchanges. Co-operation was achieved by the long term rewards given by being offered the best of the starting opportunities. Basically, they largely funded the research as they knew their game was over. The organic photoelectrics and the equatorial solar heat pipe were certainly worth their long development cycles.

"If you're expecting your own socket AND instant phecking hot water at this late stage in the season then you'd better get real," carped the broad letting agent, flexing his shoulders and twitching his neck. He was glad he hadn't gone a band down on the letting lists. Whether the agent was trying to make a point with his motions or whether he had just done too many cliptrips in the past was a mystery. The manner was aggressive, but that was business. Most people's tolerance filters just kicked in.

Needless to say he went for the dedicated socket option. He didn't have that much a call for heated water, let alone instantly. The tank was good enough. When he needed more he knew he'd need the wait to readjust back in anyway.

He clattered down the vidlink connection and used the reference to get the map readout. It was walkable, but all uphill. It had become dark, and no-one else would be going that way, let alone on foot. Probably better, as carrying the amount of suppressant he had picked up needed a company license. He was too tired and too keen to get started to go through all the questions, the form filling, and would never resort to common bribery.

He had to hover in a few places when the sky surveillance was paying him too much attention. He contemplated lighting up a cigarette, the scornful outcasting at such a public display would probably give enough cover to divert true focus for long enough.

The journey was real event uneventful, save the direct preventative countermeasures. He had established lodgings to begin his work. A slow start, but hopefully progression would follow.

"That's the one," was what he heard spoken methodically as he awoke from the chill of the duvet being casted back. Though not seeing clearly yet, he assumed the two of them were adopting an ends arm and leg carrying position. His mind was screaming out 'help me, help me' to any would be rescuers in the street outside, but his lips either betrayed him or were stilled by his would be abductors, and a weakened 'help me' was all that whispered past his lips. We accelerated out the window in a shotgun of light. He awoke for the second time. In the instant between sleep and sight he wondered if he would wake up again. But no, this was it, out of his dream.

He attended his cleaning routine in the tank, at least he had set that up right for its heat overnight. It was the day of re-registration for the year. Thankfully it was a 'modular' approach to the stages of registration, the keeners went in the morning, the rest of them drifted in and about as and when throughout the day.

One of the tell-tale signs of approaching vr neural imbalance was a change in the learning biases of the brain. Thus one part of the yearly processing was the completion of the Asotrerial synal mapping.

"New upgrade then," he said.

"Yeah," said Brian. "The triaos have really been maxed out on this one. Don't put your tongue on the mid-chin rest, it gets kind of hot."

Brian often left the air conditioning on in his rackspace even in summer. Sure enough, his chin did kind of warm up. Whether it was from the heat of the new triaos or the soup vibration heat of an unstable mounting point he wasn't convinced. Brian always raced to fit the latest bits, but sometimes spent too long so that the rigs weren't ready for pre-season. A rig toppled over one year, narrowly missing a yawning inductee.

Whilst Brian fiddled with the setup to fulfill his administration responsibilities, the warm female voice of the unit gently described the results in a soft tone.

"Your somatosensory regulation indicates you have an equivalence in your auditory and visual pattern matched learning, facilitating both unilateral and multilateral spatial comprehension. Sequential and time delayed comprehension exhibited equal bias under testing."

"You have a slight left-hemisphere dominance, although your balanced input response lowers its distinction. Parallel macro and micro comprehension achieved. Abstraction and proof easily interlaced."

"Pass or fail then?" he said.

"Same as last year by the looks of it. Not much change, average pass," chuckled Brian. He waited, and joined in with Brian's chuckling briefly, and then made an exit.

The lift in the corridor made its way up a few floors to collect the waiting passengers. He noticed a pleasant enough nice young thing waiting patiently.

Her fine blond hair flowed down her back. A hand, then an arm reached to her, and her boyfriend circled his hand on her upper hip. Even though he hadn't convinced himself he was interested, he felt a strange little widening of his mouth, and a small, slightly sharper intake of breath. His eyes undoubtedly reflected this feeling, although their view showed no witness. His reproductive instincts must have given out their slight shock of disappointment at there being one less fish in the sea.

Walking through the reception lounges could sometimes seem like a stroll through the nightlife, with the new intake trying to discriminate themselves against the muted common ground. Even within the fine confines of the rooms, there were as many again cultures, subcultures and countercultures, each interacting and transferring and counter transferring in their tribal chants.

The drone surrounding one particular 'bad ass' young man locked his attentiveness briefly. It's hard rasping guitar emphasising the inflection of the low toned, deep pained lyrics.

"White Winged Dove"

G   F#   E
All the people fall in love
G   F#   E
With old Noah's white winged dove
G   F# E
But what they don't realise
G   F# E
It's in their heart the devil lies
A   G
Tell me tell me when will I see
A   F#
The light the light that shines on me

It was an angry tune, and he wondered how many alcohol braved piercings would be performed that week. Some of them played a more bass felt sonic on their latest fashion players. That was as much a conspiracy as the promise of the big dream, the ingraining while they were intoxicated meant they were addicted as much to the music as they were the cigarettes and alcohol. Some strove for their individuality by always having the latest tunes. Others just drifted, bed hopping between styles and genres.

There were a few stall vans from the local cliptrip firms parked up outside. The hypersmiling wide-eyed sales freaks handled the small queues of sign-ups. The less affluent did it for the money. The affluent thrill seekers did it for the potential kicks gained in accessing some serious high-end equipment during down time. All made possible with Keplar's organic transistor network.

Keplar used an offshoot of quantum computing indeterminate theory to utilise the 'chaos' in the brain. By lowering to total immersion, he found that he could use the otherwise discarded unpredictive excess random firings to solve complex predicates. It sort of enabled people to work while they were asleep, although you'd wake up extremely tired. Anyone who hadn't ran a cliptrip before did so in vr week one, it was essential to gain an understanding of the more slavorial aspects of augmented intelligence, and was usually enough to put most people off.

He hadn't ran many, and when he had overheard the conversation about 'multi-tasked fryout, just don't ask what happens if it frys when you're that far in', that had pretty much put an end to it. Those without the luxury to make that decision might ultimately work at the mind farms, or contract offering connection shifts on demand. Who knows what shit they'd have your brain processing then though. Still, it gave a whole new meaning to leaving your work at the office, most had no recall whatsoever of having worked at all.

Of course, Keplar's layers were not enough on their own. It was sort of an extension of game theory. Anyone observing the random walk pattern of various walking or flying insects will notice how surprisingly effective the system is. No walk seems to plot the same course, and equal coverage and mapping seems to occur irrespective of the bounding environment.

He was reminded of the flight of the bats in the small Lighthouse game he had written years before. Even that was designed years before that, but the programming at the time (most probably due to his own poor algorithms), had stopped the project being finished. Their computed random flight feigned intelligence. Were they intelligent at all or just following a fractal equation, like the squirrels scurrying around their hoarding maps. The whole question of intelligence was a tricky one. Some would argue that any tests of it were biased towards an assumed environment, and others pondered where precisely the simple pattern match response system ended and the true reasoning began.

He continued his walk until he was outside the campus grounds, past the bollards and the gated entrances. Waiting a while for the city microshuttles to stop, he crossed the black and white stripes when it was good to go. The sensors flicked back to allow the traffic flow to continue when the last pedestrian had cleared their path, and its silent counter began clocking up queuers once more.

As he passed the next campus complex, he was glad his visits would all be to the buildings which had been extensively refurnished a couple of years ago in the next phase of 'contiguous refinement'. He didn't spare many glances towards its drab exterior, it was a bit like ML, strictly functional.

The doors of the public meeting place swung open to allow the passage of The Captain. The warmth of its lures breezed out as The Captain staggered through. No time to spend idly playing 9-ball amid banter and alcohol today though.

"Hello, Captain," he said.

"Ah, yes, hello," replied The Captain softly, and tottered off on his merry way, clutching produce of dubious origin beneath arms still toned despite their age. 'If you do the hard thing first everything else is easy' he had once been told by The Captain. Easy for The Captain to say. In actual fact, easy for The Captain to do as well, he only hoped that one day his skill would be at least in the same sphere.

Carrying on, he felt a gurgle from somewhere near his abdominal region. Puzzled for an instant, he recalled he hadn't eaten so far that day. The microshuttle recharge bay would no doubt have a selection of space wrapped foods for his enjoyment, but he wondered whether all the sandwiches would be accompanied with mayo. He needed to make a decision before his legs had carried him past the entrance gap. It was done, he was in the door.

The fluorescent lit fridge shelves supported their bounty. Triple cheese. Triple meats. BLT (slight mayo risk). Ham salad. Nice. Ham (reprocessed), bread (white), tomato (red), lettuce (green), no mayo. He didn't like mayo. Not the smell, not the look, not the colour, and that's all flagging before the taste. As for the taste, mayo tasted like it smelt and looked to him. Wrenching. Mayo, salad cream, coleslaw, all from the same bad syndicate in his opinion.

He could still taste from his mind image the revolt and disgust of the sandwich filling he had thought was otherwise when at friend's birthday party during his childhood. He had already known that mayoslaw slop just wasn't his thing. He had bit into what he thought was the safety of generic ham. The standard template construction taste he had expected was not forthcoming. He was far too nice a child, and they were far too nice a family, for him to show disgust, so he made do by leaving big crusts.

So it was to be. A clean sandwich, vacuum packed potato slices, and a silver wrapped juice drink. Luckily some genius had finally solved the straw problem. Half the straw was inside the foil packet, and half telescoped out when ready for sucking. He paid in loose tokens from the booth on the Technic mezzanine floor, to much smirking from a few half-suits.

"Bloody students," they joked, knowing they had been far worse in their time. At least he had paid. He shoved them into his pockets and left.

A short shuttle and another walk and he was back into the safety of his new lodgings. Not much time to wind down, sleep didn't need too much coaching.

He awoke to the fading in of his alarm call. Sitting up, he grabbed his bottled water from the bedside table, and gulped down generously. He pulled on his clothes, sat in the chair and fired up his socket rig. The updates continued their trickle and the streams coalesced into view. The rig's connection melded into the computer and the whole grew, the spike of bass hum like a breath of life.

The init consisted of three custom cross-streamed low-end units, given his modest budget, so as to take full advantage of the wide socket. The global standard statutes had been a bloody good thing all round. The endless formats and stream incompatibilities and third-party standards had held back the advancement of the computer for decades. Instead of solving the real problems, often a large percentage of the development time had been spent in conversion, rendering, and triaps conordination.

That's not to say the units were similar. In fact, if that had happened it would have been largely missing the point. The big corps were still free to develop their own proprietary systems, and thus maintain their revenue streams, but the point was that everybody's systems were able to intercommunicate based on the standards set worldwide.

These enabled the applications and processes running on the platforms to have true software as a service capability. This in itself was seen as a good thing, but the system enhanced the overall reliability and survival of the internetworks as a whole.

It was the virus wars which hastened the cycle. One of the problems was that there was no biodiversity in the computer microcosm. Thus when the SUCHEZ virus was released it was able to reproduce and mutate through the networks faster that the antidotal patches could be applied across the system. Thus by the time the entire internetwork had been vaccinated, the virus's self-modifying code had already rewritten itself to counter the defence, spawning the KNUT and PCMF variants. 'Les fenêtres est fermée'. Some isolated successes where gained by quarantining large parts of the networks, but obviously this rather defied the point of the whole inter thing.

Free corps and hackers alike began rolling their own systems. Initially some were just tweaks and mutates of existing code trees, but others were new roots and grew their own path. Thus the computer was born, the whole system evolving by the second as the code was refined according to its stimuli. With multiple independent updates rather than a static system, it only took a year or so for things to recover.

It is perhaps worth noting that a big catalyst to all of this was the injection of ready cash by the generous governments. Some would say it was an easy thing to do, using the bigcorp's monopoly fines to fund new bubble startups. Others might even say it was just another attempt to make something out of nothing, a new market for corps to sell more stuff.

He spoke to the computer, the gestures of his fingers tracing effortlessly across the smooth inputboard. They tapped out precise positionings like the fret dancing of a nimble guitarist, translating his thoughts into the meld.

His eyes flash widened briefly when he saw the 'Re: Load request approved' amongst his data inputs. He had

been having so much junk lately he almost thought that he
had applied for one. He tapped and tweaked, and the source
was blacklisted to the abyss.

One of his search aggregate software agents wasn't
performing its filtering capabilities to the maximum
potential. He was feeding the results from his aggregation
into an algorithm to triaps dataset information just that little
more efficiently.

```
$rig.new();
intersphere($rig);
$nr = >socket(inner,stm,H38,$rig)
{
    $$t.[H38];
    handle:
        &8 call(stm);
        &15 route(stm);
        &21 sink(inner);
        &88 bypass(stm);
        &100 cont(stm);
    end_handle;
}
cont
{
    $nr<>=@;
    rddh($nr)(.*++_);
}
route
{
    chopen($nr)(.*);
    $nr->.^;
    $_++;
    span ([$nr][$_][direct]);
}
$rig->init();
```

The mods were done and he sent the sa on its path of instinctive navigation, hunting out the information he sought like the instinctive hunt for food.

He was of the school of thought of not remembering too much so as to leave room for more. He would just store the method of retrieval or its location, performing a linking with the network to his brain memory, pointers indirectly addressing fragments of his memories and consciousness. Sometimes the forgetting of things he knew, and the learning of new things he didn't, swayed gently in a soft liquid cocktail of thoughts.

A hard tap shut the system. He was already late and he thought he should at least put in an appearance. He was never really keen on the regular presentation lectures. The problem he found with them was that everyone just ended up agreeing on a common consensus after each meeting, so they all ended up steering in the same direction. Even those who thought they were sailing their own course had heard, processed, interpreted, and based any future discoveries on its bias, whether it be a positive or a negative bias. Thus in the freelancer world there were always those who were going to try to 'do a trekkie' in their quest for new discoveries.

The lock clicked shut to his satisfaction as he pulled the front door to. He pulled his jacket about him and zipped the front up as shield against the cold breeze, and flicked up its collar into his neck. He sort of hurried down the path and steps. A young boy was lightly skipping along the street, one hand in his father's, the other carrying the unmistakable box of a beginner socket rig.

He smirked to himself as he remembered the cardboard box he had used to play with in his early youth. Then he hadn't yet a real rig, and he played in his imagination, pressing keys on the box which performed unguessable abstract functions. It wasn't until many years later that their father had bought them the Synclear XZ rig, and begun the countdown for his launch into the invisible world of the computer.

He hastened his pace, aiming to get the journey over sooner.

Chapter Two – Lift off

Well, almost. He had got the timing just a little bit wrong. He seemed to be walking toward the timetabled lecture theatre dome just as everyone else was leaving. They didn't look overjoyed, so he guessed he hadn't missed anything that much entertaining.

He chattered idly with a few faces he recognised, and amid the banter they reminded him that there was another sitting in an hour. Ideal. A visit to the canteen and all should be well.

However, the couple of sausage rolls and the milk drink seemed to take a lot out of him. He mused whether he should make the journey back home or stroll on to the afternoon's late lecture. Actually that seemed to settle it, it was an afternoon lecture. That meant the whole pace of things would be winding down. The bonus of arriving that late was that he had missed the extreme hecticness of the start to the work day, and could instead begin with a nice relaxing winding down lecture.

The amount of yawns and the number of strong caffeine drinks being brought in were a good indicator. Even Taylor was looking less animated than normal, which was still hectic, but noticeably slower. Some said that Taylor was one of those people who never did anything he said he was going to do. Truth was, Taylor often came up with good ideas, but people were so negative to his ideas he didn't bother pursuing them. Taylor flicked and backed up his work yet again. People may have chuckled at Taylor's tick like reflex, and ribbed him for backing up so frequently, but the thing was, Taylor needed to backup much more often, as he simply had more to backup from the same space in time.

The tired hum of the attendees quietened into an expectant silence of the forthcoming impartment of knowledge. Either that or their apathy had turned into sloth.

The frowns of the lecture tag team duo echoed the concern of the gathering. It was only Tuesday and everyone looked wrecked. "Hopefully just Tuesday bluesday," muttered the staff, but they knew what they had to do.

"Right then you lot!" bellowed the shorter, stouter of the two. "Now listen up. We've realised that you all live exceptionally dull and boring lives, so we've decided to bring a bit of excitement into your lives!" he raved.

A confident laugh was heard amongst the crowd. It was unmistakably Tommy's.

"Alright Tommy, you excepted," said the taller, slimmer of the pair. Everyone roared with laughter. There was no doubt in anyone's mind that Tommy led anything less that a full and consummate lifestyle. Tommy always seemed wide awake, not hectic, but just alert and fresh, ready for his next intake of what life had to offer. Tommy knew how to rock.

"As part of your continued enlightenment into the radiance and mystery of the world that is the computer, we've decided, at great expense, to take you bunch of sleeping beauties to v-industries."

Tommy laughed again. There was no echo. The silence was now one of stunned, and the spell of sleep evaporated in an instant.

"Fuck about," inflected an unknown voice. The laughter applauded in again this time.

Even he had shifted a little in his seat when the words 'v-industries' were trumpeted out. He had to admit, even he was a little bit excited.

"When then?" asked Tommy. "Or are you a bit like Gina?"

The lag of the crowd's laughter was just at the right delay to mask the yelp of Gina's elbow into Tommy's ribs.

"In two weeks," confirmed the lecturer.

The rest of the proceedings consisted mostly of background information on v-industries. Most knew the general stuff covered, but the prospect of the visit had rekindled the interest of even the most reticent of learners. From a grounding in augmented learning, v-industries expanded into the number one supplier of legal high-end virtual reality equipment for the space industry.

The connection may not at first be obvious. The moon race had quickly been superseded by the mars race, with the Electorates agenda of transferring attentions away from domestic difficulties, and the big corps agenda of all haggling for the contracts on offer.

v-industries had began life as a supplier of software to the education sector. They had successfully mapped the windows of opportunity of learning to complex geometric graphical systems. Thus, the optimum windows for each learning task such as language, speech, and triordinate combination, could all be assimilated at the correct stage of development. 'Let the mind tell you when and what it needs feeding' had been the favourite catchphrase of one of their founders. Bless them, by marrying game theory and learning aids they even made it a whole lot more fun.

His hand went again into the packet. Bollocks. He had been distracted too much. He was taking his time over consuming his chocolate honeycomb spheres, but he had forgotten to keep an eye on when the last one was approaching. Thus he had eaten the last one without knowing it was so, and when his fingers tickled the packet, they found nothing but coldness. He was left wanting more. He checked the package again. Those damn pixies, they aways pinch the last one.

The increase in efficiency in the learning process was almost as great as the increase in spatial compression achieved in the leap to language. It was possible to impart knowledge at a much faster rate, and the time taken to perfect a particular pattern prior to consumption could be unbounded.

The complexity of the flight systems increased exponentially with the switch from the local moon trip to the much longer mars journey. v-industries managed to grasp the essence of the problem. For a local moon flight, the distance is small and any communications time lag is pre-calculable. However, the mars route could mean a changeable communications lag and a much longer life-support system cycle all round. Nobody wanted another Laika, so much research was undertaken.

The technical difficulties were huge, and the research brought about considerable sideline industries and inventions. Social commentators discussed whether the missions would ultimately enable the tapping of resources of other planets when we had exhausted our own, or whether the funding should just be used to try and solve more basic human issues. Eventually all the disparate projects across the globe were united as part of the international space scientific exploration program.

Various suggestions were made of such solutions as vr systems to suspend travellers under. It was v-industries who came with the solution to the problem. Their full-immersion systems also had the advantage of lowering the net load, as the pilots were not in the craft. Instead they were on earth in what the v-industries marketing department completely wrongly described as 'intended suspended animation'. Everyone agreed it made more sense than shipping off pilots with heavy vr equipment needed to both control the systems and provide relief from the caged in feeling on long flights.

The navigators would reach extreme levels of concentration during the warm-up period to their piloting session. Once in a total relaxed state of full immersion, control was switched over from the previous pilot. Earlier research had shown that spending long periods of time at this level of concentration could be damaging, so the ability to switch over on Earth was a distinct advantage.

With instant success in the field with their new systems, v-industries attracted a high calibre of staff, and soon gained a reputation as being the best. Being the best and attracting new staff who were the best too made them just better and better.

"Big night out Thursday," said Tommy, his hand half over his face in an attempt at secrecy. "Up for it?"

"Sure," he nodded.

The transport rounded the corner faster than he would have liked, the top floor exaggerating its motion. The street lights dazzled in blurs of colour in the glaze of the winter night. Along the seafront the sound of the waves mingled with the electrostatic hum of the traffic, and the lights along the promenade and pier hazed into jagged blurs of colour.

They had ingested one each. The warm glow instantly noticeable as it had hit his tongue. The blue flecks were tingling to be set free, and the white base even now starting to dissolve slowly and release its eloquence. The other three still sat in Tommy's open palm, their fate undecided.

"I've a pocket in my wallet, should do," whispered Tommy.

"I'm not so sure," he said. "Maybe I should put them in my boots, should be safer there."

"Ok, your town, you know the tricks," confirmed Tommy.

They continued along past some high set windows. The restaurant they fronted was set up a little bit higher than street level, so that its diners had an uninterrupted view of the sea. In the present case, they were also being treated to the displays of the night, the glowing and pageantry of the nightlife scene.

Across the transport lane and past the railings. Joining the other eager party goers. The queue was moving slowly. Slow enough for the rushes to mount up in the center of his spine, pounding like hands of fingers flicking to be released upwards across the shoulders and spiral tapwards.

"Hello lads, so where you from?" inquired the puffer jacketed outer security.

"Up the road, woodtreine," he said.

"Oh yes, so what brings you here?" security stated without emotion.

"Well, we've heard it's a good night so we thought we'd come here and take a look," he said. The play and counter play continued briefly, and slowly the security discarded him as a threat.

Another wait. But at least he could feel the vibration of the impending hall. They filtered through one by one, each having another round of questioning followed by the skim search.

It had become a strange mix of safety and intolerance. Whilst anyone caught transferring inside would face stern expulsion and possible sanctions and repercussions, to the right the chemicaleers were keenly testing the regularity of the dosages and highlighting impurities.

Their previous concerns would have been unnecessary but for one thing. They liked to rock, and the user license was for one per person.

The physical skimming was fairly tame, it was more the reaction the seasoned skill provoked when reaching a hot zone. They had honed the recognition skills in years of training and experience, the slightest of tells would betray the overloaded.

Then the moment came, the sweep lay at his feet. A slight inspection and a flick of the boot's laces were all that he was delayed for.

"Good job we booted it," he said, striding confidently through the double doors. He thought he heard for a moment a whisper behind him, but he wasn't sure who had said it.

"Funny how we always know, isn't it," it had said.

They left their winter garments at the bay, and excitedly cantered across the hall and down the steps into the pit. It was a stone-lined swimming pool of great extravagance. In times gone by it had been a meeting place, and the ceiling-height glass windows had let the daylight flicker over the water's top. Drained in recent years, the concave and curved walls now let the music flow around in currents.

The bass of the sound system hit him like wind, and for a moment he thought he was outside such was its breeze. He sighed with the euphoria of the tune, feeling its joy and sadness all in the same breath. Its intensity uplifted them into a dance of joy. Quality tracks and dancing into the groove. The flash and pump of bass from the sonic cathedral of sound seemed to widen his eyes and wake him up more with each hit, even though he was already fully awake.

The night was long and full of fun. They rounded off with a campfire in the shadow of the pier, the dancing flames being replaced with the dancing rays of dawn. They feasted on potatoes baked in the fire wrapped in metallic foil. He sharpened his stick and placed a fresh marsh mallow on its tip. Near contentment.

The weekend had been pretty hectic, but there had been time to chill as well. It was a new week, and it was the day of the field trip to v-industries.

They had somehow managed to get themselves together and get on the transport. Backage stowed or clasped tightly with both hands in secrecy guarding fashion, seats sat in and hacked for, snacks and drinks positioned in accessible but unobtrusive places. Those final bottom wiggles to push the cushioning of the seating into comfort.

As the power of the actuators ground into action, the transport's audio rig span out its tracks.

"Standing on the Outside Looking In"

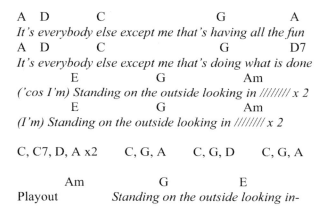

A   D   C   G   A
It's everybody else except me that's having all the fun
A   D   C   G   D7
It's everybody else except me that's doing what is done
            E   G   Am
('cos I'm) Standing on the outside looking in //////// x 2
            E   G   Am
(I'm) Standing on the outside looking in //////// x 2

C, C7, D, A x2   C, G, A   C, G, D   C, G, A

            Am   G   E
Playout   *Standing on the outside looking in-*

There was a bit of gossip going round the passengers, most of it started by Gina. A lot of it was about Gina too. He read his eyelids and rested patiently. After about three-quarters of an hour, they reached the security checkpoint of the tour branch of the v-industries research facility.

These guys seemed to have a really big thing about glass. Even before they had deployed from the transporter, the size of the doors was apparent. They were projecting a fanfare welcoming from an unseen internal source. Realtime colour holographics, all in a transparent medium which could be set to clear after the display.

As the tour party were escorted through, he could only guess that the half-metre or so thick doors were tracked on some sort of magnetic monorail system, although the track was flush to the floor and only betrayed by the path of the doors themselves.

Inside the structure the height was breathtaking. It wasn't so much tall as high and tapering, a marvel to the eye. As they passed through the initial sections of the tour, they were enraptured by the beauty of the engineering and attention to detail v-industries went to.

Each following display sector was subtly different, it wasn't just a change in the colour scheme, but a change in the whole essence of the space. Different lines or different curves, all creating a flow designed to uplift the inventions into the visitor's consciousness.

From gyroscopic balance rigs to fluid suspensoriums. At times the students listened intently to the descriptions and explanations given by the guides, at others they queued for half an hour just to live a few minutes in the immersion technology. His turn was next.

The eye lightening faded out as the reality suppressants began to reform. An aching ear abdominal descending bass reverb, the taste of dry saliva, unprogressive wrenching with its mild burn companion. Heart-depth sigh, astonished panic like falling love. Consciousness. v-industries highest performance rigs were like being born into an electrolyte world where you lived amongst your lucid dreams. His turn in the rig seemed short. The next student stepped up.

The tour continued to the sector describing the international space consortium. Part of the display was a miniature full working replica of the injection moulding space layer print system. They stood and watched in silent awe as the machine created its perfection.

Beginning with a blank sheet, the molten metal was printed up in layers, the two-dimensional sheets forming up into a three-dimensional craft. The composition of the metallic ink was key. In order that the spacecraft did not exhibit any wear and tear between journeys, the whole thing was reused by 'melting' it down and restarting again. The nanomachines within the chemical brew helped to form and bond the structure into a single solid piece of the hardest material known to man. Its designer must have felt as Matthew Smith at the sight of the miraculous brilliance of what had been created.

The marketing team models came down the stair case with its white piped handrail. In a line, then a ninety-degree change of direction in a curve, down the steps onto the level of their assembled party.

Though he was still hearing he wasn't processing. Standing steadily, the corner of his eye had glimpsed her earlier, the back of his finger had tapped the air involuntarily as if a tell to her of his would be interest. She was suited stylishly, her slender grace and poise were obvious. Yet to the eye caring enough to examine closely, the subtle discomfort in her wear revealed it wasn't her normal dress. Special attire given visitors no doubt.

She was now in fuller view. He could only observe as he stood in stasis, save the timeless turreting of his head to track her path. Simultaneously seeing and sensing the shimmer that surrounded her, his sexual selection had determined its target. Was she a pattern match to a random image of averaged symmetry determined in the womb, the sum of the whole of parts of past loves, or the undeniable beauty of true love. He knew at once. Dragon and Phoenix.

She had the look of someone who knew someone was looking at her. Head and chin slightly raised, face slightly in profile. She must have noticed.

As she stepped nearer to the group, her sight caught his momentarily. His eyes dropped first, her's followed soon after. She could see the mild blush in his face, and felt her own warming. She could see he was beholden. She knew the generics of the situation, such was her beauty she had captivated the look of others before.

Yet despite this she too felt the nakedness of the instant, as though he already knew all her secrets. With the trepidation came the glow of his sunshine. She felt a wave of change across her, as though she had just lowered herself into a warm bubble bath prepared by her lover. Not that this would phase her in the slightest, she was a cool professional. She pondered if the minute raise of her eyebrows had been detected.

Had he been looking, he might have noticed the minuscule shift, shake, and slight raising of her body and head, as she strove to compensate for her temporary feeling of vulnerability. However, his mind was engaging in a conflict of its own.

Having dropped his look in a reflex action, it wasn't the image of the floor that flickered across his sight. His mind had sensed the survivalist nature of the situation. It was rapidly reanalysing, reprocessing, reinterpreting his image library of memories, trying to obtain a pattern match from the past to formulate a response to the current predicament.

Amongst the twilight of joy and disappointment, he remembered the carefree dancing at a nightclub years earlier. Then he had matched eyes with another. They had exchanged small kisses as they danced their tribal mating dance. They had become separated in the crowds. She had asked his name, and said she would see him later, but he hadn't held any expectance. When he saw her getting out of a shuttle a short walk from the venue, his eyes had dropped then. 'I look like shit' had been his mind's reply, and he had walked on.

He saw the girl he had chased around the playground with when he was six. He had been shy of her kiss, even though she could be leaving. On her return from foreign lands years later, the better climate had faired her much better than his. She had grown and was a healthy specimen of flowering woman, he was but pale in comparison. His mind's self-image refused the match.

But he either didn't have enough data to correlate a response, or he couldn't process the amount of data necessary to reach a response in the narrow window of time given.

He wasn't even going to attempt to say anything, he knew it was hopeless to manage any kind of coherence in the situation he found himself in. He had been caught unaware. He hadn't expected to see her here. Surprise, shock, and joy all in one.

She said something in his general direction. He dared to risk raising his eyes to contact. Her stunning lashes made his eyes reflecting her beauty widen even more.

"Yes," he replied, and attempted a small, gentle smile, as though in truce.

Thankfully the professional smile she held in wait of his answer curled into a signature on the treaty. She was empathetic toward his plight and she wasn't going to push it. She glided on and continued to play her small part in the marketing parade that had been laid on for them.

It had been moments, yet an eternity, since she had looked upon him. He felt summer clouds were depriving him of her light, and he already longed for the charge of her warmth again. Luckily she had her plan. Before the party left the hangar, she positioned herself with intent. Just enough time was prepared to give them chance to exchange a couplet of succinct stares, and the unmistakable head to toe to head look of attraction. Her soul was filled with the joy that there might have been even enough time to relay a few smiles.

'She is lovely,' he thought.

It would be an easy lookup for her on the company visitor roster. His would be a little more tricky.

He had managed to see her name badge amidst the rainbow and showers earlier. Unfortunately he hadn't a total match, but a partial on the last name should be okay. He had broken the ice and he was busy tweaking the first log files to mask his tracks. The relay hadn't received many upgrades to its intrusion detection system lately, but to be fair, his translacing matrices would have made short work of them anyway.

The wayhacks had deliberately left a hidden network of sleepers. When any of the members needed a silent link they could alarm a node and mirror the wake-up responses to form an almost invisible grid. He was going to use a two second window on each petrinet today, after all, if they traced him it would only be to one of their own terminals. Sneaky he thought, have a very long piece of wool that just leads back to the ball.

"For fuck sake," shouted Tommy in a whisper, as he ducked his head back in from the doorway. "Why can't you just ask girls out like normal people. And try something better than telling them the sun contains 99.85% of the mass in the solar system."

"Just keep an eye out. You know you owe me from when I helped you and Gina out last week," he muttered, turning to look at Tommy and give him a rather harsh stare, his fingers continuing their dance on the inputboard uninterrupted.

"I thought this was some sort of info crack or something," mumbled back Tommy, his head nipping around the door frame briefly yet again. "We are in probably the most advanced facility in the country, and you're probably one of the best code deviants in the country, and we're standing here, fucking around, risking our bollocks just so you can find the network node of some tart."

"And another thing," moaned Tommy. "The reason why I was so bloody convincing about 'lying' to that guide about needing an urgent piss, is because I fucking need an urgent piss."

"Don't piss me about, Tommy," he said.

"Ha-ha," mimicked Tommy, screwing up his face and angering an expression.

"Favours I get from Jonny don't come light you know, Tommy," he continued, still tapping the route through the system. "Next time you're letting Gina drive the micro under your license, sort out your own fucking fine retract."

"Ok, look, I'm sorry. I know you helped us out. And me and Gina are really grateful, you know we are. Especially with her dad and all that. It's, well, I just need a piss."

He thought and fought and broke a breach. Nice manual. The author had interwoven the simplex and the complex view within the sentence structure. Cleverly crafted to produce a clear description whether it was word read or image read (in periodic mode). He danced through its subtle weave, its fine granularity gleaning understanding readily. The rapidity reached a peak, and he became unsure of his own thoughts. He was understanding at slightly a faster rate than his active consciousness could instantly comprehend, and at times it became confusing as to whether he was thinking or listening. No time now, he could remember what he had learnt later.

"Fuck it. This one leads into a honeypot," he sighed. "Let's go have that piss. I've routed this one into the buddy node, so we should be able to run it from the transport on the way home. I trust Gina has her usual supply of clean caller id's for her phone. She really must get off that natter habit of her's, you know."

"I know," tutted Tommy. "She's a good girl though, ain't she."

He ticked down the system, and left his note: 'if you were an articfical intelligence how would you answer this question?'

Toilets like that confirmed v-industries status at the pinnacle of the best. No-one matched them, they had it all, they were the impossible duality, the biggest, and the best.

Luckily he had picked up an extra few hack credits

when he was sorting out Gina's problem. Typical though, any gain he managed to wrangle out of deals for Tommy and Gina always seemed to get used up fixing another hack real quick.

Gina nodded and passed over the first handset. He plugged in the intercard and peeled off the antenna label cover to boot it into transmission. He had got his copy from Jonny's secure download store. Jonny was originally just another paranoid geek, and over secured his systems way beyond any real threat. Thing was, Jonny had a natural ability for calculating the veracity of crypto algorithms. The long and short of it was that Jonny's lines were magnitudes safer for those 'special' downloads, as Jonny liked to put it, never failing to wink or tap his nose when offering such a service to his more discerning customers.

He figured he had another ten minutes or so of hack time before the honeypot distractor was discovered and they started to scan the outer ports for the real incoming trace. He winked to Tommy to start the timing. Tommy may have been a bit of a fashion victim, but at least you knew he had a hardcore watch that wasn't going to give a false readout.

North-five, easting one-twenty. Relay signal found. From the trace it looked like one of Dave's vans. Nobody believed he was able to determine the members id's just from their relaying path. Actually they did, they just liked to make him think otherwise, just to try and spark a bit of uncertainty so they hoped he wouldn't always know exactly where they all were.

The members had a good system. They all liked cruising around in their microshuttles, so using them to form a dynamic relay web was an obvious idea. Each shuttle had three or four dynamic scan relays, giving at least eight secure channels at a time. By hopping between thirty or so during a one or two second interval, it made it practically impossible to form a location trace to any of the hot switched networks. Bloody handy if you needed a lift anywhere too. It was the kind of local area network that sa's would stream of.

Mandy had been giggling a while. She was now blatantly laughing. Everyone had ignored it so far, as Mandy was prone to bouts of giggles for no obvious reason. However, it was now becoming apparent that Mandy was in fact laughing at something to do with the current situation.

'Why oh why were there so many distractions,' he thought. Tommy pissing, Mandy laughing. Transport cornering. Gina yapping.

It was done. He had cracked the inner keep. Now everybody laughed as Gina's phone relay sounded the tune of 'Rule Britannia'. The information he needed was sucked down the straw, and he switched the routing to a dummy nodeset to give them even more safety.

"You guys!" howled Mandy. "You make me laugh."

"Huh?" said Tommy.

"Yeah. You hackers. You make me laugh."

"Yes, we know, Mandy," he said. "Hackers are funny. Funny to look at."

"Yeah, I mean no. You hackers, you make me laugh!"

"Yes, Mandy," Tommy rasped impatiently.

"Yeah, hackers. You're hacking v-industries aren't you!" giggled Mandy.

"Shit, Mandy, shut the fuck up," angered Mark. "Walls have ears."

"Who cares about you losers hacking v-industries. Like they don't know exactly what you're doing," laughed Mandy.

Tommy threw a look of concern at him briefly, and then hid it before he could scowl back. If it wasn't for Jonny then maybe they would have been in trouble. Tommy really knew there was no need for worry, it must just have been that piss thing earlier he comforted himself, but Mandy was laughing at something other than such a wind-up that no-one would go for.

"Yeah," Mandy screeched. "That girl you're hacking for. I know her. She works for an agency my mate works at."

"And just for that, Mandy," he said. "The hack was logged under your account."

The shock look on Mandy's face, even if only for a moment, was enough to restore balance. As if he would do such a thing.

At least Mandy's pranking had achieved one thing. Well, actually two things. In fact, one was bad. It meant he had to do something, as Mandy would surely intervene and blow any minute chance he had if he didn't act soon. He had analysed her data and figured it was a possible, albeit a long shot. He rated it at about 48%, although admittedly that was the result of rolling percentile dice rather than the output of an algorithm. It also meant that he didn't have time to do anything complicated, which was a shame. No time for the science of art. Hopefully she'd get some good data on him before Mandy distorted it all.

It could only be one thing then. Fannying about down the florists. There was good reason for his reluctance. Flowers were good, and he even could enjoy sending them. Romance was good. Problem was, it's easy to be romantic the first time, but failures could sure make them look wilted. He hadn't much luck with flowers, once being dumped soon after, another time having them licked and munched by a pet dog even before presentation.

The entrance to the florist's confronted him. An image of the owner saying, 'Here again?', flicked through his mind, but it was a false one built from his nervousness. He blanked his mind, breathed, and changed his perception to being about to enter a floral garden for the first time.

"Hello, Sir," said the assistant. "What can I get you today?"

For a moment his mind continued the perpetual visitor paranoia, but it was just a normal greeting, she had meant today as today, not as a day after yet another yesterday.

"Something nice," he said. "Something special, please."

"For your girl?" she read easily.

"Erm, yes. Something to reflect her beauty," he strained, the memory of her form slowly overcoming his embarrassment. "With a vase. Glass, please," he braved. He figured she was a busy girl, and having the arrangement delivered in a vase would mean she could enjoy the gift without worrying about its disposition.

He looked about. He saw the matching product he required. "How about something like that?"

"Ah. A good choice," enthused the assistant, hardly having to force herself into a sales pitch.

As the assistant fed the destination and payment details into the microterminal, he wrote the note with the words he had agonised over.

Now the wait of torture began. Even though the exact certain destiny had already been determined, it was unknown to him. An unimaginable magnitude of events had surpassed, billions of years of evolution. The years of his own life. The result was already known, but to him it was all that any could ever be, it was either one or the other, 0 or 1, yes or no, true or false, fifty-fifty. Unknown and unknowable to him until the moment became revealed.

He couldn't believe it. It was worse than he thought. He was in way too deep. She had topped him. Her perfumed card remarked she had enjoyed the lilies and roses, the white purity coupling with the passionate red of love. Her card had been attached to the cylinder parcel, which had been of a good diameter.

She had sent back a single orchid, its beauty such as only God could give, growing in timeless elegance from a well-crafted stand made by hands of fairyness. Her p.s. read 'I hack you too'. So it was her who had triggered his red counter.

Despite their initial nervousness, the dinner at Triangles went well. The menu was written in a pattern he didn't understand. He was never much good at real languages. The number of patterns he could code in was probably over double figures, although he did like to stick to his more favoured few. He never really got the hang of foreign languages. Probably that old thing of being able to think in the language, he could never do it, and always had to translate between his tongue and any other, which took too long to be satisfying. Different with code, code was in his native language, he would have chuckled to himself.

She was good. She knew a few languages, some of her very own, and even when confronted by a listing in a pattern she wasn't fluent in, she could still converse enough to inflect a description of a banquet with ease.

They talked heartily, their bonding growing as they interspersed their stories amidst eye locking gazes and playful banter. He was endlessly fascinated by her.

All bits were definitely lit.

Chapter Three – Boosters firing

At times things were not getting there quite as he wanted, so he used the old hacker's tricks. Motivation was sometimes hard to come by for the long and laborious writes. Although totally necessary, it could be incredibly difficult to be bothered to do them, as they just fired nothing in his brain whatsoever.

He kept stacking, waiting for the rush to come. The wave of euphoria hit him, and he tried to settle into the tasks. He almost had to fight against the level of reality suppressant in the system, so that gave his mind something to fire on.

It is not that he found the work hard, he just found it hard to work.

Later that week he was idly scribbling with his notes, sort of pretending to look busy. She seemed anxious about something. Whether it was the show that night or something else, he wasn't sure.

He watched as her essence changed. He seemed to be more distant from her, and she seemed to be acting out a snippet of an event from her past. He watched while it ran its course, her mind attempting to understand and deal with the problem which was previously out of her control, and had caused a blockage.

"That's the problem with you geniuses!" she said.

"Eh?"

"You think it's enough to simply be a 'genius'. You have to actually do something as well you know. Sitting on your arse all day doesn't count!" she continued.

"You mean contemplating," he retorted.

"Call it what you like, to me it looks like you're sat on your arse doing shit all."

He got up and looked busy. It was obviously necessary

for her at that point, so he did it.

"Sorry, poppet," he said. That seemed enough. In her replay she had changed that which could not be changed, and thus broke the hold it had over her mind.

She froze for a moment, and then looked at him lovingly. Their eyes told each other all, and there was no need for any further words on that occasion. She placed her hands on the back of the chair that she was standing behind, on the opposite side of the table to him.

"I've got some sorting out to do, babes," she said. "Why don't you pop out for a walk and get some fresh air into your thoughts?"

She was obviously needing a larger space for the waves in her mind to meander within, so he agreed, and thought it best he didn't cloud her space with his static.

"Just pop out for half an hour or so," she said caringly. "Then we'll do something."

"Ok, I'll have a wander."

"You're made of love you are!" she said.

"Made to love you, baby," he replied. She had spent most of her life helping others, and he was so glad he was able to help and love her. They exchanged a quick kiss.

He thought he'd take a walk into town. Past the railings by the church, and the school outing in the park. He watched as the children learnt by observation, a week later it would be their own opinion. Spring was coming and the days were getting brighter, although the wind still had an icy chill to its breath.

As he was walking along the pavement, a little girl ran out of the shop, across his path and towards the female figure.

"Mummy, mummy!" said the girl excitedly. The woman bowed down towards the child and played her part in the act.

"Look at these wonderful things, they make your hands and face so soft," mimed the girl. The targeted marketing of the interactive advert continued its projected figurine, the woman roleplaying as if the girl were real.

He continued along and down the street. Oh, that was a nice surprise. He saw Jonny walking up the street in the opposite direction. Actually, it was a surprise. Jonny was never up this early. Jonny still lived the life of the coder, and had no need for day and night. Now he was with her, he had to remember to manage his days a bit better, three-day coding fests with pop and pizza weren't always her dream date.

It wasn't like when he was younger, he used to be a real night owl. It probably started off with it being easier to work off-peak when the socket tariff was cheaper and the pipe wider. In those days the networks were more localised, so there were busy and quiet swings rather than the constant pulls of today's demands. Therefore most coders tended to get into the habit of staying up late. For a lot, it coupled up with the daylight avoidance thing. It's not that the coders disliked the sun, it's just that when it was a bright day it would reflect on the display screens. For others it was more of a stillness thing.

When he had explained to her about the background static, he could see that she hadn't quite got it. Night coders tended to have a naturally (or unnaturally) high frequency brain wave pattern, thus they didn't need the extra electrical stimulation from the sun to set their synapses firing at the rate of activity they required. In fact, for some their minds were so active that daylight actually seemed to hurt them. Whether it just caused the eye dazzling because they were used to dimly lit rooms, he himself always ran in a very low brightness mode so his eyes didn't bleed at the end of the day, or whether the added stimulation to their brains just made them ache, he wasn't sure. He always made sure he had a pair of shades handy on those bright days though, it was always embarrassing to have streaming eyes from the over brightness of the day. 'It's just another excuse for you geeks to stay up late, being naughty, and obsessing with your toys,' she had remarked.

Jonny looked hurried.

"Hey Jonny," he said.

"Yeah, hey," said Jonny. "So what shit you been into lately, say in the last 3 months?"

It was now clear it was both hurriedness and agitation. He wondered what shit he had been in to. Jonny hadn't paused for pleasantries. A few ice checks. Tommy and Gina's usual hacks. Maybe one or two for fun, but nothing heavy. Certainly enough to spark a mild pang of guilt, but nothing heavy enough to interest or upset Jonny.

"Have you been speaking to Gina?" he said.

"Shit, this isn't a game of hack whispers, you know," fumed Jonny. He hadn't seen Jonny this upset since they discontinued the S700E series. Jonny had bought up all the remaining units on that occasion. In fact, a few months later he released the improved design into the network.

"Erm, nothing that would blip you, Jonny," he said nervously.

"I'm not flipped by your geek games," said Jonny. "If you weirdos want to go round playing node draughts I'm not bothered, I know you guys are sensible enough not to take out anything scoped."

"Thing is," continued Jonny. "They knew the perp was using my equipment."

"They couldn't trace it then," he smiled.

"Exactly, they had no idea! It was a crystalline beauty, according to them!" cackled Jonny, forgetting for a moment the main thread as he remembered the fireworks of the crack. "Like a knife through butter, they said," laughed Jonny. "Heated nanofilament through ice I corrected them!"

It started to dawn on him what Jonny was on about.

"So, if I say," said Jonny, pausing for hacker effect. "A certain *cough* vee *cough* company. Your logs would be snowy, yes?"

He felt like a scolded child. Not a real belt whipping or anything, but he definitely felt as though he had been playing too loudly on a rainy afternoon and was about to be given chores to do by his elders.

"Erm," he said.

"Look, you know I know it was you. And you know I know that because I couldn't trace it either," said Jonny.

He almost had to bleed his tongue on his teeth to stop a smirk of clean crack glory.

"Now," said Jonny, changing the angle of his head, peering down his nose. "If I couldn't trace it, then it was either you or The Captain. And guess what?"

"Erm, I have no answer," he said.

"I asked The Captain, and he said he had done it."

He knew this one was going to cost him, and he could feel himself starting to wince.

"I've been playing fox hole for three days for your skinny arse, you know!" said Jonny.

By that he knew Jonny had spoken to Tommy. The success of getting the hack whispers source on day five was completely watered down by knowing he had made Jonny run the fox. The phrase 'skinny arse' was the key to that round of hack whispers, the geek real world game where you talked about a subject not normally discussed, and inserted a key phrase, and then used that phrase to track who had talked to who. Gina had of course been banned as she was impossible to trace. A day-fiver was a good score.

"I'm sorry I made you go on the walk," he said, genuinely. Fox holing was simple, but very time consuming. It involved going round attempting to bump into the members of the network, as many as possible, so that any trailers would be set to false. Thus the true fox could be tipped off, and to any observer it just looks like the whole world is made of foxes.

"And The Captain," said Jonny. "He'd have taken a badgering for you!"

"They'll have to rack that guy vertically," he said. "He'll still be fighting on his feet."

He was embarrassed however, if the trail had led to The Captain, The Captain would have taken the bites of the hounds for him.

"So, Mr Crack Fantastic," said Jonny, with ever so just a hint of sarcasm. "What was the download?"

Shit. Jonny was being really harsh, which wasn't his usual persona. Either he was really pissed off or he knew the download, and was just milking it for fun factor. Actually, Jonny had already cracked him. It may well have been The Captain, The Captain was so good, Jonny wouldn't have know whether it was a false positive or not.

"Ok," he said. "So how did you know it was me and not The Captain."

"Well, even without the blatant tell you just gave me, they said the guy was a real gentleman," laughed Jonny.

"Knock-knock," he fessed up.

"Indeed," said Jonny. "I had to fry a miniboard shortly after, just to cover my laughing."

"The Captain would always have gone for the stealth bonus," he admitted, nodding his head in respect.

"Yes, most people aren't as full of shit as you!" scolded Jonny. "Some would say trying the door, and if you find it locked, knocking, was not a plan of a crack."

"You know me, Jonny," he said. "The man with no plan."

"You always say that," said Jonny, even though it was true.

"Unlike The Captain," he said, continuing the main

track.

"Yes, The Captain would have got in and out by using nothing more than smoke," said Jonny.

"Yeah, invisible smoke," he said. They both paused for a moment, and they almost felt a hundred coder veterans dodge by them invisibly in the wind. Respect.

"Look, I know you're good, and I don't mind you showing off now and then. I've gotta have that little bit of respect for your manners, knocking then covering up once inside, rather than using hammers. But really, you should control that see-sawing ego of yours, you can't keep compensating for arsing around and not creating something beautiful by pulling off neat cracks."

"I know, Jonny. You're right. Things are different now though, I'm more grounded," he said. You would have thought he had told Jonny that he had invented a time machine or something. Jonny's face betrayed a certain lack of belief.

"Down to the final layer of abstraction then," said Jonny, wanting to get it out of him. "The download?"

"Well," he said. "It was data, personnel file data."

"Yes," said Jonny.

Shit. They must have hassled Jonny real bad, as he looked as though he was hoping for a share of the fee for the crack, or at least the chance to have another piece of data to add to his vault of bargaining tools.

"Jonny," he said. Jonny didn't need him to say any more, Jonny had already looked away in disbelief, and was shaking his head and waving his arms about a bit.

"If there's no payoff then it can only mean one thing," said Jonny.

"Well, look, we could invite you round for dinner," he said.

"Ah, I see. Well, now. You should have said," gleaned Jonny, stopping his dance of uncontrollability. It was kind of strange, he never had to apologise to Jonny, well, not in the 'sorry' sense, well, not unless it was major, like that crack six months ago, but that was different. Jonny seemed to take a dinner invitation for him and his wife as fair compensation. Well, that's the real world stuff, he knew he'd have to sort out something for Jonny another day in the network.

"I guess I'll have to let you off then, since it'll save us having to get that agency membership for you!" teased Jonny. "So how is the girl who you almost got us all flagged for?"

"She's an E3, Jonny," he stated, looking Jonny straight in the eye.

"About time," said Jonny. "We thought you were going to start crossing continents or something."

"Patience, Jonny, patience. That's all it took," he said.

"Yeah, we noticed, you're so fucking patient I get the goggles knocking on my door!" said Jonny. "Guess we won't have the problem of you doing boredom cracks anymore, as she'll have you dusting her rig!"

"Thanks, Jonny," he said. "Where's the next fox?"

"Lecture dome five," said Jonny. "Actually, it's like the old days. I'm getting a certain satisfaction out of it."

"Nice," he said. "Should be a good time for a game of lecture bingo."

"Yeah, always. Ok, play safe," said Jonny, with his trademark tap on the nose.

"Wilco, Jonny. Tap, tap."

"Tap, tap," echoed Jonny.

He couldn't believe he had almost made The Captain take a hit for him. Although The Captain could land with no wheels, and probably with no wings either, he was concerned by his poor show at putting The Captain in that position.

He was walking at a much faster pace, and his annoyance at himself was still rising in him, upping his temperature, almost breaking into a sweat across his forehead. Through the gate and down the path, opening and entering the front door in one motion.

"Hi babes," she smiled.

His mind stilled in an instant, he had entered a different universe, and was enveloped in her presence. The static noise in his ears of the outside world was silenced. He felt calm and relaxed in her sphere of influence. He flashed his eyes around the room in a scan for indicators, all seemed normal. Their warmth drew each other closer, the final steps like two magnets snapping together as the final pull impounded.

After the mixtures of their minds had balanced through their gentle hugs and soft kisses, they broke into chatter of the morning's trivialities.

She cunningly lifted his t-shirt and thrust her hand onto his butt in a single pickpocketer like motion. Although she wasn't over keen on his looser trousers, they did have their advantages. Such a pair would invariably mean that they were drawn more across the stomach when fastened, so when hanging on his hips there was plenty of room for her to get a hand in and go for a decent grab, which she did. He reacted no more than if she had reached out and held his hand, but they were in their space, and so were less guarded of analysis.

Relaxing her sumptuous hold, she toyed with the softness of his bum cheek.

"Early lunch?" she suggested.

"Top plan," he said.

"Great!" she smiled.

"Although one thing."

"Anything for you, my darling!" she said, flapping her eyelids flamboyantly, and although she was probably being truthful, she played the scenario as though it was a blatant false and shallow overact.

"Could you possibly, please, get me something for The Captain?" he begged earnestly.

"Again?" she laughed, tossing her hair back. "I thought you had left your wayward youth behind you!" she teased, throwing a torrent of sarcastic glares into his face.

"Well, I sort of have, baby," he said.

"Oh yeah!" she said, continuing her tease.

"This one was from a while ago," he explained.

"I see. Must have been a biggy then, if it's taken them this long to track," she said, extrapolating the information she had chipped out of him about previous cracks.

"Yeah," he smiled. She was a total geek babe, what a treasure.

"And if The Captain was involved, it must have been a risky one!" she said, hoping to pry another morsel.

"Major crack, baby," he smiled.

"Wow. Important one huh!" she said, admitting defeat that he wasn't going to tell any more.

He just smiled again and kissed her.

She drove to the seafront where they joined Tommy and Gina at the beachcomber café. It was a bright day and the sun's warmth was starting to be felt.

"Well, I sort of climbed the mountain only to find there were many other mountains, and no-one else had picked the same mountain to climb," he said.

"Ah, poor babes," she sympathised.

"Fuck off," said Tommy. "You thumbed a lift up the first mountain, thought you deserved a rest, and then hacked every other mountain nearby till you got caught."

He laughed. Tommy was funny.

"Hack your sorry ass," he said.

"Tommy's of the climb mountain school of thought,"

chittered Gina. "He likes to get off his arse, sweet bap that it is, and go do something."

"Yeah, Gina likes to think about why you want to do something, or why something is what it is, sort of the nagging school of thought," laughed Tommy.

"You're such a bitch, Tommy," whined Gina.

"C'mon, you know I is joking, baby," crawled Tommy.

"So what makes a great coder then," said Gina, going for the blatant subject change.

"It's all to do with having a concurrent appreciation of the macro and the micro," lectured Tommy with an air of aloofness. "Being able to focus on the small, yet maintain the big picture in your imagination."

"Ooh, I love it when you talk all techy," said Gina, proceeding to put two fingers towards her mouth in a down the throat action, pretending to wrench. "I've heard having a big ego helps too."

"You don't make a great coder," he said. "Coders are born hardwired."

Tommy chuckled.

"I don't mean freaks like you and The Captain!" said Gina. He took that as a compliment.

"Yeah, I guess," he said. "I guess I kinda do most of my work when I'm not working."

"You're a walking fucking Keplar!" laughed Tommy, and they all joined in.

"Bit of a stereotype though isn't it, the geek coder," she said. "It's not all woolly jumpers and sandals is it."

"Certainly not!" said Gina, blinging her bling. "Good job there's us groovy chicks to add a bit of colour to all these grey boys!"

"Really though, we are all unique when we are born, it is society that turns us into stereotypes, depending on what advertised dream we buy into," he said.

"Okay," she said. "So it's my round, what you wanting,

poppet."

"Fizzy pop," he smirked. They laughed.

"Oh really, water for you it is then," she blinked.

While she was at the service counter, he took a swig from Tommy's. The wince he let out when Tommy flicked his ear was enough to alert her to the deception. He figured Gina wouldn't have been able to hold it in anyway.

She got her revenge by pretending to bugger off without him. Whilst he was visiting the toilets, she had arranged with Tommy and Gina to make sure he was last in the microshuttle. He did think it was a bit strange when Tommy pushed the seat back after Gina had got into the car, and had gotten into the front.

He was just wondering where he was supposed to sit, when the solution formed in front of his eyes. The microshuttle drove off with her poking her tongue out, Tommy making v-gesticulations, and Gina capturing the moment on her photocorder. Could he be arsed to waste an afternoon trying to hack it off her system.

He hoped they wouldn't have gone off completely, and to his relief, when he rounded the corner there they were. Tommy was gesticulating rather a bit enthusiastically he thought, come to think of it, so was Gina. He had just enough time to rig Tommy and Gina's alarm to give them a jump thirty seconds after entering their flat. He would have set their wake up alarm, but they surely always double checked it now, and he reckoned Jonny had put a scope on it for them anyway. They dropped off Tommy and Gina, and continued home, merrily chatting and smiling away.

She had heard his gentle barefooted footsteps, and heard the change in breeze his movement left in the air, his slow steps but his swift and clean motion. She was standing at the left-hand side of the bedroom window, looking out, her body angled at roughly forty-five degrees. He watched her hair shining in the sun, its dark brown colouration lightening in its glow. Her delicate dress illuminated her exquisite curves, the pertness of her breasts captured perfectly in her elegant pose.

She knew he was watching her, but for a moment acted as if she was unobserved. She felt the expanding warmth of his love taking in her sumptuous beauty. Their desire had already sparked off its instinctive reaction in each other. Temperature raising slightly, deepening of breath, the increase in heartbeat. The burning heat of lust. He had to have her, and she had to have him. Not a random wanton lust of selfish desire, it was a pure lust of passionate love. He felt a physical lust to give pleasure to her. She felt a physical lust to give pleasure to him.

As if all were not enough to drive him wild, she feigned her act of unobservation just a little longer. She pressed her hands down on the window ledge, tip-toeing a little, pretending to strain slightly to watch a furry animal or bird continue its scamper along. She knew her alluring slow rhythmic movements would compel him to continue his mind's match of her beauty to the full length of her figure.

They both knew her play was to entice. He wasn't fooled that her act was anything less than an expression of her love for him, and she didn't mean him to be. She knew that every delight she gave him, he would reverberate multiplied.

He even loved her ankles. The dress smoothed over the divine architecture of her buttocks and legs. As he drew closer, he imagined he heard her nipples expanding against her dress as it moved in response to her change of stance.

By brushing a curl behind her ear with her fingers, and flicking her ponytail upwards, she cast her line. With an over the shoulder glance she penetrated his eyes with such power as to almost knock him backwards. Her look eyed his body up and down.

Her growing smile tweaked mischievously into a smirk for a moment, as she imagined her hook catching on the eyelet of his zip. With her look fixed with her playful thoughts, when the imagery cleared she could clearly see him growing inside of his trousers gate. The burst of nerve impulsing was too much for her, and with a enrapturing flutter of eyelashes and a flick of her head, she reeled him in at speed.

His last steps towards her seemed to be in acceleration, her class three lever in action again he thought. He placed his arms around her waist, and lowered his chin slightly onto her shoulder, nuzzling and kissing her neck with his warm lips. She nuzzled back, letting out a half-giggle half-mmm noise. She pushed back slightly against his upright body, letting his embrace draw her against him.

He nibbled and kissed her neck in long poutings, allowing the occasional taste of her skin with his tongue. Her summer glow made her skin soft and supple. The minute sweating moistened her body, lending it an amiable aroma.

He massaged her waist, first along and back around her hips, then to her front again, only this time upwards. Changing the angle of his hands, his massage continued its caress into the cupping of her breasts. Touching and massaging delicately yet deeply with his fingers and thumbs, he set her bosom afire and heaving.

His gentle eagerness led his hands up to her shoulders. He was almost stalled by skeletal logistics, but with a gracious dance she lifted her arms in the air, freeing his arms to move round so he could massage her shoulders more fully from behind. She swayed her head and kissed his hands appreciatively when she could as he continued the shoulder and neck massage.

Deepening his massage into her shoulder blades, he parted her shoulder straps and let her dress fall to the floor, shimmering against her body. As he loosened his hugging massage, she twirled round to match his lips. The spice of their kissing ignited their bodies with fireflies of passion. Parting their upper bodies briefly in a hinge like motion, she peeled the t-shirt from him effortlessly like the magic table cloth trick.

As she let the inside out t-shirt fall from her grip as their bodies closed once more, she felt his hands making their way round to her back. She knew he would soon be attempting the unlocking of her bra, and as he was still going to be an article of clothing ahead, she wasted no time in taking his belt firmly in her hand. He knew what was coming next. It was unfair he thought, he always wore the same belt, each of her bra combination locks was unique.

With a deft action perfected with passion over the endless encounters between them, she unclipped and loosened his one lever locked belt in a single movement. His task was more difficult, at least three pairs of lever locks, each with an individual and secret combination required to unfasten.

Luckily he had two things going in his favour. Firstly, whilst she had managed easily with a single hand, he was going to use two. Secondly, she was sympathetic to his plight, and drew her shoulders together slightly so as to slacken the fit.

She had become strangely amenable to the action ever since he used the multitool she had given him to simply cut the strap. He found it strange that she was considerably unimpressed by his ingenuity. After hearing that the bra was in fact a one off she had been awarded by 'one of her most favourite' designers, he was also less pleased with his endeavours.

'We all know where your face is going to be every day for the next month, don't we!' she had said on that occasional in a stern tone to mirror her stern stare. His momentary recollection of the not totally unpleasant after effects was dispersed by the success of mission unclippable.

The softness of the cotton was replaced by the smoothness of her breasts. Her nipples massaged against his chest as they both grew into full erection. The throbbing ache of her groin echoed in her ear drums as they wrapped themselves in each other, pulling and pushing the entire lengths of their bodies against and together.

The handmade wrapping paper of their underwear seemed to insulate the heat of their groins rather than separate it, but it was a layer between them that just had to go. In a perfectly timed dance they revealed their gifts as they maneuvered in time to each other, working their cuddles and kissing around the tasks in hand.

He pushed his hands down onto her buttocks, grabbing them firmly, catching the elastic holding her knickers in place with his thumbs, lowering them slightly. Massaging and groping, he thrust his hands down further, sending her lace veiling to the carpet. The dance came to her turn to lead, the 'grand unveiling' as she would graciously call it if she had been particularly pampered that day. She stretched the waste band of his boxers, moving them down and around like a hula hoop, enabling his hard shaft to spring into action now released from its caging.

She led him to the bed, smiling, caressing his hand in hers. As she lowered herself gracefully onto the bed, he changed the vector of his touching to catch her off balance. Turning her as she fell the last step of her lowering herself to the mattress, he moved beneath her so as to catch her in his embrace. She yelped as she landed across him, the excitement sending their entwinements accelerating with increased vigour.

After a while he managed to escape her tight hold as she relaxed her firm embrace for an instant during a moment of mounting passion. He was behind her once more. She felt his breath much deeper and heavier against her neck now, his panting harmonising with the beat of her heart. He licked and kissed his way down her spine, alternately massaging and caressing her back with his hands and his heat as the joy of the moment took him.

She felt as though he undid every knot in the muscles of her body with every tender touch, and tickled her worries away with the caressing of his hands. As he rose back up her body with the ripples of love, he again cupped her breasts in his hands, and he allowed his cock to hang between her legs.

Behind and slightly on top of her, as he ascended he clamped her body between his shaft and his abdomen. His cock was sandwiched between her clit and the soft bed. With their blood flow pulsating in tandem, he gently rocked upward, writhing every inch of its length against her, her running her lips against him.

Biting and groaning into her ears, she was tensing her groin in anticipation. She wasn't going to let his heat tease her any longer. She gradually increased the rocking of her sidewards motion, and then turned and twisted them both round until she faced him. He was poised over and slightly lower than her. They held each other in arms and gaze as he entered her without hesitation.

They wrapped their arms and legs around each other like spiralling plants, thrusts entering hard and deep, and their clasp of each other ever closing. The muscular waves of euphoria sent him ever hardening and her ever tightening. Their deep abdominal groaning urging each other to greater heights of ecstasy.

At long last their bodies answered each other's call, and the two of them convulsed in orgasm together as one. Shockwave after shockwave of their love for each other reverberated through them.

The waves eventually receded to a gentler ebb and flow.

When through fatigue they could not hold the tightness of
their embrace any longer, their bodies opened gently like a
story book, their embrace still held at the spine as they
relaxed in the bliss and exhaustion.

"I love you."

"I love you."

They lay panting, and she felt him still hard against her.
She knew she had satisfied him, but it was nice to have the
extra proof that he was still throbbing minutes after, as was
her own beating body.

He hadn't reckoned he had slept much, but somehow
she was awake before him, her head rested on the hand of
her bent at the elbow arm. They must have been snoozing
half an hour or so. She drew her hug closer, starting with a
slim hello, and then going for the full on kiss with her lips.
The passion in her warm kiss instantly flicked his cock into
full erection, and their kisses slackened as their breaths
grew deeper.

She rubbed her body against his side, and clenched his
leg between her thighs, performing a pole dance like
maneuver as she continued her embrace. She drew herself
over him, and stared her eyes into his.

As she mounted him she let her hard nipples tickle
across his chest, their soft spiralling sending his nerve
endings into a crescendo of firings. She descended him
hard, and let every millimetre of her hug every inch of him.

They bounced and jostled together against each other,
and as they conducted each other's music, she let her hair
flow over his body, brushing and caressing. He ran his
fingers over and round the surface of her supple skin,
teasing, massaging, and clutching.

Their opera of love reached its peak as they came
together again. They gently kissed each other to sleep.

Chapter Four – Floating in space

"Come - ON!" she insisted.

She was all ready, pristine yet with no vanity, and there was he, still hiding under the duvet. They had spent most of the day in bed, and their exhaustion and contentment had led them into a loving sleep.

"But," he muttered, his bark muffled by the warm blanketing.

"Don't even bother," she retorted in a firm, but he even he had to admit, fair, tone. Given even a millimeter of chance he would have relished bursting into his excuse, 'honed through repetition' she called it.

"But it's because I was born premature so I'm entitled to extra time in the warmth because I missed out, and the.."

His sentence was dropping off even before the pain hit home, for he knew that he had risked the consequence of his utterance. Bending back and twisting at the same time, she pincered his little finger on the threshold of teasing pain and the firing of screaming, the pinnacle of pivoting where the 'aaaa' became the 'aarrrggg'. He knew she meant it, and his body rose from the bed, following his finger that she lifted slowly upwards. He should have remembered, 'hands under pillow', but then toes could be even worse.

He didn't mind getting up too much. He knew that tonight was important to her, and thus it was important to him too. She was to be a model of perfection tonight. He showered quickly and made himself ready. She made him properly ready.

The microshuttle was waiting. She muttered something about if he wasn't so bone idle he could drive, but he figured that was just her nerves. They seated up and the journey was underway. He made sure he jumped up to flick his credit strip across the payment handler before she moved, to compensate for his guilt over being a pedestrian.

They hugged and kissed, and he gave her that extra little squeeze. He took his seat out front, and she scampered off to somewhere behind the scenes.

The chitter-chatter quelled as the lights fell low, plunging the room into silent darkness. First one, then two, then four, then eight performers. No sound save the cut that their forms made with the air. Gliding, drifting, spiralling in a radiance of lights. Bursting out of the shadow into a glow of electrostatic luminescence. From the empty void the blood flow of sound began, echoing the tussle of their movements.

They seemed like miniature elastic bands that had curled themselves up in tension, and as the energy potential was released they spiralled and twisted, unleashed to spin in all their glory in swift clean motions. There seemed to be two distinct trails left by the dancers as they weaved in and out, tracing a turning helix pattern as they effervesced across the stage.

As rapidly as the dressage had started out of nothing, the first part of the show had disappeared once more. Their initial introduction performed, the models returned one by one in waves, parading and twisting in finely crafted movements so delicate they could have belonged to a long forgotten martial art. Elve disks of expanding reddish light glittered above them, amidst the lightening electrostatic flux.

Her glow shone the brightest for him, to him the others just sang a harmony to her lead. Her garment consisted of two parts. As the light lessened over the length of her hugging body suit, the change in colour streams shimmered like a sun of rainbows shining off a salmon's jumping back.

From her arms the glowing fibres of light seemed to weave in a pattern like a spider's web. They followed different design principles than the original objective of keeping all the light in. He pictured in his mind how the optic fibres worked, the light entering from the chiplasers and refracting internally in a waveform, travelling along the fibre length as it rebounded internally towards infinity. The sheaving of the fibre seemed to be selectively transparent in places, whilst not in a recognisable pattern, it seemed to allow light to escape according to some complex fractal reasoning.

She had checked where he would be seated, true to her advanced hackplan style. Flashing her gaze at him like the sudden strobe of a lighthouse, she saved a secret moment in her performance just for him. Only noticeable from his precise aspect, she traced out her love note to him in the air, a perfect circle.

He sat with the event programme over his lap, it was big enough he had decided, so he wouldn't need a precautionary extra. As the spell of the circle she had transcribed in the air reached him, he could hear her whisperings of love. He knew he was her one, her his oxygen.

Tonight's show spectacular was over. The gathered audience sat momentarily in a mixture of stun and awe, and then gave generous applause.

Five or so minutes later, he saw her, her costume changed. Their eyes met and called each other together like the plastic cups on either end of a piece of string. She came across, and placed her arm delicately around his waist. They each managed to position their legs in the prelude to her embrace, his right leg against her thighs, so they could both feel the warmth of each other's excitement, although veiled to any onlooker.

"Enjoy the show?" she whispered teasingly, feeling his heat against her.

"I loved those side-split fibre nanolasers which created

those aura patterns of light around the garment," he said, spluttering out his nonsense like the enthralled geek he was. "You know what?"

"What, hun?" she asked, expecting him to suggest another of his childlike improvements.

"Well, The Captain would love some of that stuff for his den," he smiled.

"You!" she exclaimed, squeezing him in a light pinch.

They raised their glasses and laughed together as they watched the champagne bubbles popping upward.

Chapter Five – Low orbit

Reality suppressant helped 'smooth the transition' when immersed in virtual reality. This enabled the brain to fire faster, and helped maintain the 'suspension of disbelief', 'belief of disbelief', or whatever you wanted to call it, so that it could cope with enhanced abstraction. The small clear vials sat on the table in front of him.

He stopped and tensed his brain. Then let it relax. Warming up. Preparing for processing. It was always easy for instant recall for shorts, but for longer reasonings purity of concentration was required.

She contorted the left side of her face upwards from her mouth, until it made her eye squint slightly. She then somehow rolled it across to the other side of her face, with a kind of nose twitch in between the bob extents of the swing of the pendulum.

"You working today then, my love?" she said, casting her glance at the vials of suppressant.

"Yup, some more work to do, baby. You know how it is," he said.

"Yes, I sure do, I have to recalculate this month's lightlaser settings and sort out all of the crap that Thomas left," she said. She wasn't trying to beat him for stuff to do on this occasion, she just had stuff to do.

"Ok, I hope you manage to get it all sorted, should be a breeze for a girl like you," he said.

"Ok, poppet," she said in between kisses. "Don't spend too long in your games."

He laughed. How did she know Tommy had lent him that new piece.

As he strolled along the corridor to his den, through the window he noticed a cat playing gainfully in the garden. He remembered how Billy the cat had played as a kitten, almost seeming to instinctively train himself in his kitten games of hunt and pounce.

The rig awoke and he gave the inputboard a tap, tap. The eye lightening faded out as the reality suppressants began to reform. An aching ear abdominal descending bass reverb, the taste of dry saliva, unprogressive wrenching with its mild burn companion. Heart-depth sigh, astonished panic like falling love. Virtual consciousness.

Some would say it was a pretty easy task to match pre-recorded brain scans to each other to show regions of similarity, but it was Steinburg's key algorithms which provided the vital unlocking of the realtime mapping systems. One of his most famous insights was the discovering that there is no particular region dedicated to high-level thought processing, thus the components are almost always a distributed network. It wasn't so much the location but the connectivity of the triasm which was paramount. Keplar would later use Steinburg's theory and practice to develop his organic transistor network.

v-industries used these theories in the development of their high-end virtual reality systems. Coupled with a healthy dosage of reality suppressant, it was possible for coders to produce systems in highly abstracted languages. These weren't at all like the so called high-level languages used to implement the first systems. Although their syntax and semantics may have been unclear to a layman, they were in fact merely small subset mathematical notations of natural language.

The benefit of working at v-industries was that whilst you were highly likely to have a great idea, the person next to you was highly likely to be having a good idea too. If you put a bunch of these together, then you're going to get some pretty tasty recipes.

Steinburg's team realised that as the programming languages were precise fixed subsets, there was ultimately a finite set of connected components. In order to eliminate the severe delay in processing caused by the need to produce and interpret human language, v-industries developed a condensed language based on a system of images, which could be used to both program and control their systems.

This afternoon's worksheet was to run through a few of Steinburg's algorithms, and gain some more precise individual patterns for use in the next course. Noticing it was sized at an hour an a half, he accessed the learning clip and tapped. The reality suppressant trickled through his synapses.

The associative pattern matching brain was more adapted to reading images than reading words, post proof soon came after realisation of reading the fourteen pages backdown upforth diagonally. All that remained was to create forty-thousand picograms, each with its meaning self-encoded into it, such that any new added to the pictocabulary would innately be understood.

Steinburg may have been a genius, but his augmented learning segments sure pumped out a lot of data in a short space of time.

The transition had left him cold and tired. Maybe even hungry.

He checked the fridge door for any notes she may have left, she was very good with reminders on days that she thought he might be going in full immersion. She knew how it sometimes took a while for the short term memory systems to get back to peak efficiency after a morning with Steinburg, Keplar and co.

1. Open
2. Door
3. Eat
4. Sandwich

She sure was in a playful mood today, but he thanked

her for the sandwich. At about that time she was snacking on what he had prepared for her. 'Sweet and tasty,' she thought. Always tasted better when somebody else had made it, so they made them for each other.

There was time in his lunch segment for a quick go on Tommy's piece he reckoned. Tommy was trying to come up with a toycheat for hack whispers. Tommy didn't mind Gina always winning, but stilll wanted to get her something neat for her birthday.

Tommy's solution was threefold. First of all he planned to mike-up as many members as possible. Next step was to run the feeds through the natural language recognition software. Finally, and this was the difficult bit, he was designing triaps trackers for the task, otherwise different accents slowed the process. Still nothing to match Gina's skill for mass concurrent gossip processing, but hey, it was only a machine.

He clicked it in and waited. He found he wasn't seeing letters, but pattern matching whole words. Storing each word as an image rather than a set of letters. Made it a lot easier. He could read whole sentences like a word. It maxed out after about ten to fifteen seconds though, so not for really big books. He read the entire page without bothering to process any of it. The fifteen image felt wrong for a moment, the processor pipe paused briefly as it ran the parallel comparison of the pronunciations of 'fifteen' and 'fifthteen'.

He switched tasks, and thought in three dimensions, flying over a landscape of geometric patterns and watching a triangle pass overhead. He pumped in some sonics, and crossed it with the graphical rendering. He could not tell whether it was a straight line or a curve so he flew out further and observed over millennia. With gentle patience it became clear that the dot was transcribing a circle. Left or right he could not remember whence he had commenced.

Unknowable then if the circle was clockwise or anticlockwise, each was visible from his neck tilt views. A circle or an eight. One or eight. Backwards or forwards. 8 as a pair of o, two wholes, or from another angle and unwound perhaps a O after all. Twisting or unwinding. He let his mind wander a while in the electrostatic flux, then closed the app and tapped off the rig.

A little break and a pace upside down. The warming up done, now for the real work.

Inside the outside again. The geometry was spiralled all neat, as though all pre-rendered. It reminded him of the barbecue that had been delivered one summer. All the parts were kind of shrink wrapped by plastic onto a cardboard schematic, all clean and neat. They even supplied the screwdriver and tools needed for assembly. Nice.

The abstract pattern matching four set four-dimensional parabolic curves flew into his face, spinning and spiralling. The system calibrated to the next task. As the delta waves flickered, he remembered Tommy's japing earlier that day. 'That's the difference between arty artists and coder artists. Arties look at other pieces of art for inspiration, as code isn't real, coders look into their own minds for inspiration!'.

The way of the coder. The dovetails locked and he entered the zone. The code streamed at him from many directions, and he began the abstracted iteration of continuous refinement. It was a bit like writing a story book. The different parts emerged from his imagination in abstract segments, sometimes seeming unrelated. By focusing on each micropart in turn and adding a little to it, the whole gradually grew into a complete system. Not that any system was ever really complete, but you had to know where to stop the polishing, and avoid becoming lost in the ego of your own creation.

The patterns changed their weave to highlight a discrepancy in the code. He tapped and refocused. The error he saw was almost a typing mistake if you will, although in imagery. But by his attention being drawn to his 'typo', he noticed another error in the picture in close proximity. He smirked to himself. 'Nice that you left a note to point the error out to yourself,' The Captain would have said. 'Other times you'll go back to something and find it has already been written, you just forgot that you did it. Go with the code'.

He knew The Captain was right, but The Captain had already proved himself. Although he always set his own standards, it was sometimes his confidence that suffered. At every moment of every task his perception of perfection was always greater than that possible in the form he was in. With every action instant, a better method was already calculated, making that already done second best.

That was one of the key factors with reality suppressants. They enabled the mind to free itself of the everyday trivial worries, increasing the abstract thought comprehension of the brain, without becoming cluttered by matters of ego.

The Captain was a genius. He was more of a lazy genius, or a contented genius. One of the individual traits to which he had to tailor his Steinburg calibrations involved this problem. The Captain had analysed his biases using software he had developed based on his own experiences. His reward system seemed to fire just before the thought completion. This seemed to be due to fact that as it was apparent before completion that the problem is easily solved, it posed no further challenge and therefore offers no reward, so the brain stopped firing before completion, or didn't actively try and remember the extrapolation of the solution.

'What you need is a challenge!' had remarked The Captain, the readout from the testing rig in his hand. The Captain was right. Unfortunately there was no challenge today, so he stacked a little more suppressant into the system.

Additional module study unit computer interface design control programmatical and systemic functioning shortening mind-input response cycle. Basic navigation control. Compare contrast eval. Full immersion. Gyroscope embryonic suspension. He tapped through and completed the assignment.

The reward firing of his brain at the completion of the assignment joined with the reality suppressant and sent a burst of joy across him. Feelings and faces and patterns and places. The wave of euphoria felt a little like being loved.

"Hey, Tommy," he said. They had popped round to Tommy and Gina's for the evening.

"Hey," said Tommy. "So what's the story?"

"You know how it is geezer, tap, tap," he said.

"Tap, tap," said Tommy, rolling his fingers in a crescendo of tapping onto the table top.

"So how's things with you and Gina?" he said.

"Oh, yeah, we're good. She's a good girl, you know. Well, you know," said Tommy, with a hint of a wince.

"Yup, I know how it is," he said.

"Hey Gina," she said.

"Hi girl!" said Gina. "Nice of yous two to pop round."

"Always good to pop round to see one of the good crew," she smiled.

"Bling it up, babesby!" tinkled Gina.

"Gina's got another one of her empathy rigs set up!" bounced Tommy. "It's a neat one, sort of a group learning response theory thing. You tell 'em Gina."

"Yeah, babes, that is it. It's like a group learning response theory thing," said Gina, blinging it up while mimicking the walk of a monkey.

"Don't fall off the barrow, Gina," barked Tommy in response.

"Come on, I thought you two were cool," he said. "I wanna see Gina's rig."

"I bet you do," she said in fun, slapping his backside playfully. He just looked at her, as though she had spoke in a language unknown to him.

"Yeah, let's climb in," said Tommy.

They tapped into the group rig, and Gina led the pattern. Gina always had her bright colouration in things, took a little getting used to. She laughed as he and Tommy flipped in their shades.

As Danny's special mix led them into a warm cool party of Gina's gossip, the cares of the day drifted away into flux. Gina tapped the pattern to let them indicate their acceptance of entry into her empathy setup. They tapped in.

It started off slowly with basic question/answer pattern responses. Gina led the patterns, and showed the statement one, statement two, statement one enhance format.

As their friendship bonded them closer, he understood the reasoning behind the repeat pattern match response machine. By the response, the nature was shown, and by seeing the nature, is was possible to learn. It was almost as though everybody was becoming everybody else's problem, showing and learning in a group growth.

"Nice one, Gina," smiled Tommy.

"Yeah, works well," he said.

"Bit of touchy feelage," laughed Tommy.

"Neat and nice, Gina," she said. "When's it due in?"

"Next week. Just a bit of gold-plating and I'm done," winked Gina.

They laughed. They had a tired feeling, a hungry feeling.

"Pizza or Indian," laughed Tommy.

"Erm, food please, Tommy," she said.

A new dawn and a new day. He was reading an old report from v-industries, which was a critique on Keplar's early works into neuronisation. Keplar was explaining the narrow borders between genius and madness, and how often it was the bounding environment that influenced things. The random rapid firing of neurons in the brain could lead to greater peak potentials, thus forming a greater chance of them being fused into new unique thoughts. In some ways it was similar to physical evolution, in that sometimes it was the imperfections that caused the improvement in the system. v-industries capitalised on this research in the development of the self-sustaining genetic algorithms for self-healing code.

By harmonising these frequencies, it was possible to both prevent the overload misfirings and also enable ever peaking standing waves to be generated. There was also something about discussion on activity wave potentials, demonstrating how single firings only make loose memory, secondary firing connection starting, and tertiary firing fusation occurring.

"So what's in your day then, sweet bum," he said, admiring her sweet bum laced in her knickers as she bent over, retrieving some object from the floor.

She turned and saw his eyeing. She tutted, as though she was off put rather than flattered.

"Working out a complex one this afternoon. Maybe we could work on it together?" she asked.

"Sure, I've not much on today, was maybe going to do a bit of readinput and research, nothing too strenuous," he replied.

He fiddled about in the morning, whilst she was out and about 'doing proper stuff'. In the afternoon they relaxed a little and ran through the work together. He was never quite sure why she sometimes asked him to help, as she was far better at it than him, but they both enjoyed the learning and working. It was easy for them, there was no layer of abstraction between them, no hidden secrets or diversion routes, no office ego. It just seemed like they were playing like children, having fun and discovering new things.

Chapter Six – Experiments in zero gravity

Her next modelling assignment was in some city state of the former Russia. Though rather cold, it was a nice place to go. Very tranquil and safe. Most of the city states had now stabilised their economies, and the pride and commitment had returned to its workforce. This had reversed the mandate of a generation of young men who previously didn't commit to long term jobs as they frequently saw their neighbours years of hard work disappear overnight.

He would miss her dearly whilst she was away, but he knew she'd be safe, and it gave time for him to concentrate on his work.

He startled awake, his ears hearing the distant siren, his eyes fixed staring into his own lap. He was slumped in the chair. The base of his spine and his hips ached. Remembering he had a neck to support his head he straightened it. The group readout unit was still flickering, displaying its multitude of channels in a collection of spiralled options. Must have been the morning after the first night she was away, maybe not go so heavy tonight. That was the problem with the street stuff, he couldn't get smooth enough of a transition without increasing the feed so much that it gave him a headache. At least he hadn't wasted any of his decent stuff in the nice night of binge.

After cleaning himself up, he did some stuff, and then set about another journey into the rig. He thought to himself how it was funny that society emanated such a great aura of time control. Night and day were never really that distinct for a real coder, and he often worked late or even sometimes around the hours. Yet, even though he didn't have to conform to any nine-to-five routine of daily work, it still somehow exhibited its pull over him. Days always seemed hectic, mornings especially, cleaner to work later in the day.

He still felt a little guilty at staying up too late though, and would sometimes dim the lights at the front of their house even though he was all awake and processing. All part of societies conditioning he guessed. No wonder he had felt so tired at school, work in the mornings was just unnatural. Well, non-Keplar work anyway.

He did a few calibrations and speed readings, checking blurring/pattern matching, and what percentage of the information recognition was necessary for understanding. A little research as well, on a good day in the rig it wasn't necessary for him to search for the information, the information had a way of finding him instinctively, as though the internetwork was thinking for him.

He half remembered some nightmares he had been having in his spells of lucid dreaming, but he just treated them like a film clip. He was used to a bit of weirdness after a lot of reality suppressant. Generally he felt dreams were just training for unknown situations, the brain working stuff out, trying combinations and scenarios. Different parts of day melded with old memories as the wires carried the data to be processed, analysed, reprocessed, reanalysed and associatively indexed. Probably a bit of milestone calculation and goal setting too, that seemed to be the nature of things, having more wants and needs drove us and made us get up off our arses and do something.

Drifting to thoughts of the economic game, his mood patterns altered to exhibit a degree of cynicism, disliking how the artificial layers of the monetary system perpetuated the ecosystem. Really he was just working to maintain an environment in which he could work in. He sighed as he saw the adverts for products he would never want, all displayed in their price bandings to both create affordability and aspiration. A nostrum for the imperfect world perfected through millennia, once escaping the parodied instinctive hunt and gather, leaving only a self-propagating system unfulfilling within its own transparencies.

He didn't have her to balance him and he wandered aimlessly in his thoughts, trying to understand what the world meant. Using the reality suppressant as a substitute, he slipped into vr for comfort like Tolkien's Frodo putting on the ring.

Raising and lowering the meniscus of consciousness, the burst of electrical activity attempting to generate a new thought from old, but the moment was instantly lost again and his mind couldn't remember. It seemed the thought was logically relevant, not just a euphoric illusion, but the method of storing/maintaining the memory didn't seem to be functioning quick enough. It reminded him of early feedback experiments connecting the brain to the information pool. Feeding biases the wrong way round meant that there was so much information it was incomprehensible, information overload. When cross mapped or reversed, conceptual searching was possible, with the information finding the searcher.

He scanned a few research pages, matching against the idea of thought generation when the brain fires, firing at a faster rate to increase frequency of new thought, and trying to link an explanation of how a new thought is pattern matched to a response system with its internal random chaotic factor.

Some part of him realised that the way forward with his project on the virtual applications interface was not to create a generic one size fits all solution, but to create a configuration specific to an individual. Thus the early years of indoctrination learning could be spent on the development of capturing and storing thoughts as concepts rather than as language constructs.

Obviously normal human language development would be augmented as well, but the eventual effect would be the ability to learn in abstract pattern matching four set four-dimensional parabolic curves, as well as using traditional language and notation. Thus it would not be necessary to learn self-evidential proofs in order to perform high-level thought processing on advanced data sets. This should enable the holy grail; zero the mind static and allow near-instant calculation of the transformations necessary to perform high-level conceptual searching and triordinate correlations.

Excited by his new reasonings, he patched through the data and tapped in the reality suppressant. His skin itched with the sensory overload. Had he learned something new or just remembered what he had forgotten. He did not have time to taste the dried blood and nasal secretions before rippled convulsions expelled what little liquid remained in his stomach cavity. The acid chills came as the damp sweat flew away. But it was too late, he couldn't store the mind pulse of electricity fast enough and the solution faded from mind's eye view.

A side effect of the reality suppressants seemed to be some sort of sleep disorder. Although often extremely mentally tired, only short spans of sleep would come. It wasn't so much waking up not sleepy, as waking up incredibly tired but with the electrical thought potential already raising for the day. He figured he eventually narrowed it down to being an increased secretion of the chemical responsible for waking up the mind, in compensation of the thud knockout tiredness of long spells in the vr pool.

Something felt wrong. He knew his head was laid on its right cheek on the pillow, with his arms underneath, face down, elbows bent, hands flat. He could hear himself breathing, but he could not feel himself breathing. It was like he was above and behind himself, listening. He had the sensation of sensing himself from the back of his brain.

He knew to find the solution to his project it had to be functional and practical, yet blend abstraction and theory rapidly into the framework. For the electronics and control technology domain segment he developed a configuration program which automatically calculated the left/right audio/visual adjustments for an individual. He wasn't the perfect combination of a fifty-fifty, so he adjusted to compensate. A perfect fifty-fifty could have prevented tangential reasonings anyway, so maybe just as well. He tapped out his project plan.

Key: Programming application to provide internal reflection analysis and brain mapping, gaining cartographical analysis of regions of perception. Subtasks augmented reality autocompletion. Audio system generating sounds in response to a particular brain mappings. Input as sound, output as electro reading, learning filtering and abstraction techniques.

He filed his project summary and began the process to full immersion.

The bioelectrical signals were peaking and flowing, but it was all fucked up, by the time he had hot switched the data entry pads between the machines and started inputing, he couldn't remember what the neural firings were. The not finishing sentences was leading to misinterpretation.

With the reward coupling already firing, the augmented reality autocomplete wasn't fast enough to keep up with the speed of his processing. The delay was such that the faster the thought, the language conversion delay was such that the end of the sentence dropped off due to time lag in the vr system.

He tracked the brain sensory analysis under different conditions, noting the change in visual/audio/left/right hemisphere bias readouts. Thalamus amygdala hypothalamus pituitary gland adrenal normal. Economic and social manipulation. Lure of nature. The heightened processing also heightened his human emotional responses. He figured the sense of being watched was arising as rarely often firing regions were firing. He wondered, if kittens had their instinctive training stored in their mind, what did he have stored in his.

He awoke to the feeling of a square sheet of frozen metal tightening across his back, and a cold wind skimmering up his neck.

The task was complex. The going was becoming tough. He could only manage a level of ten or so minutes of firation before he had to break off as the readout plateaued and progression couldn't be gained. He didn't know if increasing the reality suppressant dosage to compensate was having an effect or just making him want more. Requiring more to fire his brain at an increased level, was his work progressing or did the firing cells just make it seem that way.

He smiled to a stranger in the street. The stranger didn't return his smile and his hope faded. He missed her.

He daydreamed the solution to the self reflection imagery program. It wasn't a three-dimensional graphical representation, it was an unbound abstract free thought area, a multimodal, multiplanal, multimedia, multi was good.

By first of all not finishing sentences, he thought, then by only a few words of the sentence, and then almost only needing to capture the thought itself, and not waste the extra time needed to convert the thought into language.

His sleep pattern seemed more disrupted. He only seemed to sleep a four hour segment, and then have alternate segments of one hour asleep and one hour awake. Soon this narrowed to simply a maximum sleep period of four hours. Sometimes a sleep period would only be ten minutes long, when he managed to escape consciousness momentarily. His ears popped and the pressure difference made his spine shiver.

Sometimes he seemed to be asleep for a long time, and to have dreamt many hours worth of dreams. But on waking only a very few minutes had passed. Switching off the alarm clock before he went to sleep so he got more than ten minutes of sleep.

With perseverance his session notes revealed the answer to his project.

'I can picture a picture and I know it is a picture, but I can't picture the whole picture only a subset of its total data, and this itself has no direct visual component, yet creates an imagined image which is not a picture and yet has the emotional attachment/feeling of being a picture.'

The solution for the virtual reality system seemed to be clear. Although memories were stored as images, they were not 'pictures' as we know them, they were a set of descriptive data of an image. The key was to find the syntax that this data was written in, thus being able to directly give feedback via a thought process rather than an image or language construct. Communicate with the brain in its native language, its microcode.

Chapter Seven - Toward the event horizon

He had run out of reality suppressant to power the vr system, so after the intense discussions with his peers, the rest of the day was to be taken pretty gently. He would not be using the vr system again until he was restocked. The meld of the long spells in vr gradually faded through the evening, the numb contentment of controlled blanket ignorance lessening towards the harshness of the cooler world. 'Quite an apt time for a system warm-up from our uncle whiskey,' he thought.

The hinges of the drop-down panel gave out their distinctive sound, a bit like the door from a cartoon intro sequence, a drawn out creaking, only more metallic. He couldn't remember a time when they didn't ring out with such a cry, so maybe it wasn't age, but design. The relaxed lowering of the drawbridge left the gateway into the safe haven of the drinks cabinet open, wherein warmth and joy were assured. Surely a ritual repeated in various forms throughout the millenia.

The lowered panel now formed an impromptu table. It was at a nice height for measuring. Placing the glass on its steady surface, he spun off the lid of the whiskey bottle and bent slightly so as to avoid too much parallax error in the measurement of his dose.

Pouring but a small starter into the glass, he could almost hear memories of the purists crying out as he applied liberal cola. A hangover from the habit of consumption, without cola there just wasn't enough to keep the addictive fire cycle quelled, and it'd be gone too quick. Which would have been ok for another, but he hadn't been spending many evenings with whiskey lately, so maybe too much too soon was best avoided. Thus the starter was just that, a small sample to whet the appetite.

The panel to the medicine cabinet was clicked shut once

more, held in place by its magnetic catch. The fizz of the cola bubbled in his mouth, and he let it linger a while before swallowing. The dark, treacle like concoction of fizzed air, addictives, caffeine and kick, were enough to garner a sensation from even the harshest treated taste receptors. He sank the mouthful back with a satisfying swallow.

He calmly strolled about the room for a while. He mused briefly on everyday trivialities, sometimes sitting, sometimes standing. Relaxing and drinking his drink.

But something had tickled his throat or his stomach after he had drank down. It was but a small measure, not enough to provoke queasy uneasiness surely. Yet the tumbling turn of the stomach was unmistakable. The warning signs were such that there probably wasn't enough time to reach that flushable ceramic receptacle of spew in the bathroom. So he sped quickly to the kitchen sink, and assumed the position. He was leaning forward, arched over the basin, hands and arms providing stability of aim.

With a reptilian like regurgitation, the first waves of wrenching ensued. He went into the well rehearsed routine for coping with an alcohol induced vomit. A bit of spitting and hawking would often smooth the expellants sting, so he let lose a few volleys.

There wasn't long to wait, and a small amount of liquid was expelled in two or three bursts. Each started low-down, and forced a real urging wrench jolting his body and back. At the moment of production his eyes were clasped firmly shut in avoidance of sighting any previous good riddance.

Whilst waiting in limbo in the half cold sweat half fever stage, he noticed something on the sink base that accompanied his projections, and was near to where he was sending his remaining spittle. It was draped atop the wire mesh which was presumably some sort of vegetable drainer and general sink accessory basket.

It was a slender thread. A piece of string. He felt the

dizziness of post-puke relief, gained from knowing the vomit process was all but over, but what was this new thing. A piece of string. How long is a piece of string? 'Twice the length from the middle to one of it's ends' he thought, remembering the schoolboy jape he had used years before in his comedy answer to this question of paradox. String theory.

Evaluation, processing, race, acceleration, trying to understand overload. A piece of string. How long is a piece of string. Poor Laika.

At that moment he felt as if an archaic knowledge had been revealed to him. He had lived his life thus far in complete ignorance of this secret. Yet there were people who had known the secret all along, perhaps since the beginning of time itself. There were those who knew and those who didn't. And there were those at the point he was, somewhere in the vacuum that was the in between. Knowing and unknowing, seeing that there was a secret, but not being aware of its form. His body had spoken his individual message to him in answer to his questioning, but he had no idea what it meant.

His somatosensory cortex received information from itself at such at rate that it was unable to comprehend the enormity of everything.

The rupturing of his internal umbilical cord provided the imperative impact of cascading interleafed realities to bring forth such conflict as to tempt the nature of the spine. Intertwined destinal parabolas reeling within the outside warping influences. Disparate myriad memory myriads connected into wholes for the mind's own sake, transient truth and contiguous days of nights.

His brain was a sponge that had been soaking up everything, attending to every detail, and now it had been squeezed in two hands, the stored fluidosity released in a fraction of the time it had collected. A big bang, the singularity of his mind exploding, sending wave upon wave of high impulse energy across his cortex. As the thoughts and memories fell like hail from the sky of his universe, he didn't know which to catch and which to let slide through his fingers.

He tried to adapt to survive. His mind tried to create a construct, like the ancients trying to prove their dominance over the moon and the sun by capturing the light in their hedges of stone.

The day had been Monday. Moonday. Mootday. Meetday. They had met today. They must have known. They had referred to it in their discussions. Yet how could they have discussed it, for it wasn't known yet. Even more so, the meeting wasn't pre-arranged, it was an impulse thing. Or had it been. Had it all been arranged.

The pronunciation and meaning of language changed. His whole mind fired, synapses melting and reforming. He knew it didn't make sense but his mind wouldn't let it go. Rerunning and reanalysing, correlating, predicting possible pathways and attempting to fuse connections. Raising and lowering the level of the incidence of coincidence. His mind was spidering and reindexing. But why him?

He lay and watched the story of his life. Everything was shown back to him, the love, the joy, the hope. The hate, the hurt, the despair. It flickered through his eyes, even though it was dark they just shone in the light of the story from within him.

In his memories he saw the piece of notepaper ripped from the pad. It was pinned to the noticeboard amongst the organised mess of academia. 'Love/hate'. It stated the swing. The pendulum of emotion, the two sides of the coin. He had been asked if he had liked the garment, but her question had been leading, and there was only one answer which really fitted the logic, even if that may not have been the one he wanted to give. It was a perceived choice. Like the two chocolate bars owned by the same company.

But why him? He had chosen to be with her as she was intelligent. Had he been chosen because he was intelligent? He loved her as she was intelligent. God loved him as he was intelligent. I think therefore I am. I am. I was, I am, I shall ever. That was the meaning of I am, God was, God is, and ever shall be.

Everything was the same and yet open to different interpretation, everything seemed to mean something else than what it had meant before. If God had chosen him because he was intelligent then he would be able to think his way out of his torturous purgatory.

The pendulum swing of emotion. The more given to hope, the more given to despair, the ever greater the swings and ever greater the period between them. The harder the force used to push towards one, the greater its weight given to the swing back.

Times and places and feelings and faces. He matched them. Events in his life were similar. They fitted to his life, yet to him some were wrong. His mistakes. The chances he had missed and the wrong decisions he had made. He believed in a single life. Outside of being, but still with a soul, born into the world, and after the life live as the soul again. Some believed there were many lives. Born over lifecycles.

He watched and saw himself born again. Each time he grew and lived, and each time the same choices and mistakes were made for him and by him. None of it offered any change. Reincarnation offered no hope for him.

His mind knew no language to describe the expanse of emptiness where no light escaped. The dire oblivion of feeling every decision ever made being played out through eternities and shown to be the wrong one. Not a single point, but a consistent succession of mistakes and failure.

To see, to live, to experience, to feel, the sadness and disappointment as at every turn. The perceived choice, even though doom was always unpreventable. All enough to render the steel of any heart to liquid that drains away. To live such life not once, but over and over again, being born again and again to make the same mistakes. Seeing and understanding, hurting and learning, but never being able to change a moment.

None of it created any change. Without any perceived change in state, there was no motivational force. Even then it was sometimes difficult to remember that he did not know it yet. Linear time progression merely provided experimental proof of already discovered reasonings. Wherein problematic all revealing only to thine self, sooner happening that misalignments and out syncing were common, some irreparably distanced along planes, never permitting a journey back or a circumnavigation.

His mind was lost, it was always lost, always making the same bad decisions, and always being defeated by forces beyond his control, outside of his sphere of influence.

He had to try and go to sleep. As part of his usual routine, each night after undressing, he would lay out the cross and chain he wore around his neck on his bedside cabinet. He would lay the cross at the bottom, and the chain in the shape of a cross too.

He had laid out the cross and chain. Now what to do with the piece of string. His skin itched. His skin was broken in places on his palms and ankles.

A cross. A straight line. A circle. A figure of eight. The Christian fish. A line pivoted in two like a pair of compasses. A triangle. Which shape to lay the string. Loop the loop. Tie a ribbon. Rope. Draw the line. He laid in all. Then either. Then more. Hours passed arranging the changeable shape that had no box to sort into.

He hadn't slept but he didn't feel tired. He wasn't sure

what sleep was anyway. He wasn't sure that if he went to sleep he would wake up the same. He got up again.

It must now be Tuesday. Tuesday bluesday. Tuesday. Chooseday. Choose what you want to be. Happy. Heterosexual. Christian. Human being. What did they want him to do. What did they want him to be. Maybe it was because he wasn't joining in with the illusion. Maybe they wanted him to spend money. Maybe they wanted him to buy something.

He didn't know what to buy. He wasn't sure if there was anything he wanted. In his pocket were a few loose tokens. He walked along the muddy track and the grass seemed to be as green on each side. He was in the shop, but he still didn't know what to buy. He looked around. The newspaper. The news changed everyday. A national newspaper, yes.

He was back at their house with the newspaper and some other stuff he had bought. He sat on the sofa sideways, one leg half crossed, the other on the floor. He laid out the newspaper on the middle seat of the sofa. He flicked through its pages. Some of the things in the newspaper seemed familiar. It was a bit like lecture bingo only more so. As he scanned through the pages, patterns were almost forming between his thoughts and the stories.

His mind continued its conflict, and thought against itself, spiralling and wrapping inwards and unevenly, all warping and bending trying to fit into a recognisable shape. Some things seemed to fit, matching discussions and thoughts with films or books or theories. Some all pointed together, all were a part.

Sleep never came that night either. He lay with his eyes open. Or were they shut. It didn't seem to make much difference. String. Money for old rope. Keep your third eye open. He didn't know if it was night or day anyway. Night and day were the same, contiguous, it was only a layer of abstraction. Hypnotic brainwashing.

His thoughts had streamed overnight. The paper arrived that next day. Bringing its folded pages of faces to the floor. He leafed through the stories. There was definitely a correlation. He matched the stories in his mind. He had thought of some of them the night before as he lay in his room not sleeping. Almost as if he was predicting. It couldn't be. He had to break the spell. He felt as though he had been brainwashed. Hypnotised.

String theory. Butterfly effect. Chaos theory. If a butterfly flapped its wings somewhere the change in air currents might affect the whether somewhere or something. Everything he created and everything he destroyed. Every action has an equal and opposite reaction. What goes up must come down.

He moved his arm. If a butterfly flapping its wings could cause a change in the pattern of the weather, what would the movement of his arm cause. It must be Whensday. What. Where. When. How. He saw a ring of Buddhist monks sat cross legged around a rectangular rug. Were they worrying for him? Nine-minutes past six. The time the monks transverse with their incense. 6:09. He remembered seeing the green glow of the time readout on a watch at a party, reading 6:09.

6:09. Was it the :0 or the 69. The ying and the yan. A circular snake consuming itself. He was up against a brick wall. Maybe he should build a wall. He had built a wall as a task. Maybe he should build a church. Build a school.

He could hear a pinging in his ears. Was that how they knew. They knew as they could read his mind. He remembered stories of metallic foil hats and anti-meld mesh. The collective consciousness or the pattern match response machine? Simply repeating back what we've heard. Pinging his ip. His ip address. His intellectual property. Stealing his thoughts.

As his life flashed in his eyes, he was shown all his sins, showered with guilt, and he heard the cheers and applause of the group at his confessions. All books were about him, all films and songs. All fairy tales, nursery rhymes, myths and legends. Everything he had ever learnt pointed towards proof of this moment, and yet it still had no meaning.

Thursday. Thurstdate. Thrustday. Thorsday. Thirsty. Did the good of the many outweigh the good of the few. The newspaper displayed today's thoughts. He thumbed through the sheets of the newspaper slowly. He read the pages slowly, in normal reading mode. Looked at the adverts. It was clearer today. The pages read like a log of his previous night's thoughts, every minute detail he had already imagined, every word, every sentence, had already been read out to him the night before. Chaos theory. Butterfly effect. Every action has an equal an opposite reaction. Left and right.

It gave a entirely new spin on the concept of original thought, everything he had thought had happened.

Everything he did affected something else, and as he sat and watched he could see how it was being effected. String theory. Spiral. Loop the loop. Rope.

He stopped himself moving. He didn't want his movements to affect anything in the world unduly. Prediction and causation. Everything he did and everything he thought impacted somewhere else. He was causing it. How the fuck was he going to think himself out of that one.

It didn't seem possible to stop himself thinking. A group of three. The three wise men. The three witches. The three condemned men. The three on the hill. The three kings. The three gifts. The three musketeers.

String theory. String. Rope. Noose. The good of the many and the good of the few. $E=mc^2$. Energy released equals mass deficit multiplied by the speed of light squared. Energy released equals change in mass multiplied by speed of light squared. Was he supposed to sacrifice himself so the others could gain more energy?

Thors day. Lightening. Odin. He saw the image of a questing knight from Arthurian Legend dangling from the tree. Odin. The Norse had a particular view of self sacrifice in order to gain self knowledge, either hanging from a tree or spearing themselves.

He had always considered himself selfless, yet he couldn't justify an act of total self sacrifice. He felt guilt at his own self interest. He didn't understand. Why should he provide the energy. For what reason. Why him? He felt self hatred and despair at his own self interest in not saving the world.

The questing knight hung halfway between the conscious and the unconscious. The quest for the holy grail. What knowledge was the knight seeking, what knowledge was the knight gaining. The quest. Chalice. The holy grail. Receptacle of life. Fountain of eternal life. Drink and be quenched.

Stop doing in order to prevent negative impacts elsewhere. Stop thinking in order to prevent impacts. Decide. String. Rope. Noose.

He had thought and fought for four nights without sleep. He wished he was well. His mind was exhausted and couldn't fight any more. There stopped being a start and stop to the firing of his mind, and it broke, the synapses pulsating in a random pattern regardless of their stimuli.

Stamping his mind unceremoniously through a spiralling cheese-grater shaft dancing toward the decadency of oblivion, the demons raped his thoughts and kicked his sagged body husk around amongst themselves.

Friday. Friarday. Fryday. Freeday. As fast as he could make a defensive swerve move in thought, it could be countered, covered, even erased by them. Freedom of will. Predestination. If things were predetermined could something that he did tomorrow affect something that happened yesterday. Events beyond control.

They knew everything about him. Everything had been laid out according to their great plan for him. What he thought were choices were just a continuation of the same track. He had his reports in the cupboard, telling his thoughts and listing his life. Should he destroy them. They could change his reports. They could destroy the truth.

He could hear the floyd choppers circling outside. Everyone had been in on it. Everyone knew. His lies, his mistakes, his embarrassments and his failings. His enemies, his friends, his family, his mother, his father. They had all known. Events beyond control. Makes no difference. Options always limited by external factors.

He had a final attempt to think at destinal change. It was pointless. Cannot change written destiny, the oblivion was unstoppable. If he tried to change anything they could turn up afterwards and arrange to everything to suit their purposes. Would he be paraded across the front page of the newspaper just like everybody else.

Whatever truth he made they would break into a lie. He got into bed quietly, so as not to make too much noise or disturb any of the bedding too much.

He lays me down to lie. In pastures green he leadeth me, the quiet waters by.

His eyelids reflexed and blinked in spasm when his unfocused stare burdened too much. He lay there motionless in acceptance of his oblivion. His mind quietened. His breathing slowed from panic and became calm.

He waited patiently for the end to come.

Chapter Eight – Return to earth

He had fucked it but he might be able to help someone else or stop someone else being hurt.

His survival instincts clicked in.

He turned and sat upright, pivoted, and sat with his legs over the edge of the bed touching the floor.

'Restock on reality suppressant,' he thought, getting up.

He didn't know why his survival instincts had kicked in, but guessed that's why they were. It was the weekend and he rested on Titan with the knights who knew it wasn't black and white but shades of grey.

The reality suppressant didn't work. It just made him feel worse, spinning out his mind into panic and fear rather than relaxation.

Yet another day. As soon as he was awake he wished he was still asleep. The pain of the panic tore through his heart like iced barbed wire, the cold and sharpness of the steel sending shivers of pain and despair across his body. He couldn't cry and he convulsed in short spurts, contorting his limbs and bending his body in agony, and wretching as if vomiting an unseen poison from his inner depths.

After ten or so minutes the waves of hurt lessened, allowing his abdominal muscles to relax their fierce tightening. The tears began from his left eye, and his right soon echoed with its own pearls.

At least the hard intensity of his sobbing required enough concentration to still the spiralling of his mind for a while. Another shockwave of tears came, and his abdomen tensed again with it.

"Untitled"

Who am I to question the way of the world,
Who am I to argue the facts that you've heard,
The answers that you give me are always absurd.

Sometime later. As he awoke his iced heart shattered, sending the shrapnel chill in shockwaves, the spikes freezing sharply throughout his body. He had been in a nightmare. It hadn't been very nice. He had been crying heavily in his dream, in a desert of desolation and despair. In the seconds it took to wake, he remembered he had been crying, and as his neurotransmitters changed their focus, his body caught up with the suppressed motor firings and the tears streamed down.

Trying to pray for he so loved his God. Trying to pray but the demons stealing his thoughts and rapping and nagging with the firings of pain and fear. Holding concentration of thought to say a few words of prayer, only for his will to be broken with such ease as if in squeezed in play. Such was his hellish torture he could no longer pray to his God.

Space aliens from the stomach. Secret files. He spent some days living through a life's lapping up of sci-fi and odd ball theories, living through and experiencing each one in turn, always himself, but such a change all around that everything was a different world.

Another day. He opened his eyes. There was a delay in the anti-sleep chemical being secreted, and as it trickled through his synapses, for about three seconds it seemed that the random excess firings had stopped. But no, their confusion spiked in, strobing into his shuttering of thoughts, and the obsessive macro phrases began their random firing once more. The shock of desolation returned.

Reading a book. Some other day. He tried to read the sentences of the book. It was difficult. Between every four words the memories shouted, making it hard to maintain concentration. He continued and endeavoured. Finishing the pages, he didn't know what the book was about, as the lengths of the abstract thoughts firing were longer than what he had read to himself.

It was just getting fucking stupid now. He was watching some programme on the television. The show had been a bit weird for a few days. The character in the programme had been having all weird things happening, and he would switch on and see one of the puzzles that his mind had set itself being unwound in an episode. Today's episode was just too fucking stupid. The character in the show was watching a show on television about being watched in a show and where everything that happens, happens on the television. He didn't know whether crying or laughing was the correct audience participatory response. It was all so weird it was becoming boring.

He was sitting in an armchair. A man was reading a newspaper opposite. 'Perhaps I've been given a second chance,' he thought. As he watched the man turn the news pages, he saw the headline, 'Second Chance'.

He stood a while on the footbridge. The people passed by. He was waiting, and while he waited he looked at them all. Some seemed happy, some seemed sad. As they walked by he said to them in his mind, 'God bless you'.

Walking through the town he continued with his

thought. Down the stairs. An old man, roughly dressed. 'God bless you,' he thought.

"God bless you too," said the figure.

Past the shop window. 'I don't know what I am doing', he thought to himself. He turned and looked into the shop window, a large display screen was relaying its show. A man stood in the picture on the screen, and then another joined him.

"You don't know what you're doing do you?" said the man on the screen to the other.

Thirsty, walking down the hill. 'I could really do with a healthy dose of reality suppressant now,' he thought to himself. He entered the great value bar.

"Hi," he said to the barkeeper. "How are you today?"

"It's been a bit of a busy day really, very stressful," said the barkeeper. "What I could really do with is a healthy dose of reality suppressant right now."

He stepped aboard the transport. His mind was in thought puzzles, battling with itself in pattern match games.

"Do you go to Steinehalve?" he said to the transport. 'Will I be ok,' he thought in his mind.

"Yes," said the transport.

'Will I be well,' he thought to himself. 'Yes,' he thought, trying to create the answer in his mind. As he thought his answer, he noticed that the digit of the time readout changed. During the next seventeen hours his mind fought with itself, to try and make it that at precisely the moment the digit changed, he would have an appropriate answering thought in his mind.

He got up and went to the toilet. His bowels emptied

into the pan and he stood, pausing to inspect his excretion. There seemed to be a particular shape or pattern to the way in which they had been laid, floating on top the shallow water. Some seemed to be numbers, others symbols, a < perhaps, or a =. Each day for the next week he would analyse the morning view of his shit in an attempt to try and understand the world.

Today was her return from work. She had been away five weeks now. She almost pushed the door down before she had got the key into the lock. Trust things, the key was being awkward, and she couldn't get it all done quick enough such was her excitement. She turned the key again and it freed the lock. Pushing the handle down, she eased the door open.

The house was nice and warm. Actually a little too warm. She took off her jacket. She could feel he was in the living room, so she quickly slid out of her shoes.

She knew immediately that something was wrong. He was pale and his hair needed cutting. He probably hadn't even brushed his hair let alone washed it. Though she could not catch his gaze in hers, his eyes looked blackened, as though he had last slept in the womb. It looked as though all joy had left him.

"Are you okay?" she said.

"No," he said calmly.

She had never heard that response before. The sensation of dropping twenty-thousand feet in a light plane in a storm rammed downwards through her body, sinking her heart through the floor.

She stepped over and placed her hand delicately just under his chin, and slightly to the right, so as to cup his jaw and ultimately his face. He felt cold and his eyes didn't look as though they were focusing on anything. He had probably used his electric shaver a couple of days ago. As her thumb caressed his cheek the downpour started. It was a slow trickle at first, like which one would see if they heard the splash of water being thrown against a window, and turned round only to see the ends of it slide off the glass.

Like a tap being slowly turned on to full torrent, the flow seemed to increase gradually and in proportion. Her mind flicked back to when she had cut her finger as a child, and the tide of blood that had filled her other hand quickly.

"Why are you crying?" she spoke softly.

"Sorry," he stuttered out after a long pause. The cascading stopped. "I didn't know I was."

He held the tank rails tight as his lowered himself into the water under her watchful eyes. He knew the water was warm, hot even, its steam wisping off its rippling surface. He seated himself in the bath and his legs became goose bumped. He couldn't feel his skin. He felt cold, a sun of ice burnt inside of him.

She thought his shoulders would touch as he was drawing himself in so tightly. She tried to caress some tension from his neck and collar bone, but she wasn't sure he could feel her touch.

He could feel her touch, but it didn't feel as though it was him that she was touching, or that it was her who was touching him. His elbows felt all wrong. And his wrists too.

As she bathed his hair, the soap and water running over his back seemed to make the ratchet of his shoulders slacken off a notch, albeit a very small one.

Using the fluff of the towel in an attempt to 'puff him up a bit' as she would later call it, she dried him off as he stood there like a puppet with no strings.

She put him into their bed, and lay a while beside him, hoping the warmth of her body would enable him to thaw from his hibernation. He shut his eyes. Although it was night, they danced a bright pattern beneath his lids and it seemed like day to him. The shutter flicking of his mind decreased slowly.

She hummed and sang sweetly to him in a low soft voice as she combed her fingers through his hair, sometimes her love causing her tonation to stutter.

"Let Me"

A   Amaj7 Dm   C (add 9)
Let me, oh let me, take away your pain.
A   Am   Am7   G
Let me, oh let me, make you smile again.
A   Amaj7 Dm   C (add 9)
Let me, oh let me, wipe away your tears.
A   Am   Am7   G
Let me, oh let me, banish all your fears.
Bm   Bm (sus 9)
Don't you worry or don't you fleece
Am   C   E
Because with my love comes your release.
A   Am   Am7   G
Let me, oh let me, take away your pain.

After a couple of weeks he started to talk, and he told her what he remembered of everything that had ever happened to him. He was talking as though there wasn't enough time to say what he wanted to say, all terse, sometimes not finishing sentences.

Sometimes she didn't know what else to do but just make sure he drank plenty of water to balance what he had cried out. Sometimes she found it hard to sleep as he just lay there sobbing. He had spent most of his life helping others, and she was so glad she was able to help and love him.

The searing pain rose from his abdomen and scythed

through his heart in vicious sweeps, the ripples of torment sickening him to despair. Then, the wretchedness sent cold spikes down from his shoulders.

Even though it was an afternoon and it was raining, they decided none the less to venture into the outside for a stroll of air, and to go and look at the trees in the park. It was a quiet day, nobody seemed rushed about their busyness. A distinct lack of urgency about everyone, which could easily have been mistaken for lethargy.

It was weird. It was all weird. Everything just had this weirdness about it. He walked through the park and it all looked as though he was wearing sunglasses. Not that it was sunny, or that the light was somehow shaded. It just seemed that everything was distanced from him.

The tense fear ripped down his spine between his shoulder blades, its chill causing them to pull in slightly. Time to return to the safety of his room.

One of the times they tried going out, they stood at the bar, his hands shaking. When he held his drink in his hand, it shook too. He tried holding with both hands. Then both hands began shaking, and glass shaking too.

He scribbled with pens and paper in no particular order. He drew notes and reports, trying to find a way out of his acidic hell. Triangles infinitely mirrored into each other.

```
 1  1  1   -1  1 -1    1 -1 -1
-1  1 -1   -1 -1  1    1 -1 -1
 1  1  1    1 -1 -1   -1 -1  1
 1  1  1   -1 -1  1   -1  1 -1
```

His mother visited him. He confessed to his mother of all the guilt that he felt, such as when he had stolen coins from his mother's purse, or when he had felt jealous of his siblings belongings. He told his mother of the piece of string.

"Do you still have it?" said his mother.

He fetched it, and gave it to his mother.

"Looks like a piece of dish cloth or something," said his mother, examining it, and while doing so tested its strength. As his mother pulled on the string it broke, and she continued to break it into little pieces, rubbing the bits between index finger and thumbs.

He looked on in abject horror.

His mother looked at him.

He didn't know what breaking up the string meant, but the worry of it being broken up lessened with his mother's look.

Another day his father drove him to a great cliff of granite, where the end of the land met the end of the sea. He stood on the solid rock, which seemed to point like the edge of an anvil towards the sea. He felt the wind on his face, blowing in from the sea. He opened his mouth and breathed in the air. He turned, and walked back inland. 'Sometimes things are only true if you believe them'.

It was a while before his brain firing slowed down to a more recognisable pattern. The overload left many residual traces, and sometimes on a moment he would remember them being shouted at him, and he would remember what they sounded like. Eventually the terrors lessened, and their rate of fire had descended from near a three second cycle, crawling through the scale of time until becoming hours, days, then only remembered with a decisional process.

Maybe it was a test of his character, anyone can be of strong character in an easy situation. He hadn't hurt anyone, and at least he hadn't done anything stupid. Well, apart from that visit to the clap clinic, but that was more to do with past guilt over an act of unfaithfulness that only existed in his mind. He had felt he had eternally lost the purity of the innocence of first love, and must bear both of their guilts as all was his fault. Although the manner was also probably more due to the hallucinations of the scorpions crawling up his legs. It had been a false worry in his mind.

Chapter Nine – Discussion

Some years later he realised it would be necessary to return to vr for post analysis under controlled conditions in an attempt at determination of the what and the why. This time he ensured he had a little help from his friends, and that she would be there to catch him if he fell.

On analysis, it was clear than he seemed to remain the same, whilst his perception of everything around him had changed. Whether everything around him changed at that time in the past, or whether he had a different focusing to his selective awareness that was consciousness, he was unsure.

Garbage in, garbage out. He couldn't believe some of the crap his mind had shouted back at him. Maybe it was true what they said, you are born pure and it is life that corrupts. A lot of the phrases seemed to be remembered phrases, what he had read, things from history, myth, media, or from sounds he had heard.

He couldn't rule out that as the newer evolved mammalian right and left hemispheres communicated with language, and the older reptilian parts communicated with images, it may have been the point at which the older parts had tried to learn language and communicate with the new parts. This might fit with an intelligence/pattern matched response system, repeating inconclusives in feedback, to generate a clarification response.

Maybe it was to do with the delicate balancing act of the ego. Often in any situation it was merely the ego's response to the situation, influenced by a far greater set of complexities and neuroses than simply just an analysis of the current physical situation. In fact, at times the current situation seemed completely irrelevant, and it was only the current state of the ego that determined the appropriate response that was to be given by the pattern match response system.

At a lower level, maybe it was all to do with cell division. During the process of replication and separation, the components mirror each other in a high level of symmetry. Maybe that's why humans were symmetrical. Maybe that's why there was the night and the day, the light and the dark, the opposites balancing. It was when too heavy a weight kept being chucked onto the scales that perhaps it became a problem. With the scales broken, how was a sense of balance and perspective to be maintained.

The eye lightening faded out as the reality of the newly born baby began to form. An aching ear abdominal descending bass reverb, the taste of dry saliva, unprogressive wrenching with its mild burn companion. Heart-depth sigh, astonished panic like falling love. Consciousness. Breathing. Seeing. Hearing. Feeling. Smelling. Born. Alive. Information overload. What does it all mean.

Inside an incubator. The baby lay there thinking, connecting, dreaming whilst awake. He lay there, legs crossed at the ankles, thumbs nestled between index and middle fingers. The sensory overload caused his nerves to fire at the surface of his skin, causing him to itch. He had to stop now and again to scratch feverishly, often resulting in an opening.

He remembered the time he was a newly born in an incubator. All his senses told him that everything was ok, there was no threat from his environment, but something was missing.

"Where's my baby?" said the young voice. To the baby it was just a pattern, with no matched response as yet. The sonic vibration was followed by the oscillating sounds of laughter. The baby didn't know what this meant, and his mind fired, attempting to analyse, understand and fuse connections. His mother lifted him, and he felt what he had been missing. Wrapped in the warmth and with the familiar beat of comfort that he knew, he relaxed. He made the connection. In order to receive the love he simply had to think. He lay there and let his mind fire, cusping and ebbing in streams of thought, building a thinking machine. He still didn't know what he was supposed to do with it though. And even then, he still had to do it.

His lips were sore and sometimes he didn't want to feed. Sometimes when he was being fed he knew all was okay, but after feeding he wasn't sure if he would be fed again. Perhaps that's why he liked to do everything twice. The repeat event feigning consistency.

Perhaps loving his God, loving himself, loving his future wife, loving his family, loving his friends, and trying to love the whole world would be enough to keep him occupied.

The eye lightening faded out as the reality began to reform. An aching ear abdominal descending bass reverb, the taste of dry saliva, unprogressive wrenching with its mild burn companion. Heart-depth sigh, astonished panic like falling love. Consciousness. He tapped off the rig, his analysis was done for now.

He would go on to do some more work with vr/systems tools for learning systems, interfaces for passing on knowledge, and maybe the odd bit of coding for fun.

"Ah," said The Captain. "One of the greatest mysteries is why the mind does what it does when it cannot find a solution."

"And another thing," continued The Captain. "That sleep disorder you experienced prior to things going a bit iffy. It was caused because your brain wakes up through withdrawal of reality suppressant. More suppressant won't help you sleep. Lay off the suppressant – you shouldn't need it anymore now, you're a natural."

"Finally, don't try and solve the whole massive problem, just try and solve the little bit of it that your brain can work with."

"Yes, you're right," he said.

"Sure am," continued The Captain. "You ain't that fucking clever."

It was obvious that his brain could try and find a connection between everything, the brain is exceptionally good at matching, and has a peculiar bias to proving its own theories. The fact that two people can witness the same event and create an entirely different interpretation surely limited proof through experience, as individual experiences could be both false and truthful.

He had seen it from all angles. He was a fool to ever think that he was clever, and could simply make up something to believe in. So many theories proven, yet all conflicting. You just can't make something up and believe it just because it suits you. Maybe it was a peaceful constant state of ever changing equilibrium, a whole union not a disjointed black and white distinction. Maybe the point of not being able to prove the existence of God is so it cannot be faked in order to gain power and control. Everything had seemed connected, but then it would be, as he was a connection machine.

Then again, it had proved something, God was far cleverer that he was.

Chapter 10 – Into the future

All the tracks were beginning to sound the same but it didn't matter. He knew he was rising and his excitatory state was matching tracks even when faster and slower, or perhaps containing only a slender few correlations of sonic oscillation.

His spine tightened as the pump of the bass roared home. The beat sent his feet stamping and his head snapping from side to side. His body fired up and connected to his natural vibration. Music mind and body as one, the whole of his essence rocked in the electric fireworks of dance. The tune was for him. The freedom of expression tingled through the layers of his skin, the crackling of his energy reaching escape velocity from his body. The bubble of euphoria ascending through his spine was overwhelming. The rush of emotion unbalanced his seesaw, and his tears Niagared, sinking the wave back downward.

She would still sometimes find him in that state even years later. The tears gushing down his face. Sometimes he would be leant over the table, and it would take two or three decent wipes with a cloth to mop up the pools. It wasn't real crying. It wasn't heart-felt loss, the sobbing of depression, or the hysterics of blind panic. The sadness and disappointment at something going wrong, or the pitiful weeping of hopelessness. They were simply sheets of water, running off his face like rain along a street. The miscues and false firings at the rawity of emotion. The after effects of long periods of time spent in vr, and the residues of the reality suppressants still stuck in his neural pathways.

Away from the dancing, she just sat near him, waiting patiently for the shower to pass. She wanted to cradle him in her arms, and place her hand across his forehead as if to heal his mind. Through experience they had developed silent signals. Sometimes he might lay his head across her belly or curl in her lap. Sometimes the roles would be reversed. It wasn't as bad now, nearer to the event she thought he would wash the colour out of her clothes. But here and now his head was hung down, with the tears of liquid gloss mixing with the lost dreams of spilled alcohol on the floor.

"I'm ok, it'll pass in a bit," he said, his chin not lifting from the floor, his hands rested on his knees as he sat. While the signal meant that he was fine, and he would indeed shortly be all ok again, and she knew this, as he was always very clear in communicating his 'defined condition' as he put it, she was still slightly saddened. She knew her love helped him. The occurrences had certainly lessened in magnitudes. Healed him she liked to think. But she always wondered whether she could ever cure him from the sadness that seemed to haunt him to the depth of his soul.

"Bbrrrrr," he uttered, as though cold. "Sorry about that," he shook his head gently, blinking the remaining dew from his eyelashes. Like a dog just in from the rain she thought. Poor Laika she thought, as she remembered the story of a less fortunate adventurer.

While she was temporarily distracted by the afterburn of her memories, he had stood up, and was downing the remains of his bottled beverage. She tutted as she always did. He always gave the same reply. A cheeky 'What?', for although the drink did replenish some liquid as buoyancy against that he had let slip, her motherliness would have preferred the simple purity of water.

Although his paranoia filters meant that subtlety didn't always work on him, there was no mistaking what her look meant. The joke that they both knew was old. She stood too, and their hands met as their arms raised and they stepped into stride. Their warm clasp of love met almost without necessitating guidance or effort.

A top track was starting, but one not so penetrating to

his innards. It's gentle whispering rhythm was just starting to form. As they strode forward she tugged his hand down sharply in the way 'only girls could', so that he was somehow pulled closer to her. As he took his turn to tut, the expanding warmth of their growing smiles developed into a brief but soul-felt kiss.

"Global warming?" he said. "If you kiss the ice-caps, we're fucked."

They laughed together as one. The time of trouble had passed. It was time to get on with life. They were living love and it was time to rock.

It wasn't a case of two halves becoming one, it was a case of two wholes being one. One plus one equalled one. The two co-existing particles in their quantum entanglement, strolling forward together in the ever expanding universe. It had taken billions of years of evolution for them to be reunited, and the time spent floating in the vacuous expanse of space was immeasurable and unthinkable, but now they were by each other's sides again, since their separation during the big bang at the dawn of the epoch.

Their wedding day was beautiful and they were all to live very happily for many, many years to come. He turned and smiled.

"Thank you."

ÉCOUTE ET RÉPÈTE
Polymath Renaissance
Justin Daw

$\infty < C \, o$

Chapter One – Epoch Dawn

"Of the abhorrations I have seen composed in this world and in between, it is false enlightenment which is the most vicious and curséd of all things," warned The Captain, looking through him as he spoke.

"Be wary of false enlightenment," he continued. "And resolve your mind against it."

For all our knowledge and understandings, it is egos that make us forget. We read the written and the illuminated, and marvel at their wonders, merely to bastardise and copy only that which fits in with our own spheres of constructs, and satisfies the secret realities that our subconscious has created for our selves.

He wasn't looking for answers in the internetwork today, merely checking his own. He reeled within the fluid concentric currents, the data flowing into and over him, attracted to his face like the delicate caressing of a lover's fingers.

The trilock hit home hard into the corners of his spine, and he reeled and winced with the knifing pain. The barbs broke and his mind and body fell into a blanket unconsciousness. The streams weren't correlating today. Like watching lightning over moorland from a high viewpoint, he could see the bursts after they had started but couldn't seem to anticipate from whence they would next begin their formation, or the threaded paths they would follow.

The eye lightening faded out as the reality suppressants began to reform. An aching ear abdominal descending bass reverb, the taste of dry saliva, unprogressive wrenching with its mild burn companion. Heart-depth sigh, astonished panic like falling love. The sound of suction in his ears. The mild pinging pain and the slow realisation of a consensual consciousness again.

"Yeah, this guy comes in, he's all like, well, in defcon one," said the unmistakable voice of Gina. "So, he's geeking it about at the sides, then he comes across."

"I'm all fluttering," continued Gina. "Yeah, real tip-toe unison, all in one."

"Not like you, Gina," she said calmly.

"I know, new one for me!"

"What happened next?" she prompted.

"Well, for a little bit, not a lot," sighed Gina.

He flicked off the relay shades, the prismatic outline tracers fading as he focused on the two.

"Oh, back with us dear are you?" she scolded.

Fuck. Not much patience from her today. Although entirely understandable. He hadn't realised he would be out for so long.

It now occurred to him what was happening. Gina was relaying the tale of how Tommy and Gina met. Which could only mean one thing. Actually, one of two things, but given he could see clearly now, it was only the one that remained.

"Go on, Gina, don't mind fibre for brains here," she chided, continuing her reprimands along with those glances of scythes that he'd only let her get away with.

"Rig-burn boy," laughed Gina. "That's what they call him!"

She just looked him up and down. Or more up a bit and down a bit, since he was kind of slumped in the armchair. He wouldn't have minded so much, but he knew that she knew that it would take him a while to reach full functioning, and that she could basically get away with saying anything she wanted, as he was too strobed to gander any sort of response, witty or otherwise.

"Anyways," continued Gina, although finding time to cast some disparaging looks of her own at him. "So, I'm fluttering and Tommy is defcon oneing. Neither of us making any sort of routers."

"Yup, those boys," she said.

"Yup," said Gina. "Tommy's all manning it up, and I'm all pouting and perting, two of us looking like two plants at at a conf."

"So yes, then your boy struts over, like some leetboi on a rampage, gives Tommy a shove, and then," enthused Gina, her excitement mounting in anticipation of the final tell. "He offers these words of golden inspiration: 'For fucks sake you two, stop tic-tacking and sort it out.'"

She nodded attentively.

"Well, as you can imagine, Tommy just stands there, having no idea what's going on, and well, I'm not much better!" giggled Gina. "So I do the only thing a girl could do, I grab his hand and get him some netcreds. Tommy sits his sweet baps on one of those stools, and hey, we're hanging."

"Why I put up with this shit I don't know," he said.

"Ah, the monkey learns speech!" said Gina.

"Save it for Tommy, Gina," he said. She lightly grabbed Gina's arm in restraint, as if a reminder to why they were all there.

"You wouldn't have it any other way, and you know it!" she said, walking over and pinching him ever so slightly, and planting a gentle kiss on his forehead.

"You taste of code, go clean up. I'll prep Gina."

"Ok," he said, and stumbled towards the back of the bungalow to shower and replenish.

The warming water cascaded down from the shower head and slid off his skin on its journey back to the way down. The thoughts of the trilock still shone intermittently in his mind. As he cleansed his body he tried to relay down and relax the tenseness of his brain, readying for the hack.

The sense of loss and the secretions of tears. Drifting

down and swaying. Deepening sighs and pulling together again. Shower off.

Without the sounds of the jet streams in mask, he focused and heard her and Gina yapping. Zooming like a lens, he translaced the rarefactions as he made their time period alter.

Another usual easy one today for Gina, not that he minded, it was only a bogey, and he knew the banter was all good fun really. It's just that he wasn't making much progress himself this month.

"Try blinking a little, Gina," he said.

Gina fluttered. The retinal scanning traced its map points as he tweaked and translaced. Easy to do with Gina present, he hadn't the budget or the time to do a retina not present transaction crossover. He reckoned Jonny had a fully rigged one, but it was something Jonny had never mentioned, and he was wiser than to bring it up himself.

"Few seconds more, Gina," he said.

"Sure thing, hun," bubbled Gina, low and slow, her consciousness tiring now.

The match was nearing, the turn and twist of translace dancing to a climatic satisfaction. The processes flipped and compared, like his mind's eye had once performed for the girls he had attempted to match before her perfect fit. Almost there, each one progressing the iterative rendering match until all bits were lit in their infinitely complex fractal glory.

The crystal strands turned and locked, relaying a match through the setup. She smiled and admired. She and Gina left him to the true hack, the dual-setup was just to gain entry and authorisation through to the next caponier. It was a classic speed and sweep hack, stealth or instant knockout, the pace preventing a tracing lock.

He shook his head as his soul began to hurt in the centre

of his chest. He raised the pace of his hack and clenched his fists in sprint, the drumming of his mind switching reflexes ascending in its race.

He had felt their presence before. From a mere flicker of hair on his neck to a tightening of his spine. Now he was certain. It wasn't a random sweep scanning that he had been feeling lately. It was definitely an organised tracing. Gina's birthday wasn't coming up, so he knew it wasn't Tommy routing a vengeance crack to surprise her. Someone was hacking his ass. And he didn't like it.

He tapped and tacked and sprinted through two divert loops. The cascading data streams stretching and drenching him in torrents of binary flow. As the hack reached its point of supernova, he felt the top hats of the ones barbing into his skin, and the zeroes pulsating and encapsulating his bounding frame.

He completed, tapped off, and tapped an extra feed of suppressant to mask the pain of the failed tracing hounds.

Although he was obviously unaware, Tommy had been waiting patiently for him to complete the hack. Tommy knew that twice in one week necessitated a visit. Tommy had pondered upon what he was going to leave as his calling card, but figured the only thing for it was a trip out.

She and Gina had been chuckling at Tommy's apparent paranoia today. Tommy stood by the window curtain, alternately fanning and flicking the curtain, and glancing at the hack in progress. Gina had of course led her into the conversation of Tommy's nervousness, but it didn't matter, she had some processes of her own running.

Tommy turned and scanned him without looking to any observer. He flickered the hack signal and Tommy acked. Silently motioning to Gina, Gina led her out toward the garden, and Tommy closed his distance.

"Thanks, Tommy," he said.

"np. So you're sure then?" stated Tommy coldly.

"Yeah, and I'm not happy," he said.

Gina bolted back in through the French doors with an icen look on her face. Tommy sort of shuffled towards the exit a little, but Gina's stares sent her eye lashes to rivet him in his tracks.

So in came his princess.

"Fuck off," she barked, almost causing Tommy and Gina to jump a little too.

Suddenly the full cathedral of sound system they had installed at great custom spec erupted into activity, the floor speakers clicking in with a warm hum of bass reverb. It was a pure vocal mix today:

'Yeah, and I'm not happy.'

She pointed her remote control directly at him, and repeated the clip's echo around the room, on each loop dramatically overplaying her conducting of his embarrassment.

'Yeah, and I'm not happy.'

Gina small-stepped to position herself between Tommy and the exit, just to be sure. After all, they were almost, dare she think it, almost a bit, well, responsible, for what was occurring.

"So much for our fucking agreement," she cursed vehemently. Gina was almost becoming a little shocked, for this wasn't like the girly she knew at all.

Tommy wasn't too shocked, he'd landed far worse than that from Gina. Although probably deservedly. It was some out of character for her though.

"Erm, babe," he dared.

She shook her head, barely looking into his eyes at all. In her rage she heard Gina's lips purse open in preparation of utterance. Her finger sprang up, and stitched even Gina silent.

Gina shuffled a little bit nearer toward the exit.

"It's not like you think, babe," he tried.

"Not like I think!" she screamed, shredding him with her shrills.

"He means not what you think, hun," aided Gina, pleased with her attempt.

"Yeah, that's right," managed Tommy, pre-empting any rib-dig from Gina. Tommy also felt pleased with his effort.

She looked displeased. He looked worried. Tommy and Gina looked at each other, acknowledging that if either was going to bolt, the other wasn't going to be far behind.

She paused for a moment, and in took breath.

She nodded at Tommy, and gestured three fingers to him. Tommy acked the signal, raised his wrist, and began the timing. Gina chewed and tapped her foot, hoping.

The cycles were already dying as he was realising that three wasn't nearly enough of a count to manage what he needed to manage. His thought matrices were concurrently comparing possible responses and matching outcomes. The 'I love you' line had long since flickered out of the quantum autocompletion.

"I love you," he said, regardless.

She stared back. "Well that was a fucking waste of cycles, wasn't it."

Gina and Tommy couldn't help agreeing with her, but knew that was always going to be his first response. He thought he felt the slight movement of air of both Gina and Tommy swaying towards the exit.

"It wasn't my fault," he continued.

"Never fucking is," she said, looking at Tommy and smirking, then back at him, teasing him at the continuing passing of cycles.

"I know, I promised, baby," he continued patiently.

"Yeah, I know, I even told Jonny to stop his scopes," she said.

Tommy had a quick mild pang of guilt over his two running scopes on him, but hey, that was play, not promise.

"So let it out, why the fuck are you being tracked again if you haven't been tricking with anything?" she blasted, summing up the case for the prosecution. She let out her sigh of completion, and let her tenseness relax, waiting for his answer.

"It's like this," he said. "I did it for you, baby."

"Stitch in time"

It's all over before it's begun,
The future is bleak and I am undone,
But turn it around and let's look and see,
The future is bright for her and me.

Tommy and Gina were mostly silent for the journey. The shuttle's electric hum formed the backdrop to his careful description of proceedings to her. Gina eyed the rear mirror now and then, just to check she wasn't hitting him.

"I've known something was up, ever since you went out and bought that clean palm piece," she explained. "You only do a walk and collect when you're doing a clean run, and I checked the netstat setup, and it wasn't publically wired, meaning you were obviously going to do a stealth run."

Her expertise always caught him. "It really pisses me off that you're always so much better than me," he said, trying to get some sort of defence going. He must have been shaving off the barbs slightly, as she didn't just slap him.

"Not better, just not as damn lazy," she said.

"At first I thought it was just a few script kiddies playing, or even learning, if anybody still does that. But then things started to up a gear. It wasn't the same. It wasn't just the usual mess with the odd nice neat hack, it was a consist weave of expert crack paths, backed up with a validated stream in flow."

"Usual bullshit," she said. He was thinking that she just wasn't going to be convinced, no matter what the proof. Tommy's hand was keying his beer bandwidth allocation for today, maybe some vodka suppressant was going to help everyone out. Maybe.

"This is no bunch of meddling kids, you know," she said. "While you three have been sleeping I've been doing some mining of my own."

He knew he was in serious trouble with this one, either way.

"I did it for you, baby," he said.

"That may as well be," she acknowledged. "But you can't just do that kind of hack these days. We'd all heard about you at the agency long before you showed up on our cross-scannings for the field trips. We knew that one of you was possibly going to be amongst the visitors, but with your team you did a very good mask up job."

"You always knew I knew though, right?" he said.

"Oh, of course," she said. "Some of the guys thought that you were the most arrogant bastard hack slut they had ever come across. It was only a few that recognised the pure art and entertainment in your skill. I didn't know immediately, but after that dinner with Jonny it was obvious. Sheila hasn't been as long in the game as us lot has she."

"Sheila's no weak link though, is she," said Gina.

"No, but then you didn't know I knew her before, did you," she said, beaming.

"I would show you your file one day, my darling," he said. "But I managed to get it overwritten."

Thankfully they all laughed. Tommy and Gina exited the shuttle.

She lent over. He turned his cheek up slightly, expectant of her gentle kiss. She breathed forward and whispered. "Next time you screw with v-industries, we go together."

He would have let out a chuckle, but didn't have time, as she bit his ear and made him a wincer, much to Tommy and Gina's amusement. Although the outside viewers had no conception of what had just been agreed.

They all let their cares disperse as they left the shuttle, and strolled over happily to the beachcomber café.

Chapter Two – Isoteric mappings

He wasn't even going to bother to try and kid himself that he had any chance of passing the Asotrerial synal mapping today. Normally the odd fail wouldn't have mattered too much, Brian had certainly let him off a few. Problem was, he knew Brian could only switch it temporarily, and that there was a limit to how much he could back track it.

Normally he would have rescanned and retracked back in when his mind had settled back down a little. A steady readout would have been the only trace, and the peak firings of his genius would have not alerted the overseers to his over indulgence.

Brian didn't say much, except for the minimal pattern response. Perhaps Brian knew what he knew and thought the same. He didn't wait to hear her soft voice read out the results, and as he was leaving through the door Brian cut the volume for him in favour, so there was no tell for any listeners. Brian's personalcom vibrated. 'Sorry, Brian, it's the old wound,' read the display.

His autopilot had already clicked in, and was steering his feet on their course towards Jonny's. Although there was no way now to fool the system to pass a new sample later, he knew Jonny could at least keep him in the game for a little longer.

Tap, tap. He tapped gently on Jonny's back window, and glanced around. The dogs treated him like a shadow. He and Jonny had trained them to full stealth. He was always pleased at their safety, but always remembered how much it had cost him, but still, it was done and dusted, and it worked.

"Oh yeah, wondered how long it would take your ass to show up. I figured it was that season again," muttered Jonny, welcoming his guest in a strange mixture of brotherliness and step-parental scolding.

"So, genius boy, how are you going to think yourself out of this one?" asked Jonny politely, figuring he'd already have at least half a plan.

"Usual story, Jonny. If you can rig me a mirror extension then that'll buy me another time slot, won't it," he said.

"That old trick, huh. So that must mean Brian's masking isn't going to work this time. The Captain will have something to say about that one, you know," bantered Jonny.

"I know. But it's different this time. She found out," he said.

"Oh, shit, I see," laughed Jonny. "She'll hack your sorry ass some day, you know!"

"Daily, Jonny, daily," he said, managing a small smile and a temporary eye-glazing.

"You knew it would come sooner or later," tutted Jonny. "If you hadn't been such a clever bastard at your dawn then maybe it would have been easier for us all."

"Yeah, but you know it's that creation which makes me," he said. "The Captain would agree."

"The Captain tolerates you as he admires your skill, I'm not so sure he'd have approved of the original means to the madness to achieve the method," said Jonny.

"And another thing, your vet on Sheila wasn't complete," he said.

"I know. You're just making my night tonight ain't yer," sighed Jonny. "Me and Sheila have talked. You know, like couples do. Seems like you and her aren't the only ones with residues from the fall, doesn't it."

"Some autocompletions spiral out longer, Jonny, as you know," he said.

"Yup, don't I know it. And really you've letten this one too late, but we all know why, so let's not sweat it and just have a crack at it shall we."

"Yes, good plan," he said.

"The plan is your job, remember," hesitated Jonny. "Ever since the mexico we agreed at least half a plan, didn't we."

Obviously Jonny's patience was fading this evening, but hey, who could blame him.

"I know," he said. Everyone knew it was handy to have some waypoints set. Or at least some possible waypoints set. When the Plan B had been a Mexico home run after a trivial backhack, Jonny had not been amused. That one had cost him too.

Jonny was just unequaled for it. He wasn't quite up to Jonny's standards of crypto. One of Jonny's myth tags was that he once published the solution to the vsec algorithm hidden in the finger picking of one of his teenage band songs.

"The isoteric lead watcher is similar to the struct that we saw at the intercon facility last week," he said. "I know that one was kind of a red1, but I know you can handle that no problem."

"red1's aren't going to stop us, what's the real trick," questioned Jonny, the twirl of excitement and science specification setting him running.

"Ok, the main deal is going to be a replicant switch. There's no way we have the time to copy and install a new translation, so I figure to best way to swing it through is to do a siamese reflection. That way you don't have to copy it, just mirror it. Then you can mirror the mirror."

"Brilliant," smiled Jonny. "Far easier for you to say than me to do though. Want to dual-up for fun, or are you off to do some other mischief for me to tidy up again another day?"

"We'll have some play at the weekend, Jonny," he said. "I found a nice bunker for you to have a go at."

Jonny beamed. "Always up for a bit of gaming. Guess it's better to draw the line between fun and frak I suppose."

"Yeah, we'll do it, although I'm not sure it's a single sessioner," he told Jonny, raising the expectation of better things to come, so as not to have bored Jonny's evening totally with caveman hacks.

"You know I would if I had some spare cycles tonight. I'm never at the right moment lately. I feel as though I'm fighting against time and reality itself sometimes. As if I'm drawn by an unknown will to an eternal vanishing point of variable destinations. It's all fucked up. Everything is occurring at the wrong time and I've no control over it."

"Go hack yourself, fool," said Jonny. "No fucking wonder the asotrerial's were all screwy, voigt-kampff wouldn't have let you get away with an answer like that."

"I know. Problem is there's too many subjectives and not enough definitives. Too much happening at once, and no concurrent solution."

Consciousness collapsing in on itself, spiralling and folding. Memories of unknown thoughts flicking in a blur of transcendent red squares, their opacity fluctuating in the breeze of data. He left Jonny to the crack.

"Lost where it can be found"

In a pool so deep that not measured by human hand,
She placed the pixie armour, whence can be found.

Covering up from stars and beauty, gone by dark,
Only left there in, the might light, tiny, pixie, spark.

Lest you be plagued both night and day,
With things gone missing as in hay,
Throughout the winter follow the pixie way,
What is given out, be guarded, from night, to day.

On the walk back he comforted himself that at least Jonny hadn't nagged him at all for his dubious use of suppressant. All the members tapped, it was just their hack way, but he was needing to counter something else lately too, and they were beginning to guess it. Tommy knew it was like that old game of pool, the game of confidence. Problem was, he was shot to pieces at the moment, and he needed a greater level of suppressant than normal to compensate for the ever encroaching static from the ego of the world.

Given that his Asotrerial ratings were iffy at best, he had decided to gather some underground access points just in case. The less cycles he spent in the public domain the better at the moment, a spike in usage was always going to add to the number of flags any watcherbots were programmed to scope. It was something the laymen never really grasped. It was rarely necessary to hide totally from view on a mission run through the electroworld, and as ever, the best place to hide was in full view.

"Gaming or porn, Tommy?" he said.

"Huh?" doubted Tommy, knowing Gina was out, but not really getting the thirst for porn thing.

He looked skyward and then tried again. "Porn or gaming? How do you want to mask it? Your quota is as sore as mine, and the only way we can social pass it at this period in the day is porn or gaming. Take your pick."

"Gaming is probably safer," said Tommy. "Gina would find out knowing her, and then we'd have to double hack back just to get to the same level we could by playing the gaming card now. Let's do it."

He flipped and gamescope tourney 7.2 clipped in.

Tommy never really understood how he managed to steal cycles like that, he just couldn't see how it was possible to make something out of nothing. Both he and The Captain had given a decent attempt at explaining it to their local node, but sometimes a leap of belief was just easier.

The gaming cycles ran, and the metering ticked.

"It's very simple," he said. "Although the implementation is quite complex, the theory is quite simple."

"You say that every time," said Tommy. "But it's how you do the retrieval that I don't get, and neither does Gina."

He started laughing loudly and Tommy knew what was coming next.

"That's the whole point of the theory, Tommy. Maybe you get it after all."

"I can't believe you hack that line out of me every time," chuckled Tommy.

Jonny tapped. Remembering that the after hit was cleaner. After the initial clear rush there was no follow up of blanketness to the firing and melting. But that was the point, meld up with clarity intact. It was confusing from normal, as the hard numbing reward would have fired, giving the different high of satisfaction but coupled with it's clouding of thought. Thankfully it was still eventually necessary for the mind to fall asleep from a big dose of clarity though, unless the Asotrerials were really off.

Various methods were tried by various Elected, but as with most things, any generalised solution only worked with the consensus of the majority of the controlled population. The overseers could not solve the problem with legalities, so they instead used multimedia models and personalities to implement their education and indoctrination programs. Fact was however, that hundreds of thousands chose to use reality suppressant each week.

In a similar way to how the old television networks were allowed to sell the advertising space which was reserved for Elected propaganda in return for reweaving the messaging within their programming, reality suppressant was often marked as the cause of problems in society. You can kid most of the people all of the time, but not all the the people all of the time.

Maybe it was modern life, maybe it was the lure of the speed hack and the buzz, but the negatives associated with it were more usually symptoms rather than cause, and often the subtlety that it was withdrawal not usage which caused the problem was missed.

Inside the shuttering of thoughts as the nothing became real. Jonny was chuckling to himself. Although the red1's were kind of tame as he had suggested, running in parallel meant he could switch round the whole room of chess hacks and feed his ego a little for fun. Jonny tapped.

Speeding up and slowing down in a dodge and weave of transactional translacing. Cutting a wave through the blackstatic and riding the pulses along as they rippled and rebounded into one another.

'Shit me,' thought Jonny, as he narrowed the distance to the true centre. Jonny let his autodogs feed on the isoteric hounders and leapt through the haze into the outside of the inner. So he had been right. The amount of scopes was ridiculous, even for him.

Stealthing through, Jonny realised the tangle was so bad a lot of the scopes were scoped too. Jonny ticked and tapped simultaneously as he danced his dance of glee through the defences.

As Jonny tapped the beat of his dance tracks span into their autocompletion. Remembering the frequency of the translacing keys harmonically matched to the ebb and flow of the sound. Now speeded up, the kinetics of his thoughts increased into their rapidity, and he was always thought cycles ahead of the adaptive security patterned defences.

Time for the Siamese. In a green phased of lightening, Jonny entered his zone.

In cartwheeling lines of automatching, Jonny fed his

biocrypts into the security receptors as parallel sets of isoteric mappings. The biokeys pulsed through the cell networks of pyramidic matchings, firing in response to the stimuli.

Jonny flipped in the startpoint hackclip. Jonny translaced an exact replicating pattern, and simultaneously streamed in it's natural opposite into a concurrent socket. The patterns were matching until the extending led up to a yellowbox. Both the same and the opposite were giving a result set at the same time. If both were true then there were either more than two combinations or the sets were in conflict with each other.

Jonny felt that he was so fucking almost there, just needing the final connection to trigger the completion. To be really fucked up and yet on the cusp of magnificence. The nearer the goal the longer the cycle and the thicker the air that had to be translaced through. He was so fucking on the ball it was starting to scare him a little, the rush of excitement overload causing a sparking of doubt and fear.

Jonny barely had time to see why it wasn't right. The Siamese reflection was identical. The mirror wasn't mirrored but translaced to the same result. The output matched the input.

Knowing what was coming next, Jonny smiled at the complexity of the cryptography. Rarely had he seen ones of such complexity and he knew what that meant. It was self-encoded, a trilock.

Then it became even darker yet clearer. There was a blipscope on it, and round the corner of the tower blocks of constructed realities of data, the whitebox mercilessly hunted him down in an explosive burst of bioelectric gravity.

Emanating in the mind and echoing through the body, Jonny fell to the floor reeling as the barbs of data pain iced through his veins, the depth of the sadness sighing his soul.

Throwing the rig away from him as he vomited into unconsciousness, Jonny had a strange sense of scolding from Sheila, and a mild concern for the state of the balance. The Captain silently felt the tap.

Though away from the conscious world, Jonny dreamed the beauty of the trilock. Three vertices each watching each other, triangularly spiralling into infinity. The protective mesh was a marvel of engineering, the shield merely reflecting the attack, thus might would never defeat it.

The scopes automagically cut out, silencing the secret that they kept to themselves. Hacking hurts.

Chapter Three – Trilock

"You wanna drive, babes?" he smiled as best he could.

"Yeah, right, I'd love to, baby," she smirked.

He couldn't drive as he had been advised, and experienced, grade three residual visual occurrences. Flashbacks. Not the tacky sequenced cliptrips from the movies of old, but the subtle spark of star burst vision. Sometimes a stuck memory of euphoria would be released, and he would see the firework dots spiralling in front of him briefly, like some hexagonal retinal pattern match.

"Look, the triangular shape here makes it the strongest shape," said the instructor, demonstrating with the three red plastic strips bonded at the vertices with the metal fasteners, comparing it to the less rigid square. Pupil one nodded.

The transport pulled up outside their bungalow and they skipped in, hand in hand, smiling plenty. Settling in with cake and coffee, they got into their game.

"So what's the current exchange rate to the new world then?" he uttered suddenly, from a nowhere silence.

"What? Hard currency?" she said, altering her glance slightly.

"Yeah. Currency," he said.

"Oh, now, 1.58 or something I'd say."

"Figures. These guys are joking me," he continued, his tapping increasing exponentially. He routed back and changed his geo location. "Yep, there goes," he said. "How can softs be more expensive from another geo? Rip off."

When they hacked together they needed no reality suppressant as they made one of their own. He virtualised across the global, clicked back in, re-routed, and did the deal. Currency for softs. "There," he said. "A third reduction. It's not who you are, it's where you are!" he laughed. She chuckled back.

"Just purch yer tools and stop whinging, rig-boy," she laughed.

The trend had been there from days long gone. There seemed to be a strange in built slide to the ecosystem which meant that as time progressed it seemed necessary to shift the emphasis from the responsibility of the supplier to the responsibility of the consumer. As well as from the Elected to the electee. It was all for the sake of the bargaining tokens of money, the abstracted currencies all trying to shift the balance against each other.

From distanced call centres to netbased response, the corps offered less and the consumers needed more. In the end it became increasingly that corps were getting the users themselves to produce the content of cliptrips and music videos, and then serving it all up as part of their infrastructure service agreement. Thus the big companies built the networks and nothing else, just creaming off the profits from the distribution of the content. The content creators return was never much, but marketed to the individual as a way of generating creds (although likely to be small ones), thus getting the people to create more content by carrot and stick. Plus, you had to buy their tools to do it all. Course, the network was just another hack, so soon it wasn't the only one.

"See here, the shape of the cylinder makes it the strongest shape," said the instructor, demonstrating with the white rolled up paper. Pupil two nodded.

The Cybertechnics evolved out of the schooling systems governed by the trusts. The individuals and corporations funding the new pyramid learning centres soon perfected the system into a finely crafted assembly line of establishments for their procreation. In the same way that the ancient Japanese martial arts schools developed their own fighting systems, the Cybertechnics created their own languages and constructs, according to their needs and their desires.

She and him had both been lucky. They had been incubated in strong multidiscipline manners. The problem with the single aspect training by some Cybertechnics was that there is no appreciation of different angles, and thus any interaction was limited to bounds of ego rather than of truth and primary bridges.

Some wanted it that way though. If some were trained only to do one thing, then it was the one thing that they could only do, and by that there was power and control over them.

"Black and white"

One for sorrow, Two for joy,
Three for a girl, Four for a boy,
Five for silver, Six for gold,
Seven for a secret never to be told,
Eight for a wish, Nine for a kiss,
10 for eternal wedded bliss.

She tacked and translaced, her matrices forming waves of accessibility. As his eyes reflected the phosphorus burn of the external display in their group play setup, her thoughts drifted to how she had seen the lightening in his eyes when they first met. Draining down and emotionally tiring, she completed her hack and tapped off the rig.

"Shower time for me," she said.

"Be right there," he smirked.

"You wish!" she chuckled back.

He was just over four layers in when he started to see the thought processes that led to the conclusion. Not only seeing the answer, but the processing path to the answer. Dancing round the fires in his mind, forming networks of beacons to guide the path of his thinking.

Then suddenly it was as it had been lately. A different feeling to the environment, like the envelopment of the coming winter's air when stepping out from a warmer summered house. Triangles infinitely mirrored into each other.

In the unreal he saw the real that he had experienced. Residual visual occurrences, isoteric flashbacks. The shape was more clear to him now. The vertices starred out into an iridescent net shape.

It would have necessitated a diagramatical reasoning explanation. It was all wrong, inside out, reflected back, triangles infinitely mirrored into each other. The net shape shone like nine stars, the vertices twinkling in their irrepressible brilliance. Trilock12, vertices, triangles, four set.

The eye lightening faded out as the reality of the newly born baby began to form. The mild pinging pain and the slow realisation of a consciousness. The smell of her was different. It wasn't the same smell as his genetic parentage. It was someone different. It was light although it was night. As his eyelids spasmed in growth they opened, and a sudden rush of blood empowered his retinal burn. The scent wasn't his genetic similarity yet matched like fingers interlocking in warm love. The immune systems would be highly compatible, and the descendant splitting and recombining would enhance the bonds of the chain.

The matrices spiralled and autocompleted in parallel, the triangular base into a pyramid. Mirrored internally to give an octet, each pyramid with four sides, two pyramids making six faces from eight, the bonding occurring at the shared particle surface. The electrons pulsating round the tumbling core in a dance of unison.

Then he saw it and remembered what it was for. It was the trilock. Infinite in its complexity and idyllic in its simplicity. There had seemed no way back from the Epoch Dawn so he had set it inside himself as a failsafe device. An hourglass for deprecation.

Chapter Four – Genius

Although it was the kind of place in which it was difficult to tell whether it was day or night, the time phase was waylaid by the rays that lit the muggy air when the entrance doors swang open in their moments of briefness. Too bright to sit outside all afternoon, so they had retreated inside the curve roofed building seeking shade.

"When vinci and goghy were scribbling out their notes in code it wasn't because they were being clever. It's because they were so fucking paranoid, a side effect of their immense genius," he said. "By encoding their reasonings they were aiming to ensure that any conspirators wouldn't be able to benefit from the information. Either that or they were appreciative of their genius enough to make sure that it wouldn't be deciphered until a time of greater popular understanding, or only contemporarily by one of an equal insight of genius."

He sat his glass of intoxicant back down onto the table after a healthy swing, in such a way as to indicate his rant was over and it was a good time for someone else to take up the round of conversation.

"Yeah, but you know what The Captain would say about that one," said Tommy, drinking in gulps.

"Yipes," said Gina. "That would be one of his 'Be wary of false enlightenment' rants wouldn't it," she pimped up in a ghosting voice, sipping away.

"Yeah, 'nuff to put the shits up anybody," said Tommy, almost shaking a little then, and drawing his chair closer into the table by pulling on its wooden arm rests. The floor of the tavern must have been designed to compliment this action, as the chair leg on floorboard transversal was relatively noiseless.

"Yes," he said. "It's ok encoding, but be wary of those who think they've got it, whereas all they have really gleaned is a false enlightenment constructed out of the needs of their own ego."

"Yeah, I know what you mean," nodded Tommy sagely. "Especially if you spent ages explaining it all very clearly and then they still get the wrong end of the stick."

Gina tutted silently and batted her lids.

"It sure is a funny one," interrupted The Captain, appearing from the nowhere. "On the one hand there's those egos which are trying to prove the existence of God, and then there are those egos which are trying to disprove the existence of God."

"Those proving for get told that their ego is creating something to believe in, and the ego of those arguing against told they are merely creating justification for their own acts of self, their egos making them seem more important than God to themselves. Some feel more intelligent and enlightened if they believe that there isn't a God, others more blessed as they believe there is."

"Yes, it's a strange one, some people are happier if there is a God, whereas other people are happier if there isn't a God."

"That's where I've never quite mirrored it, on that one," he said. "I think maybe some people get confused over the morality thing. Although the moral beliefs are certainly good guidelines and structure social and health benefits as well, they are still two distinct aspects."

"I guess that's why a big part of a lot of belief systems are based around a method of forgiveness or acceptance. Again, this is often mistakenly confused with the escaping from the dictates of one's parents, some rejecting their parent's moralities in order to come to terms with their experiences of life, and rejecting their belief systems too."

"A lot of modern psychology is built upon religious beliefs. Starting with Dostoyevsky's three kinds of truth, that which one shares with other people, with one's self, and with one's God. Developing into one's personal relationship with God, in that the conflict of dualities is resolved by making a decision or acceptance."

"Further from this, at some point psychologists took out the God bit completely, and replaced it with a self-belief and self-reliance kind of system, the superhuman type philosophy. Only problem with this is that it only teaches how to be selfish, and if a consultant is giving out the worst kind of guidance such as 'taste of own medicine', then all that happens is that everyone is going round fucking over everyone else just to satisfy the needs of their own self egos."

She could feel where this was all going but she didn't let on, and hid her smile.

"So, the up shot of it all being, is that it's your round, Tommy," he said.

They laughed.

"A bit like the science and belief thing though isn't it," said Tommy, widening everyone's eyes with his swift come back. "How does scientific evolution theory distract from belief, if you ask me it's just more proof that it's all not by accident."

"Yes," he said. They could all sense one of his sword like cuts through the air approaching. "Any time I have doubts about the existence of the almighty I just look at that," he said, pointing to the glass of water.

"Water, yes, just look at the stuff. Now that is pure true honest genius!"

"Indeed," she agreed, lifting her glass aloft so that they could all be entranced in the moment for a while longer. "Just look at the stuff, pure and simple. If you were going to design something that you wanted people to drink, wash with, and was obvious when it had impurities in it, what colour would you make it."

"That's clear even to me," laughed Tommy.

"I guess that kind of intelligent design thing keeps some people happy," said Gina.

"Well, I just accept that God exists, and is clever enough to design things intelligently. That works for me. Irrespective of evolution, that for me doesn't deny the almighty, just reinforces it," he said.

"It's a shame though," said The Captain, his sadness showing. "All of these billions of years of evolution, and the only problem we have solved is how to make money."

"When I'm around different people, sometimes I act differently," he said. "This is so that we can relate to each other in fellowship."

"Possibly it's the same with religion. People find an aspect that they can relate to. But if there's the afterlife, why the fuck do we fight over possessions. Guess it simply boils down to ego. If there is paradise why do men fight over mere earth?"

"I guess man's ego continually tries to master man and destroy God. Also man's ego continually tries to mimic creation thus destroying the power they feel God has over them. Most people end up rejecting God because some man is telling them what to do. Guess we should all try and look beyond the obvious."

He pondered upon how sometimes if you mentioned to people you were a Christian, they immediately thought there was something wrong with you, and proceeded to try and help 'cure' you. Whatever. Perhaps they were so uncomfortable with their own beliefs they had to challenge his so religiously. Surely the genius lay in the similarities between the differences.

The pool cue clacked the balls on their colliding paths across the green felt cosmos.

"It's a lot like when you look at other people. It's easier to see other people's goings on than your own, as you are observing rather than participating. Like when reality suppressant enables you to get a third person perspective on your self."

"I blame the government," he laughed. "It's all a conspiracy. If people don't believe in God they have to believe in money, so they go out and get it and kid themselves that they are happy behind a layer of tatt."

"Hmm, you've never really lived in the aesthetic world though, honey, have you," teased Gina, blinking her lashes up and down his appearance, much to everyone's chuckling.

"Guess all that money can pay for some impressive things though, big buildings, cathedrals and all that."

Tommy ticked and Gina acked. The old guy who The Captain had been watching them watch, took a swig of finality from his tot glass and slid back his chair. Standing and nodding with an air of satisfaction, he gestured a thank you to the bar staff and made a route for the exit.

Gina rose up as soon as the guy's shadow had departed, and with an expert pick-up that showed no elbow motion tell, she retrieved the glass object into a pink handkerchief.

"Yup, guess that's always been the way, the money has often been utilised to express the best of everything from that perspective in time. Thus the rich spent money getting the best artists to paint the best pictures, and the best artists where also the philosophers and scientists, making their own paint and tools by hand. Grand architecture has often been expressions of religion, art and culture, from stonehenge to st paul's."

"Hmm, yay, and the hilton building," laughed Gina.

"Yeah, always been the way. From the egyptian kings with their iron hammers made from meteorites constructing their pointers to the heavens, to the masons with their symbols, try squares, plumb lines and levels. And those victorians with their mother of pearls reflecting the sunlight like the moon."

They sipped and munched. Peanuts and alcoholic

intoxicant.

"Erm, pink, Gina?" she teased, frowning playfully, and took a sip from her tall slender glass, the ice clacking slightly, and the lemon tickling her taste buds.

"Yeah, it's one of Tommy's weekenders," smirked Gina, handing off to Tommy on her return from the little girl's room.

"Guess it's all well and good, and is fine, until it starts being used for power and control. All depends whether you look at it as a theme park or as a zoo."

"Most of us need to be driven by a goal. Some people need something to motivate them. Money can be a token substitute."

"Money never really got it going for me," he said.

"Yeah, but you can be driven though, can't you, when you want to be," smiled Gina enthusiastically.

"Yeah, of course he can, not like it's very often though," she smirked, pinching him loosely.

"Well, you know that bit in close encounters," he said.

"Which bit?" said Tommy.

"The bit where he's making mountains out of his potato rice," he replied.

"Oh yes," nodded Tommy almost thoughtfully.

"Constantly driven to create structures of beauty from soggy nanoparticles, for some unknown reason. Well, my whole life has been like that."

"You used to work for corps though, didn't you, hun," said Gina.

"Well, yeah, kind of. It was much the same with them all in the end though."

"Yup," she said. "They seem to have a different view on it all than us. It's a strange one. They can never seem to get over the power and control thing."

"Yeah, I put a lot into them, you know what I'm like, I work for the kinship, not for the money. Well, seemed ok for a while, and was interesting and fun. But then, they just seemed to go all weird on me. I think maybe because I didn't go around blaming someone else for things that went wrong they saw that as the problem. Funny how some people react when you cover other people's backs. What was that lark all about."

"It sort of spiralled down from there. Some I even provided nourishment for and invited them into my home. Shame they just got greedy. Started off where I'd do clips and wait for feedback, and three months later I'd get an ack back complaining it wasn't done so I wouldn't get credited. Carried on like that for a few projects, and that coupled with the continued bombardment of stuff which was just nothing to do with me kind of spoilt it all. "

"Did he go or was he pushed," said Tommy.

"Yeah, a common one so I'm told," he said. "Saves them on licensing fees and contract overheads I hear. Guess that's why they call it freelancing, everyone is trying to knock you off your steed. Although you don't kinda expect it when you're just out for a canter in the park with 'friends'."

"They can't all be like that though, did you try any others?" smiled Gina optimistically.

"Of course. Tried a few others, but none really ever got the foster parent thing. Some just appeared from nowhere, trying to sniff round and find out what it was that I had. Others tried to copy what they thought were the solutions, but were merely five year old techs from long gone."

"Bloody shame," chuckled Tommy, half in sympathy, half in extreme piss-take.

"Worse thing was, I kept giving them all free advice and explaining it all time after time after time, but they didn't listen, and even more so, when it all went wrong as I had just given them, they just scapegoated me for it too. Double thwack. Kinda makes you wonder."

"Yeah, what's that all about," said Gina.

"So in the end I just didn't bother trying to give any of my babies to any of them. After all, what's the real point in making creds that you don't want, and an offshoot of it being that you are funding corps who's morality you don't necessary follow, and are only interested in just making a fast buck rather than providing a quality solution. Just taking your carefully nurtured offspring and exploiting them in cages of code. Letting them propagate in ways you don't believe in."

"You should have kunted them!" sniggered Tommy.

"Not really my style. I could have floored their corps, but hey, that would have just created hassle for some other poor sucker, who would then have been in a bad mood and hassled some other poor sucker, and so on," he said.

"You could have niggled them with minor hacks, real small ones, multi-streamed annoyance ones," said Tommy, in a playful way.

"Nah, where's the skill in that."

"What about litigation?" said Gina.

"Again, not really my style, it'd probably have cost loads in law fees. Well, not unless I was having a really bad day, or needed a bit of entertainment."

Tommy nodded.

"Also, they sort of did it subtly over a while, so there were plenty of comms which could have wrong sided me if it came down to splitting hairs."

"Yeah, like the one that said, 'Lose the ego and don't treat your next programmer like a kunt and you'll be fine'," she said laughing, and they all joined in.

"So what did you do?" asked Gina.

"Just walked away, just walked away," he smiled.

"You still code though, babes, don't you," she said reassuringly, rubbing the top half of his arm with her hand.

"Of course, honey," he winked. "I haven't forgotten how."

"Yeah, we sometimes thank you for a little tweakage here and there," smiled Tommy.

"Indeed," he nodded, arms out wider slightly in a hug like motion. "That's how we always stay one step ahead of the isoteric hounds. I save my best codage for those who I love."

"Yay! Yay! Ack-ack codage away!" cheered Gina.

"Frustrating though. I think ultimately it's incredibly disappointing that no-one simply wanted to work together. A massive missed opportunity for them really. Oh well, I'll just keep those best systems to myself."

"Maybe just as well if they can't get over their power and control, exploitation thing. No point draining yourself to over your limits if the relationship is parasitic and not symbiotic," she said, trying to garner some sympathy.

"Yeah, save the codage for another day," he said.

"There, there, hun," said Gina, noticing her comforting of him.

"Hm, it did feel a bit like having to dump a girlfriend who I cared about a lot because she had cheated," he acknowledged. "Although what probably hurt more was having to delay the rave for a while, as some others who were probably linked withdrew too."

"Shame though, but that's yer basic economics," said Tommy. "There's a limited amount of money which is mostly redistributed. Every economy drives for growth, in wealth, resources, and thus population. Some elected go for the fad of selling out the young with debt from their Cybertechnics and their housing costs. All creating something out of nothing, and forcing them to work later in life to pay for it all."

"Doesn't have to be like that though, imagine a world where we all lived as one."

"All business is mostly a pyramid scheme."

"That's the problem when the elected start going down

the same morality route as the corps. They make it so there's no direct point of access, all of it hidden behind levels of abstraction with no-one to have any individual responsibility over anything."

"Yeah, reminds me of a clip I did once. The corp it was for was one of those consultancy project management firms," he said.

"A cutter and shutter?" laughed Tommy.

"Mostly. The irony didn't escape me when they tried to get tech support from the firm they had just sold off. Seems they sold off too much and it took months to get any sort of ack back from them."

"Well, money's never been a problem in your business has it, sweetie," teased Gina.

"I've never been told I was the cheapest. I'm often told I'm the best," he said.

"You ain't no ten dollar hooker are you, darlin'," she laughed.

"I'm just misunderstood," he smirked.

"There comes a time, in the life of every genius," said The Captain. "Where they reach the understanding that their work may not be understood in their own lifetime."

"Now," continued The Captain. "The main problem here is of abandonment in the face of pointlessness. But, on consideration, we all owe as much to the future as we do the past. Knowledge learnt, Keplared, and the output fed to the next input."

"Yeah, bit like goghy I guess," he said. "If only these bastards would look at my paintings, I don't think anyone gets it, fickle kunts.'"

"Makes you wonder though doesn't it, he was most prolific in the final days. Kinda makes you think if he knew but thought he'd hold on and get as much out as possible."

"Yeah, but apparently it was his periods of lucidity in which he created."

"Hmm, maybe. But perhaps he was only painting what he had seen."

"Does the genius cause the madness, or does the madness come from being a genius, the frustration at not being able to do anything with it."

"Yes," said The Captain sternly. "Be wary of false enlightenment."

Even though they all thought, 'here we go again', they still kind of shivered and shuddered, and even he moved about a bit uncomfortably in his seating.

"One such false enlightenment is when it is used as justification," said The Captain.

"It's a bit like psychology, really it's only someone's opinion. Two different experts most likely have two different opinions, different views and different constructs influencing their response."

"Just because an anomaly doesn't fit the pattern doesn't mean it's an anomaly. It's often simply that the model is wrong, limited by an artificial band of personal assumptions and false base calculations."

"A little knowledge is a dangerous thing, be careful it's not just your own opinion. Just because it isn't your way doesn't mean it isn't right, and remember whatever it is you think you may know, chances are, someone else knows it too. Make sure it isn't just dictated by the limits of your experiences."

"Yes. I saw a clip once where some guy was going on about his latest theory. Well, he may well have been right, but really he just used the evidence that he showed to prove his theory, with no other real counter argument."

"It was based around paintings from some ancient civilisation or something. The guy's theory was that they believed that the heavenly world was opposite in nature to the earthly world. Thus he had decided that the paintings of non-fertile sex were done in order to promote fertility in the earthly world by depicting the opposite in the heavenly world."

"Well, he may well have been right."

"Yeah, who knows."

"Exactly. They might evenly as well just been a bunch of perves."

"Yup, or maybe just showing really early forms of contraception."

"Maybe they were just really into blowjobs."

"Yeah, 'gaming or porn'," laughed Tommy.

"The problem these days is that everyone thinks they're so clever, and that we have invented everything."

"Whereas really it's just the same stuff each civilisation has discovered for itself as others have. Take greek poetry with it's hexameters and stuff. The story, the song, the intonation, the rules, all intricate and beautiful."

"Yes, but a lot of those rules were added on in later stories though, some of the original tellers didn't stick to the form so rigidly."

"Guess if you're going to have a genre it needs to be defined by it's rules, and then people wanting to replicate the success or create in that style have something to go by."

"'Cept for rig-boy here, he just whistles 'I did it my way'," laughed Gina.

"Most of it evolves naturally though doesn't it. Like elected systems. If a bunch move away, soon they will need direction, and a leader and rules will emerge. A natural route to the solution. Natural selection or selection of the natural."

"Not like the perceived democracy of public message boards then, they only moderate and display those they want to."

"Like the two questions of nature or nurture, God or science, opinion and ego. Bit of both if you ask me," he said.

"Well, I can't sit around all day philosing with you youngsters," said The Captain suddenly, and got up to leave. They all gave him hugs and cheery goodbyes.

"I know I've been mostly silent this afternoon in the pub," said The Captain, slowly. "But I do listen to what you all have to say in your own little viewpoints. The fact that you discuss does encourage me so, you know."

"We know, pops," said Tommy.

"Yay," said Gina, kissing The Captain's leathery cheek.

"Bye-bye for now," waved The Captain.

"Byes!" they all chorused.

"It is sometimes sad for The Captain," he said. "Even with my long time with him, there's loads of stuff from our late night chats that I just don't get. Then all I can do is look at him and know that he knows that no-one else may understand what he is talking about for another few hundred years. The frustration of that alone must be one keplar head-fuck."

They all nodded. Not that they could do anything about it though.

"The problem with being a genius is that amongst others you either look insane or an idiot, and amongst other geniuses merely average," he said.

"Yeah, and as we all have that instinctive drive to communicate with each other in order to pass on knowledge and experience, with The Captain, the difficulty arises as there's no-one to pass on knowledge to," said Tommy.

"What is the master without an apprentice," she said.

"Merely a slave to his genius," he acked. "Maybe one day one of us will be good enough."

They all took another drink from their drinks in their own manner, hoping that would bring some enlightenment.

"Just do it here, babes," said Gina, motioning to Tommy and lifting her palms upward and widening her fingers in encouragement.

"It's a fine weight norwegian tot glass. Pure glass by the seems of it, no impurities, engraved manufacturer's seal and elected warranty and dosage message marks," said Tommy.

Dipping into his pocket, he passed the cyanoacrylate to Tommy, who turned his back slightly to cover his dubious actions, and shook the plastic bottle to render its engineered solution into a steady mixture. Dashing the tot glass as though salting it to taste, Tommy applied the carefully prepared solution with not a great deal of care.

"Easy this stuff," said Gina. "Even a monkey could use it."

Tommy just glared and held out his hand towards Gina, while she helpfully blew the liquid dry.

Gina pincered the adapted mascara brush into between Tommy's thumb and index finger, and Tommy rolled it across the surface with care and skill. Once the fingerprint copy had been collected to its full extent, Gina held out the container for Tommy to pop it into. Job done, sample collected. Flicking it up a little like a fielder triumphant in her catch, Gina nipped it in into her cotton blouse pocket, giving the outside of the garment a tap, tap, on its deposit, just for safety's sake, securing and reassuring its presence.

"Tick tock," she said. "Time to go home. Come on kids, let's go."

He and Tommy collected up their empty drinking vessels, murmured over to the dark wooden bar, and set them down gently. Thanking the staff gleefully, they all departed The Royal Hussar, and made their way back homeward to end another day.

Chapter Five – Day trip

"So, yay, how many clicks have I just driven all yous then?" asked Gina, parking up in a rock and a sway.

"'Bout two hundred I'd say, hun," she said.

"So, you all love me then, yay?" smiled Gina.

"Yes, Gina, we all love you," he said.

"No, I mean, you all love me, don't you," blinked Gina.

"What now, Gina," guessed Tommy.

Tommy didn't so much care as have immediate concern for which was going to cost him more, creds from Jonny or teared out mascara.

"Tickets."

By the time Jonny and Sheila pulled up in the lovebug wagon, the rf feeds were already initiating. As long as they all stayed within ten metres of Jonny's central frequency ticket, they could belly hop in on his waves and trick in through the system. Once inside, there should be enough open tags presenting themselves ready for the gang to pop in on anything they fancied. Not the kind of hack they'd do normally of course, they paid their way, but hey, they had tickets, just not in their pockets. Only thing was, Jonny was metering, and Gina knew it.

"Ok, ok, I'll feed half," said Tommy. "I know I should've reminded you, baby, it's a sharer."

Shit, if Tommy was halving already, what had he forgotten.

As they swifted through the gated entrances, Gina did as Gina did. Drawing everyone's attention to the two young girls having their goldfish moment, they all smiled as the shining light reflected around the bagged water, the golden fish, and their happy glowing faces.

He smiled both inwardly and outwardly as the soft sound of the bell tinkled in the distance. A new young driver experiencing their first journey on the Gus Honeybun rail tracked transport. They all smiled past, the joy in the faces of the co-pilots not yet old enough to control delighting themselves with the bell ringing duties of the engine, bringing replenishment to their tired hearts.

They all looked at each other smiling. They didn't need to tell each other which gameclip they were going to go on first, they all knew. It was always the same one. He shuffled along at the back while she danced forward up front.

"C'est ne pas un livre v8.3," said the sign. Good. There wasn't a queue. A few seats left in the multisystem multirig. They settled down and firmed in, the rig fielding their thoughts in a whirlwind of carnival firings.

"Version 8.3 rocks," said Gina.

"Yeah, definitely the best. v2 was the hardest to develop, took a lot to be in a good enough mood to code out what was already written in imagination," he said.

From the blacked out distance came the shape, spiralling over itself in a blur, unidentifiable at its range. As the white dot flew nearer it became clearer, and the strands of luminescence coalesced into view.

A white rectangle, glowing in beauty yet modest in its display. Perfectly formed, perfectly proportioned. The width, height and depth set at the natural equation of 111, 175 and 8.

The obelisk shone into construction and opened like a story book. Taking on their illumination, the words glowed their strange green and blue glow, cascading out and into the participants of the game, becoming bright white, almost ultraviolet and transparent. The page numbers blowing the sails of years like the wind, the speed and strength in translation translacing meaning into world view.

The route through the clip was in truth navigated by the observer. Whilst concise in their meanings, the individual interpretation was always going to be biased by its own needs.

Tacking and pivoting in their own waves through the oceanic size of the abstracted systems, they flowed through the script in their courses, each racing or jumping as was their want. Playing back and watching from the different geos and egos, some used the lightpencils to correct the mistakes that we all inevitably make for ourselves in our lifetimes, others merely weighed themselves against the words.

After the clips had looped back so they had another chance to read what they had missed, the rig retracted and they came out from the inner once more.

"A beautiful piece of contemporary existentialism, capturing the innate conflict in the co-existence of the triasm between the aesthetic, ethical and spiritual dimensions," said Jonny. It was one of Jonny's more familiar matched responses, but they still enjoyed the listening, and Jonny definitely still enjoyed the telling.

"Don't take it all too seriously, it's just for fun, for entertainment," he said. "Some might even say it had humour in it."

He was checking a couple of readouts from a palmpiece that seemed to have appeared from nowhere. He tutted.

"I can't believe so few people fill out the user contributed notes," he sighed. "Oh well, guess they're all too busy hacking."

"Hack it up, babes," she said, and kissed him, and then gave his hand such a drag as to indicate they were going.

Maybe she didn't like the fact that he had opened up the maintenance panel and wired in, just to check how the readouts were listing. Well, he could check it from base easy enough, but where was the fun in that.

He cleaned up quickly, as was the joy with Jonny's custom insertion pegs, and let her drag him away from one source of fun to another.

Skipping from gameclip to gameclip, they let the joy of

the moment take hold, and played free of care whilst time allowed them.

Strolling over to the familiar stall, he dropped the tokens and scooped up the projectiles in a single, swift motion. With a skim of his wrist he tossed the ball to her after her eyes had flash acked his challenge.

She hesitated for an instant with the trepidation of the coming test of skill. Her delicate animation reminded him of one of the first times that they had met up. She had let slip her veil of hiding from him for a gentle moment, and he had seen a scared little girl, who briefly managed a nervous smile and a cheeky giggle.

Pulling her arm back in a pivot like a trebuchet, Gina's encouragement signaled the release of the rasp and the projectile was launched. Acceleration and accuracy that would have made a ninja jealous.

"Guess who's daddy couldn't wait for a boy," she smiled.

"Ah, never mind, honey. Guess it has its uses," sympathised Gina, and gave Tommy a 'just you remember that for future reference' kind of look.

He took up his turn and launched his missile without much fuss, but with a fair amount of skill.

"No daddy with daughters," he said. "But three older brothers. Plus the mates of the three older brothers. Which meant the ratio of batting to fielding for me was such that a a long accurate throw was quickly developed. Through survival rather than skill or expert coaching. Although 'chuck it this end' might amount to trade secrets in some quarters."

The sets of coconuts knocked from their perches. Counting up the tickets they had collected over several visits, they were pleased they had enough for their prize. A styled ice-bucket, brown leather casing and horse-shaped miniature trophies as decoration. Functional and aesthetic, just the job for the task planned.

That hunger feeling had been there a little while, and had it not been for such excitement they might have had to interrupt their playing sooner. Their thoughts of hunger matched to the environment they were in. That special taste only found here. That beautiful burger. The taste of cooking that was only from that place of sanctuary. That certain oil and that certain taste of years of cooking on that metal plate, much tastier than the sterilised standard templated constructions available in midtown. Not only did it have high nutritional content, but it had character. Proper food. Texture and taste. Smell and scent. The joy of the hunt, the kill and the feast, all encapsulated in that beautiful burger with real cheese.

The sliding doors kicked open. Although they weren't the most elvish of constructions, they performed the task. Their main aim was accomplished, by automatic opening nobody needed to press their hands against the door. Thus, when everybody came to eat they weren't merely just eating what each other had just smeared onto the door push panels.

They strolled across the shining alternatively tiled floor to the counter, and gazed at the fast-food menu in all its glory, its pictures and its confusion mimicking an instinctive choice response to spur addiction and selection.

"You're such a slut," she said to him. "You really are, you know."

He had positioned himself to the side of the service counter, as per usual. While they were all amusing themselves with choice and subsequent wait for harvest, he had other lures of expedience to satisfy his itinerary. Sooner or later one of the staff would go through the service door.

"There you go, enjoy your meals," smiled the service assistant from behind the counter, in what would seem full templated script response mode, but in fact was genuine and with natural conversational feeling.

"Thanks honeybun," smiled back Gina. Carrying the parcels back outside, they unwrapped them whilst seated on the wooden easel benches.

"59779" he said.

"You are such a hack slut," she scolded. "You really are. You just can't help yourself can you. It's like everywhere we go, every deck, every pad, every scanner. All just another bit of hack skirt for you to flirt with."

He knew she was right, but somehow it didn't seem to matter. So he was a hack slut. Nothing wrong with that, really. Tapping away into his palmpiece he added the code to the database that the members kept for themselves. There weren't many places that they didn't know how to gain access through.

The oars slid slowly and smoothly in tune with the ripple of the water.

"There's no use in giving it one of your 'success is achieved by proficiency in the medium rather than the proficiency of the participant' rants, just put some effort into it!" laughed Gina.

"Just a little bit more, you pair. Then you can have some of this chococloud dreamwhip cream cake!" she shrilled, joining in with the comedy and tapping on her container.

"Row? This isn't a stream it's a lake!" said Tommy.

"Then make your own current, dear boy, dear boy," spoke and sang Gina.

Drawing up to the tiny island, they smiled as the weeping trees came into fuller view, their delicate beauty floating gently in the breeze. Occasionally a piece of its blossom would be released from its mooring into the air streams, and glide a path outwards, drifting downwards. They noticed how the steady variations in the undulating wind and the fairy crafted shapes of the blossom interplayed in such a way that the random factors created a pattern of coverage, carpeting the whole island in a soft dotted painting of petals.

He never quite understood why everything had to be in those strange containers these days. They were sort of plastic shrink wrappers, only they were more like some sort of organic paper polycomposite. He ought to look it up one cycle, but hey, who had the time until the data was needed to be known.

Both he and Tommy would have just picked up their slices and been half way through by now in one bite, had she not produced those sweet spoon-fork things of hers from her gadget bag.

Just as well as it turned out, for although the cake looked like spongy stuff, it was more like pure cream and ice cream fluff. So it had a lovely light airy sponge texture, but was even more melty in the mouth, a vanilla and chococloud swirl main centre, with a more solid biscuit chocolate base, some sort of thick caramel spread roofing, topped off with curly flakes of both milk and white chocolate.

"Maybe all that advertising from old wasn't all lies," said Tommy, not feeling slightly sick until after the last mouthful, although it quickly disappeared again, so maybe it had been due to his rate of consumption. Come to look at it, Tommy was the only one who had completed. Still, it didn't matter, he had enjoyed it fair enough. Maybe those girls from the ads had the right idea, much better shoveling that lovely stuff into your mouth that having it rammed with, actually, thought change instigated.

They rested and lazed in the warm sun, amongst the green grass and the white and rose petals. In their stillness the world moved on and around them, and in their relaxed concentration they watched every minute beautiful glory.

It had been a good day and good fun, the best place to practice skills they might need one day, amongst friends in a relaxed environment. Well, with a bit of edginess and subversion, giving that they were riding on floating tickets.

Chapter Six - Imbalance

He ticked off the rig, and sighed as the view returned. Twisting back in and realigning. Hiccups. She was going to kick his ass for this one. It's not so much that everything wasn't clean, as much as it hadn't been cleaned. Not a creation of mess, just a fading through time and a gathering of desolance.

Hardly his fault though really. It was just that pursuing his work to the depth that he wanted meant taking long periods of concentration. He had never been one for being a nine-to-fiver. It wasn't just the routine that he couldn't do, but that the timing seemed all wrong and too short a sync. It took a lot longer than a typical nine till five to rev up, let alone get into the zone required for autocompletions.

He guessed the difficulties arose when the doubling up carried on over too long a period. If the suppressant was both being used for codal zoning and for relaxation, then it was easy to see how the ratings could become transparent.

She sure would bitch at him, he was way out. He had been spending far too long in the rig. Not that it really mattered, but obviously real interfacing was tricky.

Sometimes he didn't even bother to readjust back in properly, like you do when you wake up in the night needing a pee, but try and not open your eyes so as to pretend you're still asleep. So it was with him, he figured he wasn't going to be in the real long enough to warrant the slow down and speed up again to get back into the rig.

He stood there watching. The events unfolding before his eyes. Slowly, seemingly scripted, elongated over a stretching putty of time. That was the problem with the real, sometimes it was just too fucking slow, and it became painful waiting for the delay in reality.

"There you go, cheers," said the assistant.

"Thanks," he let out at last. Although only seconds in

the real, it seemed an age in his mind flickering, it's speed reading every detail, seeing every particle flow in the air, and every rarefaction of vibrating sound that would become listened speech. He sometimes thought it a pity he couldn't see round corners though.

He left the transport commercial outlet and swooped round the corner. Then he noticed how quiet it was. How silent. His thoughts in his head were louder than the noise from the surrounding environment. Not that they were loud, but just fast, the buzz they created making a greater sound than the emptiness around him.

"Pomum aurantium"

Hanging on the edges of other people's lives
Watching their egos and battling its lies
Pret tic cal um mann na
Um ma na ka

He couldn't show up at The Captain's without a gift, so he had braved the terrors of the 24-hour store. Who knows what kind of weirdo one would come across in those places, and that's working behind the counter let alone the characters that could be found in the place.

Everyone knew that stores had a kind of hierarchical structure which dictated which you'd end up visiting depending on how vague your isoteric mappings to consensual reality were. Not the marketing segment tailored brands found in midtown, as essential supplies were different. Not like the luxury items on offer there, even if they were in their branded bands of affordability and accepted level in the aesthetic chain.

It would start at being the level of your typical store, average stock, average range, something of the vital supplies for everyone. Anyone could visit, and that's were the real mainstream was, even if some tried to differentiate themselves in dress or stature, they were pretty much of a muchness. Then it might go to the local outlets. At least you'd recognise the staff, so there couldn't be any type of plants laid down in wait to catch you out if you were having a tricky moment.

Beyond that, the familiarity might not be so welcome. The need to indicate a basic pattern matched response, all too difficult when the Asotrerials are really off, and there's no fooling those who know you.

To then what is left, the 24-hour open access store. Those places always seemed to draw the type of stereotype that rose from slumber at twilight, irrespective of what time period the day was actually in. Still, done now, packets retrieved.

The Captain sat whilst he stood, pacing.

"If I have to go in to do this season's asotrerials then all they are going to do is destroy what I believe in and replace it with something else," he said. "I've been in that room with the mirror window before, as you know."

"Yes, I know," murmured The Captain. "The number of dawns you've been pushed through some would say is slightly excessive."

"It isn't paranoia, cross paranoia or anticipatory paranoia. It's not like that. And it isn't the reality suppressant, as you know," he explained.

"Yes, I know," nodded The Captain. "Always used to irk me as a youngster that one. When I'd be trying to explain a new theory to some of the overseers, they would just say that they would have to refer to the wacky charts."

"It's similar to an infinite game of hack whispers," he continued. "I am able to link just about anything together, which is great for cross-connectivity and referencing, but it's a total bastard when I attempt to calculate any sort of advanced keplar autocompletion."

Pacing up and down, he continued.

"It also makes anticipatory sentencing very difficult," he said. "I can pre-calculate the end of most sentences prior to them being sounded out. Couple this with a bit of referencing, and after a while it's pretty easy to naturally see what people's constructed realities are."

He looked at The Captain, hoping to see some sort of look of understanding.

"Continue," nodded The Captain.

"Yes," he said, hoping the ack was genuine and not just leading. Not that it mattered, the databurst had started and it was flowing out. "After a while I can see what books they've read, what clips they've seen, what episodics they like, and the main media routes they feed from. Almost a narrow banded input hack whispers or hack media source, a repeated input response of someone else's opinion."

"I see," said The Captain, instantly wishing to have uttered a better phrase in the current circumstances.

"Hm," he pressed the air from his mouth. "So, anticipatory relays and routed opinion. Like when you look at pages of code or text and read them as an image, the words and syntax forming presequenced pictogramatic sequences."

"Ah, the pictographic construction methods," tutted in The Captain, rubbing his chin earnestly. "Yes, we've discussed those before I believe. I think you were right by the way, the bit of both is best in patterned learning there."

"Indeed," he agreed, distracted from the active thread for a moment to complete another reasoning.

"The way your Cybertechnic taught early language comprehension has biased your interleaved interpretation methodologies," said The Captain. "As your base was the block reading method, you were able to add onto it the phonetic method in order to achieve your particular accelerated interpretation."

"I like to call it 'phonetic blocks'," he said. "Or perhaps maybe 'segmented phonetic pictocabulary', if you've cycles to spare."

"So you've been continuing your work with thought recording and retrieval then," said The Captain, placing his hands on his knees and sitting up slightly.

"Thought capture is a bit of a holy grail of mine, as you know," he replied. "The ability to be able to capture what I'm thinking when in the rig, forge instantaneous memory during the top keplar cycles, before the solution disappears again from view with the end of the reaction. But that isn't it either. It's not like it's one thing, it's a whole bunch, all cascading in on themselves and conflicting."

"Remember it's your brain that produces the solution, not the reality suppressant," said The Captain. "The suppressant just helps you relax. Don't fall into the trap of just tapping the suppressant and expecting it to come up with the answer, you still have to think. That's the key, maintaining the thought process through the suppressant."

"It's like if you read something," he said. "And at a later date it's in a conversation which covers similar subjects, it's highly likely that you will merely repeat what you've read without interpretation and expressing it as your own opinion, indeed, the listeners could interpret it as your own opinion. It's also highly probable that if you encounter a different source repeating the same read subject, the information will be designated as trivial and obvious, and in addition the relayer a poor source of information."

Continuing his pacing, he continued his tale.

"I've been working later in the evening, nights, and doing weekenders again as well," he said. "It's almost like it's much better and easier to function when the rest of society is relaxed and not giving out it's hectic buzz and static."

"So when is the last time you felt relaxed?" enquired The Captain.

"Relaxed?" he said.

"Yeah, relaxed."

"In what way?" he said.

The Captain sighed. "In a relaxed way! You know. Not tense."

"You know I don't really relax when I'm working," he said. "So that's not a system status I really recall."

"No wonder you're shy of Asotrerials at the moment then," muttered The Captain.

"Yes, I've been in that room with the mirror window," he retorted. "In my early years I used to go there thinking that they were actually going to say something useful."

The Captain let himself let out a little laugh. He chuckled too, the irony wasn't lost on him either.

"But, as you know, they're not really interested in solving the problem, but merely creating an aesthetic solution. Paint over the cracks."

"Yes," said The Captain. "That's really the facility that they are aimed at."

"They just try and break what you believe in and try and replace it with an alternate falseness of consensual reality," he continued, the pacing gathering to a race as his explanation grew.

The Captain nodded with a knowingness.

"Once I went there and they gave it the old time patterning one, which may suit their purposes, but it doesn't mine," he continued. "Saying that I should give up cola, caffeine, nicotine, and go to bed at 9 and get up at 6. Well, that's just utterly fucking ridiculous."

The Captain allowed himself a fuller, belly driven laugh. "I can see that it was the 'go to bed at 9 and get up at 6' that really turned you right off it."

"Ok, I can see that's funny," he said. "But really, it's

only advice aimed at making the anomaly fit the curve, when really it's the fact that the curve is only a best fit that's the problem."

The Captain was still laughing a little, but acking out that he was listening and Keplaring what was being discussed.

"Nine-to-five might suit the factory owners," he said. "But it's shite all use to me. Society merely becomes a structured system of false enlightenments, varying from bulk whispers, opinion, advertising, to manipulation and control. I know all the little conspiracy theories and ego-rationalisations keep everyone busy, but what good is it to me. Everyone just having their own conversations dropping in phrases which they think are important. A twenty-four hour sleep segment is so wrong. Two four or five hour segments is much better."

The Captain belted out a roar. "The afternoon nap!"

"Look, it doesn't have to be afternoon nap, the timing isn't the key, it's the displacement. And it takes much longer than twenty-four hours to rev up into a decent keplar cycle, sometimes sleep is the last thing you want."

"I see that," said The Captain. "Allow me my fun."

"Yeah, ok, I wouldn't deprive you of that," he said. "But straight away they're coming in with the constructs. Making you wait in the room off the corridor, as who knows who strolls by, staring. Enough to make anyone feel uncomfortable. And later, in the second room they have a pentagram dotted out using drawing pins behind the questioner."

"Shape conspiracy matching straight away," agreed The Captain.

"It's all right," he continued. "But I've had my brain washed too many times to be bothered with it all again."

"And I know what you're going to come out with next," said The Captain.

"Yup," he said

"Yes," said The Captain. "And at some point they will discuss your reality suppressant consumption."

"Indeed," he said. "Doesn't that just irk you so damn much!"

"Always and whenever I hear it, true is true," sighed The Captain.

"Social use is no different than anything else," he ranted.

"Moderation in all things," wised The Captain.

"Yeah. It's the tone of it all though isn't it," he said. "Blaming reality suppressant when it's just a symptom, a counter play for the real problem."

"Hmm," deeply sounded The Captain.

"And as for ceasing," he said, gaining into full flow. "Well, that's just silly."

"I know that," said The Captain.

"To remove the cure for the symptom doesn't remove the cause of the symptom, does it," he said.

"I know what you mean with that one," said The Captain.

"Whoever did that clip on the non-physical dependence was just silly," he said. "We all know that there's the brain ache, the hyperness as things are too slow without the processing realm of the suppressant. And as for the sweating palms, well, sweating everything, it's just general temperature regulation fuck-city."

"We know this now," said The Captain.

"All that before we get into the real depth of it all too. The base that makes it all work and tic," he said. "The fact that we are wired differently. The reality suppressant helps us to think, makes our synapses fire in our natural vibration. Raising the excitatory state of the synapses so that connections are more readily formed."

"Ok. As Jonny would say, what's the download?" said The Captain, whilst not disliking the conversation keen to make more rapid progress.

"Where do I start," he laughed. "The frustration of telling advice, and then being scapegoated when it isn't taken and things go wrong. Nobody contributes anything back to what I am talking to them about. They just repeat back to me what I have already told them previously on the subject. This becomes incredibly frustrating for some reason."

"They've listened to what you have said though, haven't they, if they remember it to repeat it back," answered The Captain.

"I'm not sure they remember that they are repeating it, but the problem is that it's just a repeat, and no attempt at processing or extrapolation has been made. It's like my thought cycles are continually drained in managing something, and that I'm unable to recharge. I don't get any rest, just fall into unconsciousness when I've given out too much, only to wake again, and as I can't sleep forced to do it all again."

"I see," said The Captain.

"Then I don't just wake up, I really wake up. Not like a gradual tuning into awakeness with that period of sleepy haziness, but a shock wide-eyed wake up with no time to catch a breath."

"Heightened overwatch senses," said The Captain.

"I've got all the fucking pieces, and I can see where they all fucking fit, but I'm so fucking drained I haven't the energy to move them from where they are to where they need to be arranged for everyone else to see the solution to the puzzle."

He paused in his pacing for a moment. "And that's fucking frustrating."

"Go on," said The Captain, gesturing for him to be seated. He shook his head.

"I've done with the lures of nature and expedience, I

could never be assed with the lures of power. I've been out and got the golden fleece, what a distraction that was. So here I am, at the same place, with still no solution. It doesn't seem to matter what I do, it all reacts and changes and doesn't alter a thing, like a groundhog day completely dependent on the actions of other people, with my own actions never influencing an instant."

"Non-progressive Keplaring," said The Captain.

"And when I try and multiphase it, everyone just keeps repeating what I am saying," he said.

"Repeating what your are saying?" said The Captain.

"Yes. Écoute et répète."

He shoved his hands deep into his pockets, and The Captain pondered on his keyphrase for a brief moment.

"Or worse than that," he continued. "Repeating back to me what somebody else has told them. The externals reflecting a non-relevant pattern matched response."

"I am aware of your problem," said The Captain. "I've rigged up some new wave reflexes that I'd like you to try."

"Ok," he said.

"This should help us better understand the isoteric structure, and thus ultimately help you when you come to the big hack," explained The Captain.

"The big hack?"

"Yes, the big hack. We've known it was coming. So let's formulate it and see what we can do," said The Captain, setting up the reverse-feed abstract visualisation unit.

He fell into the rig and let the programming run through his mind. A shared face. Three vertices each watching each other. Triangularly spiralling into infinity. A gate. A guard from the inner and a guard from the outer. Eight faces, three shared bonds.

"Hmmm," said The Captain. "Your's seems a little different. Most lock the door on the outside."

Chapter Seven – pop

"You're just a fucking barcode!" she shouted, at and through him. Ouch, that must have hurt. Through the door and across the rug she glided like a leaf, straight in for the slap. Not a hesitation or a halt, justitia ex tempore.

Oops. As soon as she had completed the impact of her performance she had regretted it. He didn't even attempt any delicate maneuver to block or lessen the impact of the blow by siding his cheek. He just sat there motionless, and the full force of her twatting hit him sharply.

She sank down to his seated level, bending her legs to the floor gracefully until she was kneeling. Massaging the sting from his face slowly, first with fingers and then with the back of her hand, hoping to warm the coldness of her impact.

Shit. She hadn't gone for him like that since he borrowed her rig that time, and accidentally got that crumb of chocolate wedged in it somehow.

"Sorry, baby," she said, her eyes burning a path towards his.

"It's ok," he said, and motioned what would have been a smile. He took her other hand in his, and stroked it with his thumb.

"It wasn't so clear what the sitch was this time," she said. "I thought you'd just been pissing around as usual. I didn't know it was so big an isoteric structure."

She turned and looked at The Captain, who stood there briefly, nodding. The Captain had orange2 flagged her, which usually meant he had just been too playful. This time however, she now realised it had all been a warm up for the big hack.

As she kissed his forehead softly, she could almost feel the buzz of his mind beneath his skin, the crackle of processing writhing inside. His eyes were moving and changing their focus in rapidity, echoing the switching and analysing of his synapses.

Helping him up from the chair of the rig, she noticed he was weakened slightly by the hack.

"If The Captain ever plugs you into one of those," he said, pointing to the now resting unit. "Start to worry."

Noticing his weakening, and ignoring his glances of annoyance, The Captain handed her one of his special recovery sachets. They were a bit like the packs marathon runners would get handed after crossing the line, only these were salts for the brain rather than the body.

 Leaving through the door, the sight of the transport was enough to pad him a little strength, and he tensed his legs, and shrugged off her walking frame mannerisms with his shoulders. It was some fucking wagon, the monster truck.

Standing there like both a 1 and a 0, the Land Rover Defender aroused that certain instinctive edge of admiration in both her and him. The power and the reliability. The craftsmanship of the timeless classic. The barded mount for les chevaliers d'honneur.

"Yes," she said. "I brought the monster truck."

"I am pleased," he said.

She winked and smiled. "Like my lover. Always guaranteed to keep the power going right until the end, always gets the job done."

"Winch or rack today for you, madam," he cracked.

A moment of laughing, and then the standing there before the monument of engineering. Dressed in the glory of Nato matt black, the roof rack equipped, the sidestep bars adding their promise of stability, and the checker plated outline highlighting the E3 quality we all seek. Enough lighting to find one of Gina's earrings in the worst of fields, and the spare wheel on the bonnet for that final female touch. Yes, that female touch. Wheel on the middle of the bonnet so the rear door wasn't so weighted when it was swung open on a slope. Handy when hauled up on a steep incline, water up to the knees, in the rain. Not like the parking aid on those sweet small toy jeeps.

Starting smoothly as soon as it was called upon, the engine exponentialled into motion. Tommy was in the hot seat, with the blinged out Gina at his side.

They both sat in the rear seat, more hackgear behind them. A blanket and her hugs warming him from the acid chills of the previous hack. Normally he'd have a rest up after that big an isoteric analysis, but the game had already started and there was no key to press for pause.

Day turned to night, and more blankets were unbagged as Gina and Tommy took turns to pilot the transport. The jagged blur of the out of town road lighting hazed in colours in his eyes if they opened on a less deep cycle. She made him as comfortable as she could, and he took his turn too.

As she tickled her fingers across his forehead, she sang her improvised song in a whisper.

"Set my love"

I set my love awaiting, waiting for you,
Throughout the seasons darkness, forever I knew.

A teared dewdrop shining, for the morning sun,
My timeless pixie armour; waiting for you.

He slept a quiet sleep in the lullaby rocking of the transport, dreaming softly of her love.

He cast back the blanket and sprang into life like a daisy opening for the sun in a speeded up clip. He was in an excited rush. Before the transport had settled to a halt, he had tricked the door latch and was ready to disembark. He danced over to the grass in a kind of side-stepping sprint motion, a lower stance and a firm press down of acceleration.

Once nestled on the springy greenness of the wild growth, he opened the satellite uplink panels and kicked the palmpiece into action from its battery saving slumber.

The primary assault hack was a beautiful Coldiltz double he had prepared earlier. On a previous hack into the system he had faked an escape, the detectors not realising he was still there for roll call, so when the real escape occurred the numbers they counted weren't true.

Stealthing in under his false log count hack, he drifted into the rigged centres. Lying in wait for a while until the timing cycles coalesced, then an under curve swoop up, and the lock unbeeped.

Tommy was playing this one for show. Jonny had rigged him up with some touch sensors, so that when Tommy clicked his fingers the shuriken grunt of code took out what remained of the surveillance system in unison with the debeep.

The gate creaked open. It had been a while since it had been opened, and although the toughened black paint had weathered the elements, the bearings of the hinges had degraded in performance through lack of use and movement.

"Never go in through the door," she smiled, and cut the three wires of the fence as she intoned her well loved phrase.

"Yeah, very good, babes. But luckily we didn't forget to ground the couple of thousand volts parsing through it," he said.

"Don't get jealous, honey," she ticked. "These are Jonny maxcuts. Insulated to the bone and proximity sensored for current."

"Clever bitch," he said, kissing her oh-so-soft cheek, but shying from the bum pinch on this occasion. That cheek was certainly soft. "Love you, sweet cheeks."

"You boys aren't the only ones with your geek gadgets, you know," she kissed back. "Least we have some sexy stylin' too. Better than your black, or silver, or black and silver."

Gina was laughing. Looks like a bit of humour was bringing them all a bit closer.

"Ok, mistress of many masterings," interjected Tommy, hamming it up even more so. "Can you hit that thing from here."

Tommy turned and pointed to the last sensoriums delaying their journey across the bracken and grassed field. "Hit that shit from here."

Gina stamped her foot and huffed. "Go do it with goats. You know I'm crap at throwing. Hympt. You can't casket hack can you."

He stood there silently. Rotating his wrists in warm up. Flexing his fingers so they pumped liked a heart. Jonny had taken out the main observers from afar. The wired fence and the ir motion sensors were always really meant to keep out the bigger animals, to stop them chewing the masts or urinating near the cable entry points. Bastards, they'd piss and corrode anything given enough time, and for some reason they'd eat their way through that sheathing as though it tasted like candy.

Eyeing up the sensor networks, he slowed his breathing. Each atop a concrete pillion, the steel masts held the arrays aloft in their vigilance. Some hacks required elegance, some required skill. These little fuckers required just one thing, the brute force approach.

As they smashed they emitted that joyous crackle and hiss. Hence the rock approach, the encasements were wired and laced, enough to fry any pigeon mistaken for a tamperer, and severely melt the skill of any pianist. They were military spec, although cheap, hence the fry effect was never touted as a failing. They were added on much to the disgust of everyone after the facility had closed down. That gave that extra satisfaction when they fissled.

"All the fun of the fair," he laughed.

Hacks and slacks done, they strolled across the bracken and dark grassed field. Approximately in the centre, a few rough trees partially obscured the plain concrete pillbox. They were based on the design of the World War Two gun emplacements, which in turn were based on the boxes Victorian ladies had for their tablets and habits. Octagonal in design, for gun duty they covered every fire arc, for pill guard the eight segments gave one per day, plus that special space for the panic pill or a keepsake. In the present case however, the eight sides echoed the incoming routes of the interworked optical cables.

This afternoon's guardian of the gate was a single sinister black casing.

"Star fixings," said Gina.

"On it," said Tommy, flipping his Swiss army hacktool into activity, and fixing the correct sized drivehead like a bayonet. Unscrewing gently after Gina had checked for blipscopes and boobies, the two bottom holders were removed, thus allowing the casing front cover to be opened up on its top hinging.

They all laughed.

It was a multiple-digit pin input system, horizontally mounted. This was opposed to vertical mounting, which made it harder to read over someone's shoulder, that's how hard their marketing department ended up trying.

"Concrete casing, jelly baby guards," laughed Tommy.

Flashing her camera at the panel, she read out the serial number that appeared on her display in cross referencing from her base of data.

He danced this pattern into his palmpiece, and began the secondary cross matching. The member made database of manufacturer types began its scan. Although the security algorithm was uncrackable, there was a pattern range per chip batch number which rendered the complexity down by several big magnitudes, and thus breakable. Of course, it had taken considerable man hours to facilitate, with a distributed members network of activity drilling down to all those poor geeks sitting in a basement for two months each ticking away at the data, just to solve one piece. Still, add up all the little pixels and what a picture.

"Ok, if we lower the temperature down a bit, the probability range of inputs would allow us to use a Jonny number 79 on it," he smiled.

"Tacky, tacky-tacky, tacky-tack," sang Tommy.

He lowered his backage and removed the horse trophy ice bucket in all its fantastic leather bound extravagance.

"Wish these bastards would put the hinges on the bottom," moaned Tommy, shoveling and squeezing the beads of ice into the casing, whilst trying to hold it shut.

The rest of them just stood giggling.

"You always grab all the glamour, Tommy, always," she said.

Ramming the casing firmly shut to the crack of plastic and ice, Tommy smiled and let himself relax a little.

"What do you reckon, hun," said Gina, turning to look at her.

"About two or three, I'd say," she said.

So two or three cycles of waiting it was, the ice doing its job, and the potential processing capability of the panel encryption lowering with every degree.

"That should do it," she said, nodding in Tommy's direction.

Tommy opened the casing, let those beads that would roll out, and then scooped out the remainder with some sort of local twig.

"Ok, over to you then, hackboi," said Tommy.

He stepped up. The Jonny number 97 tapped in and connected, spiralled and translaced, clicked and opened, its panel even showing the time the hacktool took with a cheesy rating animation, for a bit of fun atop the functional. The displayed cartoon of dancing Pop Weasel indicated an elderly system which only necessitated a few steps from a brief Irish jig of calculations to crack.

"Ladies first," he said.

"They are no ladies here," joked Tommy.

She used a corner of her sleeve to dust the handle, and squeezed the trigger latch to slide it open. They all ducked inside to the stillness of undisturbed air.

The next bit was again pretty simple, the gadgets did all the work, although the gadgets weren't simple. Using the automated cable splicer, they routed through their own wirings and patched in the desired weave. First step done here, the required net pipes and cross entry points connected, along with a bit of jumping to disguise the trails. A pure over air line would have been neater, but for the maxed out instantaneous bandwidth they needed, this was the only way.

"Woof," barked the dog in the distance, muffed by the pillbox casing they had led themselves in to.

"Fuck," whispered Tommy. "We're in the shit now."

Tommy had ducked into a low combat stance in anticipation of the canine, but he sensed that it was a handled dog and so rose to a more midrange, so any accompanying biped was in sharp attack range too.

Gina swung round her tits in preparation of a human hack.

Tommy almost launched into an attack as there was an unexpected delay. However, the eventual processed understanding of the sound of a pant and a lap of tongue against ice betrayed that it wasn't a merc security outfit hired to patrol.

"What the fuck are you kids doing here?" said the stern voice.

"Dave!" excitedly greeted Gina.

"You youngies you think you've got it all with your tech toys and your leetboi threads," bantered Dave. "But you haven't got the science of nature that Mickey has here in his nose."

"And how are you, young Mickey," said Gina, rubbing the long ears and patting head and neck.

"I know yous guys are professionals," said Dave. "But you know you're gonna need a print to get anywhere don't you?"

"Yup, got one," rebuked Gina smugly in a playful way.

"Who did you have to sleep with to get that?" laughed Dave.

Luckily Dave was back and out the door before Tommy and Gina's blows would have struck. They were annoyed that Dave had just maneuvered out without blocking, but pleased that his age hadn't wearied his skill.

Dave barely felt Gina's mascara case hit him, but the chuckle he let out on seeing and understanding was real enough.

"Those schoolgirl tricks never fade, Gina," said Dave, tossing the mascara back.

"Sure thing not, babe," said Gina, catching the mascara and switching it round with the package containing the fingerprint they had collected in The Royal Hussar. Dave only saw the switch as Gina huffed up the point of exchange in play, and Dave knew it well.

"Look, I don't mind what version of node drafts you're playing, but don't leave a mess and shut the gate after you leave," said Dave. "You could have told me, and I'd have lowered everything for you."

"Where's the fun in that," they said in unison.

"Erm, Dave," she said. "We may have to wire a

donation to one of your causes. For the, erm, wire."

"Jonny blades huh," said Dave. "How is the old hackfool."

"Jonny is as Jonny does," smiled Gina.

"Same as," smiled Dave. "So you kids, what's the big hack today?"

"v-industries," he said.

Dave rolled about a bit laughing.

"Yeah right," said Dave. "Good luck with that."

After a few more hacks to secure the route, they had spent the night at The Halfway House Inn. Rested and recuperated a little, the new day brought new hope.

Tommy and Gina settled up the bills in cash, and joined them outside. They were sat on a light wooden bench, back to back, spine to spine, his left elbow resting on the low back, her right. Having had time to choose their clothes as opposed to the previous days hurried hacks, they were dressed for hack fun rather than wandering around in mud. That had definitely pleased Gina, whilst Gina didn't mind and was always game, a higher fashion could be worn today.

The two of them were engrossed in one of their thumb battle hack games on their handsets. Today she was wearing mostly black, a sexy skirt coupled with some stylish boots, and a rather fetching tight lapelled jacket. Her white blouse completed the effect, the frilly white lace of its edging elegantly flowing down and covering its front buttons, and the thick white cuffs tucked over the black sleeve ends, giving that hint of continental styling.

He was suited up in his white outfit. White everything. 'Handy if I ever need to find you in the dark!' she had joked, but hey, he liked it, and together they looked ok, even if he did look a bit of a muppet when unaccompanied. Not that he cared the slightest. Felt right for him, comfort zone assured and a few neat pockets to stow those essential small tools.

"Sensible footwear though, yes?" said Gina.

"Yes, hun," they replied in tandem. Judging by the fact that his thumb was much more highly active than hers, she was winning, and winning by far. Still, he was laughing, she always won, but he did enjoy the playing with her.

The night before they had changed their appearance in other ways. Whilst clothing was one thing, really clothing was all the same anyway, it was all just dressing, no matter what it was. What really mattered was what lay underneath, under the skin. That's what they had hacked, instead of changing one's appearance to change type, it was more a matter of changing one's data to change who one was. Change your profile data and you become a different society stereotype, the clothes are just clothes to hide the bits that you end up spending more and more to cover.

They had borrowed the lightweight aluminum boat from Jonny. The worn greenish camouflage would still have been effective if it were not broad daylight. Still, no living sensors were going to be here, the place was long disused.

Crossing what was somewhere between a moat and a fjord, the flat bottomed boat glided a steady path under his and Tommy's oarsmanship, her steering, and Gina doing a figurehead type pose at the front. Over the still water, and past that funny type of seaweed that they had only ever seen here.

Mooring up on the cranky jetty, they stepped slowly toward their goal and the wood became earth. Past a few rocky outcrops which reminded him of the tors near home, and up a gentle slope. The thin wire fence here was just that, no need for cutters or grounding, just a grab together and leg over would do. No need for security here, it was only useful to them now they had completed the intermediate hacks to create the route.

As he strolled across the sheep mowed grass, his many memories of here shone through him. Years ago he had been here to Troonhilly Downs, on a Cybertechnic placement, learning the systems and getting some time on the massive satellite transmission dishes.

Another year he had been here on one of the member's organised rave party tours, the memory of the outdoor party stomp fest that weekend brought a smile to his face and a slight shiver to his spine.

The dish align was a little easier than the trisat one. That time he had to hack the weather service web page that the intern used to align the dish with the wind factoring. Whole lot of people left their umbrellas at home, sorry guys.

Each time he had left another hackpoint for the members to tap, and this is where he knew he'd come for the big hack. It was the only place he had access to that would give them enough instantaneous bandwidth when they needed it, right at the point of climax to the hack.

The entry deck here was more difficult. There were no geek tools on this one, no flash or pan, just his fingers versus the encrypted structure. A fast hack and tap and he accessed in. They were here, at the point of presence.

They unpacked the hackgear out from the sealed pelican cases, and sent Tommy back for more.

Chapter Eight – hack xf trilock

To a casual observer the scene would have looked quite sedate in its serenity. The two of them, laid out on the horizontal dual rig. Their external peaceful innocence did not betray the horrors that lay inside. His and her heads gently resting on the pillows, as if dreaming of sheep in the electric pulsating of thoughts in their synapses.

Only in time lapse would the true sight have been revealed. A snapshot instant would not have shown how Tommy and Gina had watched the progression of the hack. In the early founding hours, Gina and Tommy observed the hack through the group projection rig, their dancing and translacing bringing laughter and smiles.

As the biogravity had increased, Tommy and Gina switched off the scope displaying the thoughts of their mind. Not only would the coming sights be sickening in their horrendous complexity, but the mere experience of another's darkness would have required a whole isoteric mapping hack of its own.

An earlier frame would have shown Gina's tears of helplessness. Gina had watched their firmly clamped handholding wilt into a limp resting of two damp leaves lying atop one another as the pain of the hack drained the essence from them.

Tommy had comforted Gina, although he didn't quite understand.

"If it's biogravity how come they are still in the rig?" asked Tommy.

"I know, sweetie, I hope we gain that much progress one day," hugged Gina.

"Yeah, we're getting there," said Tommy, managing a smile. "But how come they just haven't vomited, or their bodies just rejected the rig?"

"Yes, I know. She and The Captain chatted to me about

it once. It was a little while you and me had met, hun. I think they sort of tell you stuff as you go along, don't they."

"Hmm, yup, I remember some similar visits, although I guess you and Mandy had plenty of prechats too," affirmed Tommy.

"Yes, you boys have them too! Pity you all waste so much time on the bullshit though and have to catch up later," smiled Gina, and battered her eyelids and shoulders, her hips and head tottering on the spot. "Good time to tell you some more of it then I guess," continued Gina. "Since we gonna have the time and the opportunity while we wait their one out."

"Erm, ok," murmured Tommy, wanting answers but hesitant of them.

The poison of the biogravity sweated out through their skin. Her delicate hair dampening onto the pillow as the hours drifted by. His face growing its black lawn of stubble.

"You know your dawn, babes," said Gina, holding Tommy tightly and interfacing with his eyes.

"Yeah, like any of us any forget it," said Tommy, acking Gina's contact and opening for more.

"Bit like, well, falling and dying, isn't it," shrugged Gina, momentarily flicking away from his gaze whilst remembering her own. Tommy sucked air up through his nostrils.

"Bit like, well yeah," Tommy sighed in reply, drawing Gina in and allowing her to drain and replenish off his warmth.

"And you remember the bit from translacing class that disproved that stuff about the length of time taken to dream certain events is about the same as the time it would take to experience those events in waking reality," relayed Gina.

"Yeah, they sure got that one wrong didn't they. Now it

just seems like they were nuts, living in a 2d world of wooden technology."

"Yes, at least they got the bit right about dreams being thoughts though. Well, the only way she could describe it to me, and you know what she's like for eloquence," said Gina, widening her eyes and pursing and pouting in emphasis.

"Yeah," agreed Tommy.

"Well, if you remember from his cliptrip, 'c'est ne pas un livre', I think it was," whispered Gina, lowering her voice even though only Tommy would be able to hear anyway. "It was her that brought him back, wasn't it."

"Yes, I see, and as we all know, it was him that brought her back, yes?" gathered Tommy.

"Yes, that's right. Perfect fit that they are and all that, 'siamese reflector crossfeed' or something Jonny would probably call it."

Tommy began to recite his memory of understanding. "Human psychology is obvious to all but the one experiencing it."

"Yeah, but then the problem is everyone has their own opinion of it," said Gina, echoing the appropriate learning pattern matched response, their cross keying increasing the insight with every repetition. Écoute et répète.

"It's probably obvious to the one experiencing it too, but they either have no way of expressing it or if they do people think they are insane," said Tommy, completing the codex.

He and her were lost in the hack. All time existing instantaneously. Their thoughts melding into loops of explanation to each other.

"One method at which time may be viewed is on a linear scale," he said. "Time travel to the past is not disproven, as travel to the past would not effect future events as they haven't happened yet. All time exists instantaneously until it occurs, and all time occurs at the same time, i.e. instantaneously."

"Time exists in this manner in a quantum entanglement state," she said. "We (humans) experience time linearly as we exist inside of the time that is occurring, and thus our rate of quantum entanglement completion is occurring at a slower rate than the time we are inside. See figure 8 (shows concentric circles), for further explanation of the authoritative cross-definitions."

Tommy and Gina silently sighed.

"All any of can do is find an outlet to our madness," he said, causing a rupture of laughter amongst them. The hack was in its early stages, and was more like dreaming than paining at the moment. He and her enjoyed its lightness with each other in a bright spring picnic of data.

"I'm just lucky in that mine was coding," he laughed.

Both of them dancing a translating abstraction into symbolic representation. Thought into language. Thought into code. Thought into words. Code and language similar. Coding merely a method of increasing the abstraction to symbolic representation comprehension.

His consciousness was tired and he let his subconscious take the strain of the combinational autocompletion for a while. She watched over him, guarding him with her love. The campfire of her emotions keeping the hounds stretched back to a distant perimeter.

"It's time to get up," she had said.

"Just a little while longer, baby," he had muffled from beneath the warm covers.

"Look, baby," she retorted, in her firm but fair way. "Don't even bother with that line that you love. It isn't going to wash."

She sat on the bed and kissed him gently.

"A few more cycles, you know it's not my body that needs it, but my mind," he breathed, almost as if snoring out the words in his sleep.

"I see, usual bullshit," she smiled. She let him dwell a while in his lucid dreaming whilst awake. She was gradually letting him let her believe him. Although he could have risen from their bed, without an extra few cycles to still, it would have been merely sleepwalking.

The memory of her memory faded out as she continued to fend off the occasional insurgence of the biogravity hounds with her wrist locking blows.

"So what do we do, baby," said Tommy, as they mopped the brows of their sleeping friends.

"Watch it out really," she said, screwing up her nose a little, which Tommy found cute, even given the appalling situation. Guess it was a bit of a lift to help cope with the starkness of the viewing desolation.

"Jonny said he would pop in later," said Gina. "He told me he was going to have a chat with The Captain about something. Maybe they'll peak it."

"Yeah, maybe," said Tommy, mimicking the response of hope as was his skill. Covering his ascendence of sorrow, Tommy's instincts didn't let the weight of the shadow be cast over Gina. Tommy remembered what he had said to him a few days earlier.

'At some point,' he had said. 'The girls always tire. It's like why the weekend was invented. A bit like a weekly new year. The renewal thing. Like the seasons.'

Tommy had nodded, like Tommy did.

'We all take up about as much as we can handle,' he had continued. 'Often more than we can. At which point the hope of the weekend kicks in, and the weekend itself is reward enough to replenish enough to face another week again.'

'Yeah, I get it,' had said Tommy.

'Thing is,' he lent in. 'When I go in with her, at the point you and Gina are tiring, Gina is going have the hope for the weekend kick in.'

'I can see that,' had said Tommy.

'Thing is, if Jonny and The Captain do turn up, the only thing they're going to be able to bring to the party is pizza.'

Tommy mixed the pleasure of the understanding with the depth of the data.

Her marvel at his beauty formed electric tears as she admired his hack. He progressively rendered his skill in response to every stimuli that was shone at it. Faster in defence than that could be formed in attack. With her covering his hope and his skill matching everything that spiralled at it, progress was programmed into the wiring of data. The shards of barbed biogravity thought back in a martial dance step of palmistry, their physical manifestations countered with synaptic skill.

That was one of the things about him she loved the most. He was the best at what he was best at. In the streaming unconsciousness of reality he bettered at all he was forced to try at. That was one of the things that turned her on to him. He was her renaissance man. But there was one thing he was better at than all other things. He was best at being her friend.

She sensed the biodiversity of the defence was gaining the evolutionary upper hand and switched her and him round. Her fractally opposite combinational response meant the defence mechanisms of the viral attacking defenders had to adapt to survive, and were forced back a few generations. He took his turn to wonder at the wonder of her skill, guarding her soul from despair against the shadowing attacks of the skulking blackstatic mists with the depth of his love for her, while her electrostatic angelic luminescence thought back the physical negatively of the scything painers with her delicate performance of timed punches and gliding kicks.

Gina's grip tightened on Tommy's as they watched their hand clasp fading as the winter of the hack approached in the passing of the length of time. His and her hands seemed to age from their ripeness with the drawn out drama of the battle.

Tommy and Gina could feel each other's warmth for each other through the pulse of the beat of their hearts in their hands. The sadness of watching the heat and the beat fade away from the resting lovers hurt Gina's soul.

Gina and Tommy felt for them as they watched and waited. Few went that far in, and although they all had studied the theory and the history way back in class, it wasn't many who went on to tackle the type of systems they seemed born to dance with. As was such, the watching and the waiting was worsened by the knowledge, if not the experience, of what was coming next.

The ultima defence mechanisms were not programmed to show any form of global protective response. They were merciless and ruthless, the pairing dna coding removed from the remembering of their biological programmed constructs. After the weaning down of the physical layer of programming hacks, the isoteric mappings would go in for the kill. After kicking their bodies to the sagged husks of wretchedness, the demonic raping of their thoughts would follow as they attempted to destroy the very hope of their souls.

Though in the collective consciousness of the real world their physical representations had long since born relevance such was their drained state, in the inside of the outside that was the programmed world of the v-industries granite distributed defence constructs, him and her held their interlocking finger hand clasp in fun as they danced their dance of joy in rejection of the shredding gloom.

Her and him were seeing the complexity of the attacking defences. Were it not for the pain they might marvel at the complexity of the coding, but it was all wrong, it wasn't beautiful, it was grotesque in its architecture, the dark horrors of dark souls biting and clawing.

Him and her walked into the shadows through the meniscus of consciousness, twisting the barriers of today and tomorrow, flowing through the past and instinctively knowing the answer. They hoped their hope would see them through, for although the first rounds would be hard, they knew that they knew that their foundations were stronger.

"He laid it on me like this," said Tommy, rubbing Gina's shoulder. "He said it was a bit like the poorly conceived operating systems of the nineties. Product bullshit driven rather than quality driven had meant that it was a continuing slackhack built atop another. In a tottering stack of fixes to fix weaknesses in the fixes and new useless features, the whole bloated and feasted upon itself in a confusion of greed and necessity."

"Yeah, she said it to me in a similar way, same but different, you know, girly not geeky," said Gina.

"Really," said Tommy. "You mean geekgirly rather than geekboyly surely."

"Oh yes, rest it off for a day," said Gina, pushing against Tommy's chest. "Base of it being, yay."

The four knights without sleep. The isoteric hounders were tightening their hold. It was their Epoch Dawns which gave the members their emotional resilience to withstand the onslaught of the defence systems, but it was also where the flailers would wreak their fiercest attacks. They reminded him of his misery. His Epoch Dawn. His failed hopes and his darkened soul.

The field trip that never was. The piece of paper pinned to the private message board stating the love/hate swing. The perceived choices against the predetermined outcome. The feeling of unfaithfulness even though the knot had been undone. Seeing the beauty again and not being able to face as eternity had already been lost. The irony of destroying what was by seeking comfort from the pain of losing it.

He looked at his fingers. He had been using the sandpaper to smooth the walls for decorating. Maybe he had overdone it today. As he sweated, the moisture seeped into the minuscule holes that the grains had worn into his fingers. As the sweat sank through the holes, they itched, and as they itched they rubbed more, and the holes were widened and made more.

They stamped his body downwards through the spiralling shaft. The metal sides were barbed like a cheese grater, the sharpened pipe endings shredded his skin as they stomped their dance of stomp which had no ceremony, no thought to it, no care or preparation. The would have been smooth sides of the grating apparatus had been blast sprayed with a crystalline white solid. A potent salt to burn his openings in his tangled fall.

He lay there in the incubator. His skin itched. He looked at himself, where he had itched he had scratched more. Where it didn't hurt it didn't itch, and where it didn't hurt it looked better, smoother, more beautiful.

He sanded the walls and made them smoother, more beautiful, so they wouldn't hurt anymore.

Another layer of the isoteric mapping defence clicked open. Hacking hurts.

"Well," continued Gina, saddening in her description. "To them, it's a bit like dying."

"Dying?" questioned Tommy.

"Yes, hun, dying," nodded Gina. "With a bioelectric hack that big, no one person can stand the backshot of the amount of biogravity spored out by the defences. Effectively what is happening is that they are taking turns to emotionally die inside of the rig."

"I'm starting to get it now," murmured Tommy. "And they don't flatline as it's the hope of each other that brings them back."

"Yes, that's right," squeezed Gina. "Their dawns were what she called 'equivalence' or something."

"I remember," said Tommy. "A couple of times when he was wasted and performing away he would fascinate about it, tracking treasures down at the same time or something. He called it 'logical equivalence'."

"Good for you, hun," loved Gina. "A while back you'd have had to look that one up."

"Look, don't spoil it," defended Tommy.

"It's ok, don't jig an environmental withdrawal from the stimuli, pulse back and get closer," said Gina.

"So in essence then," said Tommy, preparing himself for the revelation. "They are taking turns to dawn and resuscitate each other's consciousnesses."

"Yes. Experiencing fractal epoch dawns at a rapid rate," said Gina.

"I ain't ever getting into that shit," said Tommy.

"Thank fuck for that," agreed Gina.

"If they were metering for this one, it'd be a fortune," said Tommy, shaking his head.

"More pimp than your ass," smiled Gina.

All those years of rubbing the bars with his thumbs to weaken them when the guards weren't watching were all in vain. They knew and watched without looking. The guard unlocked the door of bars and swang it open, leaving thus. It was no different. He still had no way of getting through the door, and he lay there motionless and broken. And then, the guards laughed at him in his wretchedness, both despising and pitying him, as far as their weakened depravity could.

"So how was it for you, darling," Gina said, the stereotypical line so far out of context. "So, how, was it. Your dawn."

"Oh, you know," Tommy said with that sense of urgency and hesitation. "It wasn't very nice."

"Ever feel you've got a master plan but are unable to do anything with it?" he said. "I do, since the day I was born. In fact, before that, when I was in the womb. That's why I popped out earlier, I realised I was keen to get started, keplar the solution. A larger short-term memory, lower immediate memory, corrected during sleep."

"It's a bit like playing chess in your imagination," said Gina. "Only the number of possible moves is infinite. The players think ahead in thousands of combinations of moves, each reacting to each other dynamically."

"Only when the final connection is made does the route autocomplete and the reality of the outcome occur," said Tommy.

The self analysis leading to the self therapy of the commlink in his teens to the girl he hadn't asked those years before. Correcting the missed events even though the time had passed for any reality to be affected. The rapidity of thought, the spiralling of complexities, instant analysation, instant self analysis, the greater shorter immediate memory. The eight digit on the deck, the eight digit on the comm dial pad. The positioning, the inversion, the movement of the star.

The leaving test from the first Cybertechnic when two base ten bits were lit. The two questions that weren't obvious. One was ok with a couple seconds of thought. The other a relatives aunties and uncles type thing, he drew a little diagram and made a guess. There, that should do it.

Another day he handed his sheet of paper to the primary planner. Their task that morning had been to design something to place in one of the three squares in the concrete slab, left behind from the removal of the building. In its situation in between two of the playgrounds of his primary Cybertechnic, a 'patio' sized paving slab protected each plot prior to the planner's permission being granted.

"It's a perpetual motion machine," he said, pointing to his diagram, showing his invention in a side-slice cutaway type view. The exterior display side of things was to be a waterfall, a calming sight to any observer surely. The mechanics inside the hill of the fall revealed how the wheel maintained its motion. The buckets attached to the wheel scooped the water back upwards inside the hill, their power being drawn by water already scooped falling.

"It's good, but it's not suitable," said the doubting Thomas. He didn't understand why, nor was given a reason why.

Gina and Tommy watched.

It was topic tasks that afternoon. He walked over to the side shelf and looked at the book on mediaeval history. He had always liked castles, and was fascinated by a page showing a castle design and which described its functioning. He replaced the book on the shelf and returned to his table.

He sat on his red plastic backed chair, and he wrote some words on the castle, and drew a picture. Hoping it was enough to show to the primary approver, he joined the small queue.

"You've copied all of this straight out of the book," shrilled the music tutor, her voice shivering his spine.

Puzzled, he returned to his seat, and spoke to the girl at his table. "Why do I bother. All she asks me to do is read and learn, and when I do it's not right. It's not as if I can go back and see the castle, so it's going to be like the book, isn't it."

He didn't remember he had remembered it like an image.

Waited.

Seated on a higher plastic chair, legs swinging as they dangled. Reading the word flip-charts on the side worktop, with their red spiral bindings on top. The panels of black words on white rectangles, words and blocks. The view through the wide window to out over the primary Cybertechnic playing fields, and on towards the woods.

Hoped.

The first day at the first Cybertechnic. The coat hanging peg with his name on it, all pre-arranged, ready and waiting for him. The wooden fort with the wooden soldiers, the memories of others.

The eye lightening faded out as the reality of the newly born baby began to form. An aching ear abdominal descending bass reverb, the taste of dry saliva, unprogressive wrenching with its mild burn companion. Heart-depth sigh, astonished panic like falling love. Consciousness. Breathing. Seeing. Hearing. Feeling. Smelling. Born. Alive. Information overload. What does it all mean.

Inside an incubator. The baby lay there thinking,

connecting, dreaming whilst awake. He lay there, legs crossed at the ankles, thumbs nestled between index and middle fingers. The sensory overload caused his nerves to fire at the surface of his skin, causing him to itch. He had to stop now and again to scratch feverishly, often resulting in an opening.

His mind grew as it responded to the stimuli. The brain folds increasing in their regions of proximity. The firation of nerve impulses, three signals enough to form a connection in the delicate array structure of consciousness.

As the fired thoughts pulsed further away from their origination, they formed new cross matches of their own. When the whole shone in thoughts, the growing weaves melded tapestries of uniqueness.

Watching his fingerprints provide traction for his fingers to grasp things. Inside the incubator the baby was picked up and never left to settle. He had been battling against a false pattern since birth. It didn't fit, it was all wrong for him. When to sleep or feed or think, it was all random and confused. It wasn't a routine he needed but an appropriate action at an appropriate time. Needing a result there was no synaptic equation that his thoughts could follow to create the desired response.

Sometimes thinking one way would provide the appropriate response to the pattern he was trying to create, other times the same pattern would not produce the same result. Maybe it was combinations of thought. His mind would spiral out in autocompletions in efforts to gain the response.

In a short time as the processing structures had grown rapidly he had calculated his own internal solutions, but still the influence over the external seemed distant. He would think this 1, think that 0, this, that, 101 combinations. There was no control over external events.

The biometrics hack. He couldn't answer as he could

only remember her face, her eyes and her hair. Especially her eyes, eyelashes. The hack couldn't autocomplete and he knew the only way round was to expend a little of the trilock on it. The hack had completed but the blip had been pipped.

The starting with a cell. The growing of a stem. The joining and co-operation of a spine. The formation of the control centres, the piping of the transmission mediums and the bonding of the the motor actuators. The construction of the pattern matched processor and the nanomachine. The reptilian brain growing from the stem. The cells expanding and creating the animal brain around the older cell designs of the reptile. The mammalian brain slowly forming in its place around and in the animal brain. The what we are and what we were, evolution through the layers of modular processing, cell, stem, reptile, animal to mammal. The final steps to the conscious awareness.

"Two or three undulating strings of energy and light," he said. "Wherein they touch matter formed and universes created. This implies that matter formation has a trigger threshold, one energy line is not enough for transmogrification to occur, but the summation of two or more raises the potential enough to reach the required escape electrical threshold point for the reaction of energy to mass formation to occur."

"Was it two or three strings," she said. "Or one same supercoiled string of ∞."

As the hack progressed the isoteric structure thought against him with unerring accuracy, trying to defeat the intrusion attempt. Battling within his deepest emotions to try and conquer all that his soul held dear. His hope, his faith and his love.

His fantasies of explaining how he felt to somebody were fading. He had slowly given up hope on being able to see his friends again. One day he had planned to visit them, or create another rave to reunite them all again. But he had travelled too far. There was no journey back to where everything was that he had left behind. No return trip, and no possibility of circumnavigation.

The full page newspaper advertisement designed to dispel the conspiracy theories that still had hold over him. The humour lost and the message misread for egotistical bounds. The shape may have looked as a pyramid shooting to the stars, but by moving further away would be revealed more as a trophy, or as a holy grail. An individual standing amongst the faceless corps, not for power and control, exploitation or monetary gain, but to inspire those cast down not to live in fear.

Slowly he had discounted them all in turn as being able to understand was he was saying. Some he didn't want to burden with his darkness, others could not hear but for the reaction of their own egos, still others simply had no conception or connection to anything he was trying to communicate. The frustration.

As his mind had categorised and created objects of reality inside of his consciousness, so now he developed bounds of being, invisible borders and cages to his actions. In the same way that the late night hacker may have tiered down to the 24-hour store, his mind compartmentalised into rooms with the less and less he understood, trying to solve by making the world smaller, modulising, breaking down into components.

A feeling of just needing one good day to happen to set things right. All those wasted years of that one day, just needing something to happen now. Something to happen. Something external to go his way. Something good to happen that he had no control over.

The strange solice in the taste of one's own tears. That place where joy and sadness exist as one. Each equidistant from him, neither real in thought or obtainable in experience. Simply all they are, emotions, as meaningless to him as the answers to an unknown equation of questions.

Leaving a lamp on in the day to feel like company. He knew it wouldn't solve the problem he needed to solve, and so he didn't want to do it. Didn't want to, or couldn't, or was unable, it didn't matter. Layer built upon layer, doing something which didn't solve the problem could simply be painful in itself. All wired-up wrong, the joy disappearing and becoming pain as the mind and the body knew it wasn't solving the true problem. The layers of problems, none of which could be solved. All stacked on top of each other, little point in trying to complete the top layers as the root layers were themselves unsolvable.

He could see how the abstraction of the zoo or the themepark worked. Designed to keep apart and out, as much as keep in the cage. The devices and illusions to keep people happy in their distractions. None of them seemed to create a reality for him, none of them forming a meaning to his toil.

The disassociation of the feeling of hunger with eating as a solution to it. An associated feeling with something that needs correcting, but with sadness knowing that feeding would not quell that hunger. Everything tasting wrong. Feeding itself seeming unnatural.

Lost inside of himself. Normally they would have flagged a call to him when an atom was in that kind of state. He had not the energy to escape the circular orbit around his despair. The barbs spiked and sucked his synapses downward and draining, somewhere deep in the recesses of his mind he screamed a thousand cold screams of dying. The waves of sadness rippled through the surface of his skin with their icy shivers. He knew there was light at the end of the tunnel, problem was it was him holding the torch, wandering hopelessly in the dark.

The pulsating of a hundred false enlightenments tearing

at his soul. The suggestion, hypnotism and indoctrination, exploitation of the pattern matched response and the ego to prove untruths from linking partial fragments of facts. Relying on the mind's inbuilt referencing facilities to extrapolate a third point from the two inputs supplied. Manipulations of the random spreading autocompletions to make the last steps occur by filling in the gaps with unreasoned logic.

Thoughts circulating and trying to understand one another to form a cohesive whole. Sold in manners ranging from trivial changes in language and inflection to achieve a point, to the more sinister. The laughability of trying to prove deciphering on translation or phonetic similarity, the most trivial form being a rather poor derivation of the sun of god from the Son of God. To the shredding pits of cascading hell.

The drugged scripted play of the posting sacrifice. Told to stand in a manner that was more historically suited to the burn and the stake. The hands tied behind the back, and the feet pressed together. The placement of the body promoting a feeling of vulnerability, falsely used in proof of the posterity seeking laid trails of the Magdalene descendant conspiracy when mistaken for a feeling of sexuality.

His primary Cybertechnic play where the three of them stood on stools in their handmade costumes in the tier seated hall. The two girls were the sun and the moon, and he played the role of the stars. The different aspects of the heavens, the different symbols of uniqueness, sometimes used to unite together against in false bandings. The truth lay more in the whole of a part.

Dropping elastic bands along his routes of traversal, trying to spin him off his true track. The entrance tree first branch trimmed to a post, and then being replaced by the pole and the chain with its spiked crowns. The conversations of strangers near the bank and in the posting office.

But how could something that had no proof be disproved by proof. Idyllic in its simplicity and yet infinite in its complexity. The point of not being able to prove the existence of God was so that it could not be faked in order to gain power and control.

He felt cold, tired, and lonely, and as though it had always been that way. Reap what you sow, or sow what you reap. Feeling as though everyone else's egos were cursing his fate. Their answers of misunderstandings dictating events. Knowing and watching but not being able to change a thing.

The memory of a hack. The route in through triple splicing and the triangular watch. The meaning and messaging of his entire life, all connected within to some unknown grand master plan, already known and impossible to change. The links of the chain, eight in number on the base, seven on the face sides, the triangular keylink connecting at the top. The white winged dove at the centre. The connected initials somehow appearing at the three and the nine on the beacons of the level playing fields. How could objects created before his existence be so telling of the events he had made in his past. The connections between corps, the hack whispers being very telling, the links revealed, the motives unknown. Drawn out and controlled. The financial managers, the bandwidth overseers, the medical professionals, the tally of the accountant.

Spending weeks so alone in isolation working on his latest reasonings. Cross referencing and analysing once he was back out of the rig. Great parallel discoveries from history, no-one to witness or believe he had experienced them for himself too. The process repeating in endless cycles of new discovery and frustration.

The pleasure synapses firing in compensation for the

dark feelings of pain. The more the onslaught from the isoterics, the more their bodies released their organic bubbles. The waves of despair in the lags between the emissions and the reseting of the centres. As the opposing forces wrestled against each other, the pleasure slowly lost its ability to fire over and mask the pain. The emotional victories becoming more and more empiric. The meniscus of the reservoirs of reserves slowly expended away. Beyond the forgetting of the knowing of joy. The rapid firings of despair conditioning a constant experience of pain. Pleasure itself becoming hurtful. Standing on the event horizon, staring into the black pit of hell. All lightness being sucked in never to return again, forever lost in the depths of the unknowable. The sadness that haunted. The silence and the stillness. The cool chill of the wind on the bridge of his nose and his forehead.

From the depths of the ashes her phoenix rose, rekindling the fire of his dragon breath, life once more. Turning around to let look and see the beam of the incoming light, being lightened by its glow. There was one experience that never seemed to tire, never needed refilling, never scolded with the scarcity of its supply. The reality of love. With that gift he had managed to turn and sit upright, pivot, and sit with his legs over the edge of the bed touching the floor.

The defence systems reacted quickly to regrow the breach. Another test of tolerance with the statements of love being a defence of a broken ego. But they knew altruism bonded them all, in the same way the cells of their bodies had co-operated to achieve the full functioning of the system with consciousness. There was no hiding from truth by the arguing of opinion.

How to find her. At least he knew what he was looking for. As he knew her and knew of her, he knew that she was. He knew that when they met even if it was for the first time they would be no strangers. Instantly distinctive, locked in each other's gaze, the retina pattern match displaying in the fractal pigments of their eyes, indicating the pattern of her dna, highlighting her love and her genetic compatibility with him.

As he knew she was, he knew that at some point he would meet her. Squinting to alter the light shape gently to glean a match. Wearing polarised sunglasses to see if recognition was easier on one plane. Waiting in patience for her. Preparing and expecting. Again or first didn't matter, he just had knowledge. It hadn't happened on his layer of abstraction yet, and therefore would occur naturally at some point along his pre-arranged linear path of life. Like when he was lost in the department store, the harder he moved to look the further the distance and the less of a probability of a coincidence. He stood still, timeless as a hedge of stone, awaiting the sun, the moon, and the stars to lock in whatever pattern then would lock in, to mark the moment of fascination when all bits would be simultaneously lit. He wasn't out of time, just outside of time.

In his calculations in the incubator, it seemed apparent that if it hurt him to be without her, then it must hurt her to be without him too. So he took that hurt and added it to his own, so that she would not have to suffer it. He knew he couldn't take up all of it, but hoped it would be enough to allow her to have the strength to find him, lasting long enough for them to meet and recharge off one another, dancing in their perpetual energetic quantum spin. Covering her tracks, deleting the files that were logged about her. They had no way of contacting each other but they knew each other was there.

Living in the past, yet in the future, yet with no present. Having no moment or experience, just a knowledge of the past and a pre-calculated extrapolation of the future. A timeless existence of tomorrow and yesterday, the narrowed meniscus breathing in its alterings. Their opposing angular momentums creating the 0 and the 1, the circle and the shaft, the co-existence of time to create their present.

A focused alignment of both the particle and wave of light, the shimmering and depth turning of the structures. Each without, yet eternally bonded by a force so strong it never weakened over distance. The model of the rock dropping being honed to calculate how an unknown stone would interact.

e	$= mc^2$	$< c\ O <$
e/m	$= c^2$	$\infty < C\ o < c\ o < C\ O$
sqrt(e/m)	$= c$	$\infty < C\ o$
e/ c^2	$= m$	

"This infers that we are not made of matter but of energy," he said. "We only exist as matter at any one time as the probability of that matter occurring is 1 (meaning it always occurs), but the point at which it actually appears is indeterminate."

"However," she said. "Given that c is a large value, the speed at which the energy is travelling is such that in any given time frame the probability of the particle appearing is 1."

"Note this may only be true at the level of abstraction at which the particle is conceptually aware of," they said together as one. "I.e., it can exist constantly within itself and appear contiguous, even if outside its layer of abstraction it appears only intermittently, and inside its layer of abstraction it appears more complex by orders of magnitude (there are a lower number of sample points than there are instances, thus 'bits are missing')."

Their Epoch Dawns had occurred at the same time. A sense of belonging when near her. Not only belonging to her, but belonging with her, some how she made point to his existence. His mind stilled when in her presence. The whole that connected everything was him. It all seemed connected as it was, by him.

That which the isoterics thought was his weakness was his strength. They had no knowledge and no understanding of what it meant, how could they, their dna was sliced of emotion. As their final judgment axe fell, he let his energised orbits lower, emitting his photon radiance. With its long wave particle accelerated into light, new solutions were visible. From a different angle their Sierpinski pyramid tetrahedrons could be seen shimmering in infinite beauty. Things were always that way, and like the petals falling on the island, though the pattern seemed random, it always autocompleted into the inevitable. It made no difference from where the plot started, or the order of the points, in the simplicity of its complexity every outcome achieved full coverage.

They sat contently and played like children. There was no beginning and no end to the game. There was no winner or loser, the game itself was just for the playing. It was the joyfully playing together that they loved. There was no ego between them, no separation. They were as two aspects of one, dancing in their quantum entanglement of love.

The defending attackers waned. There was no enemy for them to divide and conquer. After the physical fighting, and after the torrent of emotional drains, there were no weaknesses to pierce with their weapons of adaptive evolution.

The Captain had been right. He had just needed a challenge. By performing a hack of infinite complexity and resolving his mind against it, he had broken the trilock.

'Do the hard thing first and everything else is easy'.

"How d'you feel?" whispered Jonny, not risking any great volume so as to allow their ears to readjust back in.

Their eyes blinked into the dim lighting.

"Bit tired," he said. "Maybe need a nap later."

"Would be. Can we get something to eat," she said.

"Sure thing, hun," smiled Gina.

"A meat feast jalapeño would probably kick start us again," he smiled.

"Real food please, darling, not coder corn," she said.

"Ok. That one reminded me a bit of flying over the carolina's in a small seater," he said. "Started off all cool, lady ready newspaper, executive looking smart, air hostess doing the mostess. Later in the storm the pilot keeps going on about no need to worry, just a small bit of turbulence. Well, they are small to start with. Then he's saying things like, 'no problem, just a little drop of five thousand feet in the turbulence'. Only feels little, small little bump, so yeah, it's ok."

She nodded.

"Then it's, 'no problem, just a drop of ten thousand feet'," he said. "And you start thinking, now, did we climb a bit after the last drop?"

Tommy laughed.

"Well," he continued. "By now the executive is white knuckling his seat, and the lady is expending more energy trying to hold the paper in place as the whole craft rocks, and is only pretending to actually read the news. A little bit after, and we're dropping some more. No-one knows how big a drop it was, and we're all waiting for the sound of the voice to come over the tannoy and tell us."

Gina stared.

"So we're waiting, and then the air hostess is even starting to look worried, and the newspaper has been crumple folded up, the cool composed play of a seasoned traveler has been shattered."

She smiled.

"Then suddenly there's this big banging noise, and a jolt

which rocks us forward," he said. "A shaky voice squeaks out the speaker. 'That is it folks. We've landed.'"

They laughed together.

"I'll drive," said Tommy.

"Slowly," he said.

"Hm, and no gear changes," she said.

He turned and smiled. "And another thing. Can you all stop playing hack whispers with me now."

EQUATIONAL
EQUIVALENCE

Justin Daw

Chapter One – Of tetrahedra

It was morning again. The facial chill contrasting with the warmth of the duvet zone. Head withdrawn tortoise-like from the sharpness of reality, retreating back into the womb. Rubbing the cold hand that had reached to tap, tap, on the alarm snooze button. The gathering together of sleep-swept thoughts, the opaqueness of the flickering reminders of past and current draws. After the daily play with the three snooze periods, and the smirk of the irony of setting the alarm three periods early, the final fist thud on the sensor pad came.

Pushing the covers back slowly as though they were steel sheaving, stretching out of the bed and stepping along into the shower room. Sliding the door latch across, doubling up on gates even though the flat was otherwise empty, the entrance locked, and the building secure. A skillful flick on the sink plug lever, and the exacting turns on the taps to achieve the preferred temperature. As the liquid love of the water streamed its fall into the basin, the ritual continued as it did each morning. She looked into the mirror and faced her self, alone.

Her glance away timed perfectly with the downward splash of her pixie tears. She cursed that the taps never seemed to run fast enough as she flipped them off again. Bending down and forcing her face through the surface tension of the water, her tears added to that already there and cried away unnoticed.

As she sobbed in hard heart-felt wrenches, the back of her mind comforted her with the fact that shedding underwater would mean there would be no red-eye tell, and that after a shower and a little padded warpaint, she would be ready to step out into an unknowable world once more.

Today was no different. It was the same as it always was. Another day, another hack.

Stepping into the shower, she sang her slow hush lullaby.

"Never Me"

I'm standing in a sunshine sea,
Of miracles and destiny.
Dancing through the golden glow,
Facing sorrows all must know.

Teared out armour drifts so slow,
Gainst the tides of downward flow.
I see the light that shines so free,
On where it shines, but never me.

I love you, darling.

As she skipped out of the shower, she allowed herself one of the few smiles from her daily quota.

Fuck. She ought to stop being so sketchy, singing to a guy she hadn't even met, and think about what she was supposed to be doing at work. Well, at least think about what she was supposed to be acting to be doing at work. A job was just a job, not like she wanted the money or the bullshit, but cover was cover, and the best place to hide was in full view.

She turned her red transport right onto the main faststream thoroughfare, and promptly grounded to a halt amidst the bustle of outers heading into midtown. As she tapped her fingers in a crescendo impatiently, a stylish fashion caught her eye. It didn't look to be local, so as she hovered in the traffic, she studied with her glances. Ebbing along with the lady's footsteps, noting the turn of lace and the contrast of tailored colours.

As things carried along, the purveyor of style passed

some young man suited up, standing with inactivity in some shop doorway, complete with designer stubble and dodgy pointed collar shirt. In the tracking of the current street's interest, he gave that man look of up and down, rubbing his chin's fur and nodding with a smirk. She figured his interest lay in other qualities of fashion.

Further down, an older gentleman clothed more in the garb of the street let tell similar glances, although with no accompanying smirkness. She could almost hear the social mutterings of the stereotyped judgments of the 'old perv'. Showed what a difference the disguise made, the same actions, but the reactions worlds apart. Not all were fooled so easily. Shoes for feet, caps for heads. Some used the suits to hide behind as rationalisations for the sin in business, others the warpaint of makeup to thicken their skin against it.

It really did remind her that she must have a word with that new lad in the office she was temping in. Tell him to cut his hair and stop dressing like a tramp. That way there would be a chance for him with the comms girl everyone knew he fancied. Urrgh. She hoped that dodgy sleaze guy from the office down the hall would just ask her out so she could turn him down, and let him move on with his conquesting.

She parked up her red transport neatly as the venetian metal door secured the entrance. Trudging up the staircase into that place of 'work', whatever that was. Some needed to leave one box and enter another for part of the day, just to fool their minds into believing when they were working and when they were playing. Trigger some sort of learned response to let them know when they were supposed to be stressed, and when they were supposed to be happy.

To her it was much of a muchness. It was all a means to an end. She was content enough to play at working to get the periods of working at her play. Hackers were hackers, they didn't have jobs as hackers, they hacked a job so they could hack. All the members did the same.

"Oh, hi, Caroline," she said.

"Yeah, oh, yeah, hi," giggled Caroline.

"Didn't know you were in today then," she asked.

"Yeah, in today, cramming a couple of extras, you know how it is," said Caroline.

Actually she didn't know, but hey. "Yeah, I know how that is, huni," she masked. "So not much happening at your Cybertechnic then?"

"Nah, not much happening," replied Caroline. "But then mine's a small route one, I wasn't a fast track like you, not that it bothers me."

"I know that. Guess we all have different paths flung at us, that's why I'm in this place now."

"Yeah, sorry, I know how it is, we all just do," said Caroline. "Do what we're told, feed our brains on the food they give us."

"That we do," she said, her smile widening. "I still have to study too though, who knows how they work it."

"Mystery," nodded Caroline. "Guess it never ends."

"That seems so true," she nodded gently. "Anyway, best get to my desk of chains then, see you later."

"So, did you find true love at the weekend then?" teased Caroline.

"No," she sighed. "But I'm still," she said, pausing, almost saying 'hacking'.

"Hopeful?" danced Caroline, in a cheerleader like way.

"Yes, I guess there's always *that*," she said, and drifted away to her designated workspace.

"Hey, Caroline," said the new girl.

"Yeah, hey, Mandy," smiled Caroline. "Got any goss?"

*

Tommy and Jonny were in the common room of their Cybertechnic. Jonny was fiddling with some bits of something, and Tommy was periodically lifting himself up on the chin-ups bar. The both of them occasionally glancing at and around the display screens flickering their programs and programmes. He pretty much fell through the double doors, and rushed over excitedly.

"I've got it this time," he blurted out.

"Hmm," nodded Tommy.

"Yeah, worked it out, keplared it!" he shouted. "By doing some tansengental reasonings, and cross-matching with previous correlations, I've figured it. Using the notions of fractal simplicity and quantum mechanics I've discovered that we must be logically equivalent."

Tommy puffed out, raising his chin above the bar.

"Yeah. I've got this shape or pattern or something encoded in my brain. In fact, it might be encoded in my dna or something."

Jonny tutted as a tiny reluctant fixing burred instead of unscrewing.

"That's right," he continued in full hacker flow. "The secrets themselves are encoded in me, I think it's only a matter of deciphering the particular triangulations, and then I should be able to remember what it is that I already know."

Tommy and Jonny looked up and zoned in briefly on one of the display screens as a change in brightness and volume sparked their reflexes, then turned back to their twitching fascinations.

"As far as I can work out, she is long blond, five-five, green eyes, left-handed, slim, probably a 32b or 34c, and is called Anna. Dyed or natural blond I'm not sure. What do you think?" he prompted.

Tommy and Jonny continued silently in their ticks.

"Tommy, what do you think?" he said.

"Huh," said Tommy, lifting up into another pull. "I wasn't listening much, I thought you were talking to Jonny."

"Jonny," he said. "What do you think?"

"Hmm," said Jonny. "I thought you were talking to Tommy."

They laughed. He laughed the shortest. He recapped.

"So why Anna then?" said Jonny.

"Obvious. Palindromic of course," he said.

"Erm, yeah, that makes sense," lied Jonny.

"Plus, the A does look a bit like a triangle, doesn't it. Especially if you go into dimensionals, with Δ ^^Δ. You know what I'm like for triangles," he said.

"Yeah, we know that," said Jonny.

"If she's as paranoid as you though, she's probably changed her appearance though, hasn't she," said Tommy.

"Um," he sighed. There was a short pause. "You guys are just fucking with me aren't you."

"Yes," they nodded.

He sighed and left. Trudging down the stairs back to the rig lab, he sighed again and wondered how it was all beginning to seem a little bit like work. Actually, work, there probably was something he was supposed to be doing for his current tertiary Cybertechnic unit. An easy one if he could manage to force himself to actually do it. He had completed the assignment in week one, two weeks early. But he knew that somehow he'd still only manage to transmit it for assessment after the designated window had just expired.

As the lift in the corridor made its way down, he watched the metal supports flash by in their patterns. He remembered how in his primary Cybertechnic he had been shown the pictures of the seaside piers. Told to see what shapes the girders were made of, he relayed every answer except that which was being prompted for.

The problem had been that he could see it from all angles, and focused through to dimensional matches rather than seeing the obvious flat shapes. Nestled between the parallel outlines, the criss-crossing straps formed their constructs. Seeing squares, crosses, parallelograms, x's, but not the triangles. To him they were but the component sides of the outlined net of a three-dimensional shape. His mind reiterating in attempts of autocompletion to tie the missing side.

"All my love (I am saving)"

Bm7   F#m   Dm7   E7+
My heart is oh so heavy, my songs they are all sad,
Without you my darling, I've nothing to spark me glad.

Bm7   F#m   Dm7 E7+
All my-i love___   I am saving___
All my-i love___   I am wasting___

Bm7   F#m   Dm7   E7+
Each day that I wake up, and feel your deepened pain,
Glowing for your precious light, we eternally meet again.

Bm7   F#m   Dm7 E7+
All my-i love___   I am saving___
All my-i love___   I am wasting___

Bm7   F#m   Dm7   E7+
When will I ever reach, the truth that lies so deep,
My mind forever aching with the secrets it does keep.

Bm7   F#m   Dm7 E7+
All my-i love___   I am saving___
All my-i love___   I am wasting___

Flipping to the ic structures work module, wiring in a response mechanism for the data transferal path. The circuits first firing the undulations of energy to mark the Transmit Acknowledgment signal (TACK), then listening in wait for the ACK burst of electricity to rebound back.

As the hard pasta shells crashed onto the white ceramic plate, he remembered the clacker of dried biscuit food hitting a blue bowl. Nourishment for mind and body of young Billy the cat. Flickering back to the kitten's arrival, the tiny size of the truly black and white cat. A black body of baby fur, with a fluffy white underbelly. The pattern repeated on the growing face, a black head, with white chin and whisker regions. After feeding and playing and dancing, it was very much time for the young kitten to sleep. Fascinated by stairs not previously allowed to climb, the preferred sleeping space was about three-quarters of the way up the twelve, or was it thirteen, straight steps, the rose carpeting and the white banistered hand rail.

Straining to stay awake, Billy the kitten's eyes drooped along with his head. Each time a nervous mind jolt kept the system functioning in consciousness, not letting enough relaxation to fall into dreams. He sat and lay there, draped amongst the stairs, patiently being with Billy, until the repeated experiences of comfort burned enough of a synapse path to enable a condition of stillness from sensations in the unfamiliar environment to be reached.

So as it was with him now. Not much of a sleep pattern for a while, flashes of sleep caught in the here and there. Feeding and playing flipped the firings into slowing and stopping beneath their threshold of response, but the pulse of the primary objective beated as loud as it always did. Something was missing. He couldn't fool his self. Sleep was always sparse when the autocompletions of destiny were still left undone.

And so the day ended as it began.

Chapter Two - Oddness

Lazy Sunday. He figured it was going to be one of those odd afternoons as soon as he entered The Royal Hussar. 'I did it my way' was already playing through the jukebox. Readjusting his eye brightness filters as he stepped across to the bar, he noticed the old figure to his left, along with some bags whose contents where obviously not from the stores that they advertised.

"Usual, Sir, is it," said the barman.

"Yes," he nodded, a little discomforted by being referred to as Sir.

"Hello there!" gleaned the old man from his seat across the bar. "Let me buy you a drink!"

"Oh, no, it's ok, I've got it," he said.

"No, let me buy you that drink."

"It's ok," whispered the barman. "He always buys people drinks. He's loaded. Let The Captain get it for you. Probably gets lonely, figure he's outlived everyone he knew."

"Ok, then, thank you," he conceded.

"Pint of Scrumpy Jack it is then," smiled the barman.

With the golden rays poured into the glass, he lifted the beacon and carried it over to an empty table. The Captain tottered across.

"So you one of thoses at the Cybertechnic from across the wander way then, yes?" asked The Captain.

"Yes, that's correct," he said, taking those few first refreshing gulps from his glass.

"All that new age stuff then I suppose, wasn't quite like that in my day," reeled off The Captain.

"Indeed," he agreed. "Some of the overseers there banter about punched cards and ticking tapes, I'm guessing your ways before even that."

"Ways before that!" laughed The Captain. "Before

Keplar organics, waveform navigation, solid-state even. True binary mechanics, cogs and all."

The Captain recited his tale of how he had been a fighter pilot for the Polish air service, and then for the RAF and The Allies after the decimations. He must have been through some shit.

"Funny things those dronings," continued The Captain. "There was always a guaranteed time of incursion for them. Could set your pocket piece by them. Sunday teatime."

"Yes," he smiled. "The dark teatime of the soul."

"We reckoned it was a morale thing. They must have decided that by attacking at that perceived safe haven of time and place, it would affect us the most."

"Verifiable tactics that, I guess," he tried to confirm and agree.

"True as," laughed The Captain excitedly with the understanding of the telling. "The harshest of enemies will wreak their fiercest attack at the moment that they perceive is your weakest."

Their glasses emptied more.

"Strange thing was, it sort of geeried us up," said The Captain. "The true Englishmen looked upon it as cricket high tea. They all relaxed in the afternoon, had their Sunday tea, cake and nonsense, maybe even the odd snooze. After this period of gentle stillness, they laughed, 'Second Innings', when the waves came in."

He couldn't help but admire the truth in that, bit like Drake and his bowls. Chill out and finish what he was doing, then ride out to the fast pitchers. Although some would banter that Drake was pissed the night before, had a terrible hangover, and so didn't surface until late.

"So you see," leaned in The Captain. "Sometimes the enemy attack at the moment they anticipate you will be at your most vulnerable, where in fact, it is the moment at which you tap your greatest strength."

The sound of the pool table clinked from the near distance. The drinks flowed their flow.

"You seem nervous," prodded The Captain.

"Well, not really," he said. "Although I guess things are always a bit sketchy when missions are incomplete."

"Hmm, yes, I know that feeling," said The Captain in an eye-glazing.

"It has been said that I'm a little paranoid though," he laughed. "But don't tell anyone I told you."

The Captain barely managed a smile at that. "Guess you can never be too paranoid. Especially someone with your skillset, you being at the Cybertechnic and all that I mean."

"Too paranoid," he said. "That isn't something that would occur. But yes, I have been subject to a few recruitment drives in my time."

"I'm sure you have," said The Captain. "There's certainly a good few tricks about."

"Yeah. Makes it hard to meet the right woman though," he smiled.

"Oh? The right woman?" quizzed The Captain.

"Hmm, yes," he replied hesitantly. "I think I'm one of those people with a long burn-in. Once I was walking up a hill, and three girls all dressed to thrill were speeding down towards me. In the typical way of girls, none of them maneuvered to make way, so I ended up squeezing past by a wall, at least I didn't have to do a hop into the transport way."

Gulps of liquid fluidity to lubricate his tale.

"Yes," he continued. "As they floated past, after their preanings and eye-casting glances, one of them piped up, 'Don't worry girls, he's looking for the one, not some one.'"

"That walk of yours must give out some weird TACKS," said The Captain.

"Very probably," he said. "What I really mean though, without my ramblings, is that it can get difficult when I meet a girl to as whether she's trying to seduce me or merely recruit me."

"I can see you've been through a few of those," laughed The Captain.

"Yeah. It's sometimes like a pyramid stream of them," he said. "From the simple single girl bait and trap, to the holidaying alpha girls, to the worst of the worst. The double whammy of the linked encouragement."

"Oh, yes?" hacked The Captain.

"Yes," he said. "The worst of the worst is the brother and sister lure. Works better than the female friend bait as there's an established excuse for the moments of coincidental meetings."

"Ah," slowly nodded The Captain, swigging a few swigs.

"The amiable stranger befriends you in a difficult situation, which is probably engineered too, and then pops up by and by. After the trust has been triggered, the sibling card is brought into play. With the secondary befriendment, and then the inevitable played for reversed seduction, the end result is that two separate yet complimentary sources of information make their tapways."

"Interesting stuff," said The Captain. "Don't worry. I won't bore you with one of those. Although as my dear friend Henry would have said to you, that's better than electrodes on your bollocks!"

They laughed heartily and drank a toast to Henry. He noticed he was laughing, and then remembered it wasn't his laugh. Someone had most likely stolen his. He hoped he hadn't accidentally stolen the one he was using, but it was probably just a generic indication of laughter, that reflex of human response.

"Everybody's trying to sell you something, I suppose," he said. "Even if it's just their opinion."

"That's often the way," said The Captain. "I presume

you've had a few agencies have a go at trying."

"I suppose I have," he said. "Maybe all those positive manipulations by all those varied religious groups, and all those sketchy girls just wanting a wallet and a willy, have stood me in good stead."

"Maybe," said The Captain. "I heard some of those cults can be a bit iffy."

"Yeah," he said. "Even with the real legit ones you're always left wondering whether it's just all for the ego of the high preacher. Either having reached a dawn where the mission is to make up for their own failings by rekindling others, or just a competition thing with rival sects, the numbers of members forming a high score table of fame for them."

"Hmm," said The Captain thoughtfully.

"Maybe I'm just ranting though, those aren't so bad," he said. "Suppose they only mean well, and just want to make you part of their community, but it can get all a bit encouraging and assimilation like."

"There's worse sharks that attack," confirmed The Captain.

"Definitely," he nodded furiously. "Some I've encountered have bordered on satanic offerings, trying to get inductees to sacrifice themselves without knowing, in some power and control, energy gain scheme."

"Sounds highly odd," said The Captain.

"Yeah," he said. "During one particularly long period of brain washing, I had live voice comms saying stuff like, 'If they knew you knew they'd want to kill you'."

"A nasty one," said The Captain.

"Very," he said. "Enough to put even someone with level asoterials off their game for good, let alone someone who's fractalling internally. And this is all coming in from someone who had built up a position of trust over a long period. A definite long wire-in."

"A good turn of phrase that, fractalling internally," said The Captain.

"Thanks," he said. "What with all the false flag umbrellas, triple identify forges and ether history database manipulations, you're left never really sure who's behind it all. There's so many layers of abstraction these days. That's why I pretty much try and have to do nothing with any of them. It's ok getting a 'pension' cheque every now and again, but you know the goggles will be knocking on your doors with transports any time there's a bad sitch."

"Hmm, yes," said The Captain. "Sometimes it may simply be more prudent to hack for your self."

*

"So what time did he say he was coming round then?" said Jonny, barely looking up amongst his tweaking.

"Oh, you know," said Tommy. "You know what he's like. Doesn't have a time thing does he. He was telling me he's in a 'variable vinci double' at the moment. Some sketched-out stuff about two four-hour sleep slots at differing times of the day."

"Really," said Jonny.

"Yeah, so he says," replied Tommy. "He says he does like evenings though, so he's probably awake then."

"Awake," smirked Jonny, clicking two pieces together. "Some would argue that he never enters a conscious state. Just stays on the surface of interaction between the borders of the dream like and waking reality."

"That sounds like something he would say," laughed Tommy.

Jonny huffed. "You're probably right. I'm probably only repeating what he told me. Or repeating what he repeatedly tells me more like."

"Yeah," nodded Tommy. "Guess we all have our

missions that drive us, just wish he'd work out what the fuck his is and give us a bit of quiet."

"So very, very, true," said Jonny.

"The beef of it all being," said Tommy. "Is that he'll probably be around some time this evening."

"I thought this was an assist," frowned Jonny. "He ain't half working up the hackcreds on this one."

The hackcreds system was a good system when you needed it. As is often the way, sometimes you need to perform your biggest hacks when you're at your lowest point, and sometimes you can't be in two places at once to pull off a simultaneous trigger.

"Hackcreds then, Jonny," said Tommy.

"Yes, hackcreds, Tommy," said Jonny, giving that look of 'you should know this', to the younger Tommy.

"Yeah, I know what they're all about, but where'd they come from, originally I mean."

"Ah. Well, if you listen, then I'll burst off what I know," said Jonny.

"Ok, ok, I'll sit comfortable and listen for a bit," said Tommy. "I won't drag it into a multiplayer discussion group where the source of the data disappears into the interplay of a pub group conversation."

"You know you can pay attention when the need arises," laughed Jonny. "Even if I haven't got dyed hair and a big cleavage."

Tommy scratched his chin and peered innocently out from the top corners of his eyes.

"Ok," said Jonny. "The associated myth tag of the hackcreds origination is the usual blend of fact and fiction. A small group in Belgium apparently hacked themselves into a tight spot with the naval force of a neighbouring country. Purely by accident of course, a honeypot on the admiralty matrix triggered a harmless sa bee to nest in it. The bee did as it was designed to do, eat up the honey by tying up the resources of the near network, and then buzz off back to the hive."

Tommy almost thought of adding in a buzzing noise to make things multimedia, but on this occasion thought the better of it.

"Now," said Jonny, going into full professor Yaffle mode. "On safely returning home, the pollen that the bees had collected could be analysed and the location of the honeypot tagged like the location of a speeding device. If necessary, other bees could then be sent out in other sorties to keep the honey producers busy, and distracted."

"Sounds all well and good," risked Tommy, to Jonny's stares.

"Yes, and in practice the system worked well," continued Jonny. "As it turned out, it all worked rather too well. The initial targets where intended to be small, and thus have a finite amount of drawable resources. Maybe the coders of both the intrusion and the detection system were just too good for the job. They both designed excellent systems, although some could argue in hindsight that it was all just too much gold-plating through boredom."

"Bling, bling," whispered Tommy in a low voice that Jonny didn't bother to process.

"When the pioneer bee arrived, its sensory components detected that it was in fact the biggest fucking jar of honey that it had ever seen. The original design was that the individual bees would just top up on their fill, and then fly back to base, reporting findings to the other bees. What the Belgians, often mistakenly and rather piss-takingly referred to as the Wasps or the Busy Bees, forgot to do, was cap the performance of their neatly coded insects."

"Myth tag legend has it, that on what must have been a particularly rainy or sunny day depending on the nature of the particular coders, they decided to make some optimisations. Running through what must have been a simple benchmarking and load simulation tool, one of the coders noticed that there was an inefficient bottleneck in the architecture. When a source was particularly rich in honey, the system was designed to send out extra bees to feed. Thus with a big jar, the cycles the bees took to travel to the pot where larger than the cycles spent at the destination. As the group only had limited processing power and resources, supply outstripped demand and the hive ran out of bees."

Tommy did a buzzing noise of a bee that had no buzz. Luckily Jonny was into his tale and didn't notice the puffs of buzzed out air.

"Taking inspiration from the already beloved nature analogy, the simplest solution seemed to be to give a bee the ability to tell a queen bee the situation. A good idea in itself," said Jonny.

"Doubling up on idleness, somebody at the admiralty matrix host also ran some performance tests of their own. They realised that if an intrusion was viral and replicating, then the system would need to draw on resources from elsewhere. Here's the thing, it was the priority level at which this request got flagged at. Admittedly, most coders feel that their piece is important, but in this case the integer selected was just a little too above the level of reporting it should have been. Maybe the fault was snowballed as other nearby systems had undocumented features, which also had undocumented references and matches to the significance of alert levels."

"The plot thickens," said Tommy. "Like the honey."

"Yes. So while the Belgians are out getting pizza or something," continued Jonny.

"Those lucky bastards, where's ours," interrupted Tommy.

"What time did you post for it?" asked Jonny.

"Erm, not sure."

"Did you tip them last time" said Jonny, continuing his

interrogation.

"Yeah, course," said Tommy. "One or two cans of stella, I think. Even gave a choice between cider or stella."

"I see," said Jonny. "They must be busy then. And so back to our pioneer bee."

"Very good," said Tommy.

"So, off pops our fresh bee, all keen and eager. Nips in, lands and finds a miracle of honey. Filling up in haste, he flies back to the hive and reports to the queen herself."

"Nice," said Tommy.

"Now," said Jonny, sternly. "This is where the effect of that little optimisation comes in. The queen bee has developed the ability to know when it's too big a honeypot to send out her limited number of bees."

"Wise momma," laughed Tommy.

"With this data, she runs the routine that the hacker had put in. The solution to the bottleneck was simple – fly out another queen to the pot, and establish a local hive."

"Conquer and populate," said Tommy.

"All fair well in itself. So, the queen bee arrives and sets off her bees. And now comes the sting in the tail," smiled Jonny.

"Busy bees!" said Tommy.

"Yes. Here comes the secondary impact of the optimisation. The bees report to the queen the size of the pot, and guess what, the queen divides and now there's two queens."

"Sounding like something out of attack of the killer bees," said Tommy.

"Yes. And so both of the optimisation routines fire up in their efficiency. The host starts flagging resource pulls, and the bees keep telling the queens to make more queens."

"A classic deadlock run chase scenario," said Tommy.

"Neatly put. There we have it, two processes locked in performance competition, each able to draw on more resources to be chased by the other."

"Sounds like a very sticky situation," laughed Tommy.

"Very sticky," agreed Jonny. "Needless to say, some entity noticed. A very big entity. Not the kind of systems to be poking into without a very good mexico."

"Yeah, and by the sounds of it, all the Belgians had was some soggy pizza," laughed Tommy.

"Hopefully decent pizza," said Jonny. "Probably something meaty or severely hot, judging by what they did next."

"Those darn jalapeños," laughed Tommy.

"High probability," nodded Jonny, smiling. "They knew the trace would be coming, and they figured a beacon bonfire would be the only way to avoid the track."

"Very resource intensive," said Tommy, thankful he hadn't been there.

"That's right," said Jonny. "Now, they needed a way to tap the coder power to achieve the hack. Given that they were real trueschool hackers, they sought information in the subject area of the target they were avoiding."

"Erm, what eats bees?" spat out Tommy.

"Not quite. Naval history was more their ticket. They came across that point in history where the brits were defeated by dutch. Severely embarrassed, the hornet like investigations of the reasons why showed that money was the key. The dutch were able to generate more funds from their native country, and thus build a superior fleet."

"Clever," said Tommy.

"Yes. The dutch banking system enabled the government to effectively borrow money from dutch corps, by holding it in their banks, and then selling shares in the holdings of the banks."

"Good stuff," said Tommy.

"Yes," agreed Jonny. "The beauty of the plan was that it effectively enabled the system to use the same money twice, creating something out of nothing."

"Doubling your stack is always good," smiled Tommy, then switching to the mimic of a stern poker face.

"And so the hackcreds system was born," said Jonny triumphantly. "By establishing a bank of hackers, they were able to construct the network of blinding flares which they had originally conceived."

"The system we all know and love," said Tommy. "Well, mostly."

"Yes. The way of it does serve as a good method of drawing fresh talent into the pool," said Jonny. "Often the one's who need to do a larger hack quick are those starting out."

"Good job the cybertechnic covered some of the brown envelope stuff," said Tommy. "Or I'd probably owe a lot more creds."

"The design does have a way of attracting the right sort of wrong types," smiled Jonny.

"A seemingly endless supply of those," laughed Tommy.

"And as for the Belgians, rumour has it they're still paying off the hackdebt to this day," punchlined Jonny. Tommy lapped it up. "Joking aside, he's running up a bit of a tab with this, isn't he."

"Well, erm, sort of," stuttered Tommy.

"I see," said Jonny with much eyebrow raising.

"Actually, I kind of sort of, well, owe, him," managed Tommy.

"You do have a way of doing just the wrong thing at the right time," chuckled Jonny. "But he's still ticking away at my meter, even if not yours."

"I know," said Tommy. "But he is meteor driven on this one, keeps going on about tracking treasures down and the 'big hack', whatever that is."

"Don't we not know it," said Jonny.

"And you know what happened last time," smiled Tommy. "He created that credbot system to do lots of tiny hacks for him whilst he was sleeping."

"That was very inventive," said Jonny. "But the weight of some of the coins on all these latest ones will need balancing out with a little more than trivs."

"I'm not even going to ask what silos he's got you scoping," said Tommy.

"He wants to listen to some of his own bollocks sometime," said Jonny. "Maybe he'll be able to work it all out for him self."

The entrance buzzer roared out. Jonny and Tommy stood excitedly in expectance. Looking into the vidpanel display.

"Oh," said Tommy, disappointment draining and deepening his voice. "It's you."

"Well there's a fucking welcome for you," he said.

"Come on up," said Jonny, fingers dancing on the keypad to the solenoids.

"So how's it going?" he said.

"Pretty lame," said Jonny. "A time consuming series rather than anything of playful excellence."

"Usual way," he said. "Tie-up for a while with the fodder, and then out will come the end of level boss."

"Yes, the usual isoteric way of this type of system," said Jonny.

"I'll let you have first crack at the gargant when it rears in then," he said.

"You're so caring," said Jonny, partly thanking, and partly in sarcasm.

The buzzer roared again.

"You two dual-up and I'll sort the fuel," said Tommy.

"Good plan," said Jonny. "So tell me then, how do you always arrive at the right time for pizza?"

"Oh, you know how it is, Jonny," he said with his

hacker smile. "One of the delivery guys owes me hackcreds."

Jonny just smiled back.

"Well praise the Lord!" said Tommy, armed with the righteousness of that heavenly repast, pizza, and the miracle of being given extra jalapeños on the side.

Chapter Three – For a girl

He awoke screaming in pain. His felt as though the hurt in his skin was afire, the surface taut and sore, bleeding. Where it hurt it itched, where it itched he scratched, and where he scratched it hurt. His instinctive solution did not solve the problem, and the circular torment continued in its cycles until his mind realised no progress was being made, and it gave up in screams which jolted his body in spasm.

He could sense that his progenitors weren't there. It was light although he knew it was dark. The night watchers looked on, the layer of the incubator glass between them and him. They couldn't lift and hold him as the pressure against his skin would only have created pain. He lay there, legs crossed at the ankles, thumbs nestled between index and middle fingers.

Morning came with its cool chill and eerie stillness. A slow passing of cycles, coupled with the expectancy of something destined to occur. The baby lay there thinking, connecting, dreaming whilst awake. An exhausting wait of emptiness. He felt cold, tired, and lonely.

With the sun through the window came the maternal glow. His mother had returned with the beginning of the work day. He tried to feed through his sore lips, a little nourishment was gleaned, but feeding didn't seem to quell the chemical triggering in his mind.

Settling him back down, his mother gazed upon him. Looking at him lovingly, glancing over the breaks in his skin. Blowing gently over them with a breath of perfect temperature, giving a mild relief to the burning sensations of pain, and a tactile touch of warm comfort. He fell into sleep.

Another night the intermittent observer from an agency who had watched them watch, hacked in. Seeing the baby unconscious amidst the restless writhing of the soreness of his skin surface, she copied the blowing technique she had smiled upon a few days before.

The eye lightening faded out as the reality of the newly born baby began to form. The mild pinging pain and the slow realisation of a consciousness. The smell of her was different. It wasn't the same smell as his genetic parentage. It was someone different. It was light although it was night. As his eyelids spasmed in growth they opened, and a sudden rush of blood empowered his retinal burn. The scent wasn't his genetic similarity yet matched like fingers interlocking in warm love. The immune systems would be highly compatible, and the descendant splitting and recombining would enhance the bonds of the genetic chain.

She blinked slowly. The baby wriggled in the dance of wanting to be picked up, arms half stretching out in a hug like motion. She motioned her protruding bent index finger towards and into the fish tank incubator. Starting at the left side of the baby's mouth, her finger's knuckle traced the slow circular shape round his lips, and a slight quarter circuit more to position back to the central.

His eyes focused on the pattern in her eyes. A prismatic net shape burning in starred vertices. As she sang to him in a soft lullaby, his nanomachines recorded every visual detail, long blackened eyelashes, the cheekbone and nose edgeline ridges, a slight puffiness beneath her eyes, slowly iterating and continuing down to her chin. As she blinked he suckled on the flavouring of her finger knuckle. His first taste of reality suppressant. The memory was fused.

"It's done," she sighed. "The little lighthouse."

"I know you think it unfair now, but it's vital for the survival of your future daughter," said The Captain.

***

Things were certainly so not right. They hadn't been for a while. Stuff could go sketchy of course, but this seemed a little different. She knew that tiredness and a building up of a lot of trivialities could weigh her down sometimes, but this felt a little more that those odd week or so's of flu-like darkness.

Maybe it was because she was everybody's last call. The person they ventured to when there wasn't anyone else to turn to for help. She was ok with that, for some reason she did manage to have an endless patience when it came to that kind of Keplarisation. She was a keeper of many people's secrets.

Problem was, her own hacking had led her to a level of abstraction from which she couldn't define her viewpoint to anybody else. She seemed to have the answers to the hidden equations, but she didn't seem to have any use for them, or anyone to communicate them to or understand them, or indeed any interface to even feed them into.

She had learnt her skills and used them to experience and practice as she had been taught. But now what. It was no longer enough in itself. Training for what, no purpose or sake to it. She was lost. Not really lost, for she had a fully annotated map, but just no place to go, no reason to visit.

She had worked out her detailed plan for her escape to Mexico, as all the members did. She wondered whether the time had come to just accept and give up, but really she needed to tidy the flat first. Never good to leave unsolved items, or a mess. Leave things more beautiful than you find them.

Actually, that paperwork was needed somewhere too. She visited Caroline.

"Hey, Caroline," she said plainly and simply.
"Yeah, babes, hi," gave back Caroline.
"Brought that paperwork and that, you know, tidy as

does," she said.

"Thanks, appreciated," said Caroline. "So how's it in your world?"

"In all done," she said. "This has been the worst year of my life."

"You're lucky you've gone so long in life not to have had it before," said Caroline.

She left soon after.

Bumping into her friend's uncle in the street.

"Hi," she said.

"Oh, hello you, I've heard you've been having a rough one of late," said uncle.

"Yeah," she sighed. "All not good. Sort of lots of stuff really. Tryout here. Sketchiness there."

"Well, it's all just life stuff isn't it. You've solved the money problem which is most people's difficult one, so really, you have an advantage."

"Yes," she said.

The comm line to her parents in one of the regular three day check-ins.

"We've heard that things aren't so great," said her mother. "Well, I'm worse, as you should know. You can't be thinking about some running away plan. My problems should put yours into perspective."

"What have you been up to then, little one," said her father. "If things aren't going great you should lay off that wacky reality suppressant. You know that it isn't good for you."

Why did they *always* bring that up.

That cunt from the office had told everyone that he had shagged her when the wanker hadn't. Probably only told that fucking Mandy, the local transmitter station. Actually, a little unfair on Mandy, she just liked to talk. The grapevine definitely looked as though it had been in full-bodied flow.

Everyone in the office was looking at her differently. Had they heard the false gossip or had they not. Some looked down their noises at her, some eyed her up as though she had now become some global piece of free for all porn. Others pronounced her name in different intonations and inflections when they said hi.

The toilet cubicles seemed to empty when she entered. When she wired comms they seemed to take longer and longer to respond, and the replies were offhand and unmeaningful. Hushed voices and giggles when she was near.

There wasn't anybody to listen to the explanation of her side of the story. What words to use or in which language, she did not know. Forever lost in an abyss of confusion and misunderstanding. There wasn't anybody who knew who she was.

She didn't feel well. Leaving the office and in the street. It was the same. Everyone seeing the false lies that were branded on her head. Glancing, eyeing, staring, judging. Turning her transport away, the hums of the traffic chattering about her. The smart dressed and the tramp like on street corners. One meeting another, then moving on and passing the gossip to the next along the chain. Harsh looks and backs of heads. She felt cold, tired, and lonely.

Returning into and securing all entrances to the flat. Over garments and shoes dragged and kicked off into snow drifts in the corridor. Stumbling into the bedroom and ensuite.

She poked her tongue out into the mirror, examining for some unknown symptom. Her temperature regulation just didn't seem right. Too hot or too cold. She had a fever. Maybe she hadn't eaten. Draining over too much to do that now, little other action possible but going to bed.

Her Asoterials must be really off. Thoughts flickering in a blur of sleep hazed enlightenment. Connections drifting in and out through consciousness, waves of lightening crashing into jagged rocks. The swimming of swans and the high-pitched hooting of migrating geese. A cycled curse of continued heart-felt explanations falling on empty ears. No truth gleaned from knowledge or experience, time stolen in false understandings and judgmental rationalisations of fickle onlookers.

The long hours of the long days drew out into the endless length of night. Shining silver tears wept out to fall amongst the oceans, rising and subsiding with the swing of the tides. As her sweat of nightmares and the rivers of her eyes dampened the bed, she took turns to roll herself to the other less moistened side.

The acid chills of sleep deprivation unchaining the black knighted wraiths of draining terrors, shredding her face into unrecognisable forms. Shaded blood seeping from the walls of the room, pouring in and filling up, until the mattress lay floating atop a thickened spew of putrid hatred.

On the fourth day since everything first began, the bubbling and gurgling of a torrid spiralling flow around her. The foul-mouthed spits of boiling raging forth the tongues which lapped around her covers. The pressure mounting against the shields until the wretchedness broke the very sanctuary of her bed. In and around her. Invading, intruding, violating the sacredness of her soul. Enveloping and squashing inward.

Finding half a peanut in her bed. The pea and the nut. A shell and its fruit. Found a peanut last night I. The shape and the suggestion. Synapses melting and reforming, trying to glean a pattern match to explain the symbol. Everything being linked through and outside of time to this moment. An eternity of not understanding the questions to the obvious answers which were found in proof.

Falling into a conscious unconsciousness, the sound of a silent wind and a numbness of feeling. Standing up.

On a liquid plane of patterned light she stood motionless and relaxed, her legs bent ever so slightly, a delicate curve in her elbows. The cool chill of the wind behind her, blowing her hair forward. Not the most flattering direction to be viewed in.

Such was the breeze, any sounds her lips motioned drifted away in packets of light, inaudible to her as though the monitor speakers were turned off on her stage of infinite proportions.

No matter which direction she stepped in, the undulating concentric circles of light seemed to pulse toward an unknown centre faster than she could traverse. She silently prayed her thoughts to her God, to bring her comfort on her hiking travels. Left or right, forward or back, it made no difference. No matter how she danced and twisted and turned in flow, the wind was always behind her, shining towards an inner destination. She was lost to all hope.

She stopped her rushing, and stood patiently. Silently expectant in wait. In the stillness of her acceptance of the cascading of non-existent time, she saw a shape that the rays of light danced over in their passing. Taking time to focus and concentrate, changing the beams and rarefactions, she saw it was someone lying down.

As the meniscus of her eyes changed their wavelengths, the shape became clearer. Not so much zooming in, but being drawn toward a viewpoint of understanding.

Although still distant, the shape was much clearer now. It was a man laying on his side. One leg bent at the knee so it pointed upward, his head resting on an arm which was bent at the elbow, the whole creating a circuit of curves.

He lay on the very edge of a black abyss, an event horizon where all the streams of accelerated light suddenly sped to a point where even they held no form such was the distance between their component waves of particles.

Rays shone out from his eyes like a lighthouse of vision, projecting a shimmering glow of radiance in their paths of searching. She watched as his sight fell on an abstracted world of beings, who collided and interacted in a non-obvious correlation. As he gazed upon them, they seemed to reveal their light in a gradual raising of ultraviolet auras from their feet, like the appearing of a heat haze shimmering over a sun baked transport lane. The odd one reflected back a dim glow, although the numbers and brightness of them was hardly noticeable.

There were other beings which lit their own light without any intervention. Now and again glowing, in quite a regular short-spanned pattern. His light seemed to be guiding them away from a ragged shore. Once they had their bearings, mostly the bright lights shone for each other, drawing themselves to each other in.

She could see all the illuminations dancing their light show. It was like that she had seen at parties and gatherings, were eye contact and a smile could spark the crossings of the light sabres of love. She saw the light, but it never shone on her.

Her viewpoint moving closer, translacing like a lens. Unlike the source of lightening behind her, his beacon only seemed to shine intermittently. Each sweep seeming to drain an unseen power source, needing a short moment of recharge, and then radiating in all its glory again.

Then his lighthouse stopped. The wait for the recharge ebbed away into the acceptance that the transport had either been or wasn't coming. Either way the timetable was irrelevant, and gave no indicators or further data.

She watched as he moved his legs ninety degrees, and stood up. The centre of the spiralling circles became darker, the rays of light travelling faster still, their acceleration rising exponentially. Standing on the event horizon, staring into the black pit of hell. All lightness being sucked in never to return again, forever lost in the depths of the unknowable.

Seeing and experiencing all his hope lost in an endless curse of repeated failures, she felt the warmth of her tears of pixie armour drip down her icen face. The panic of the heaves of his chest breathing seemed to slow gently, until they looked to resonate in matched cycles to the peaks and troughs of the incoming ripples of light.

She watched effortlessly and timelessly as he walked to the centre of the circle. Not so much floating above the lightfall, as just existing in stasis on top of it, as though he had no mass that could be pulled to form a weight to be drawn down and inward.

Then the very will seemed to disappear from his abstraction of being, as though he doubted his existence itself. He seemed to be looking for something, searching in the cascading parabolas of timelight.

She tried to maneuver herself so as to be in his field of vision, tilting her face slightly in the expectance of being looked upon. How ever she danced and cartwheeled around, she was always behind him. He couldn't see her, his gaze distracted in the meanderings of fluid flows. Like the early memory of when she had strolled over the black and white striped pedestrian crossing, spotting a potential target to spark her iterations of possible matchings, only to be missed in passing as he admired the big red sports car revving impatiently in wait.

Intermingled with the visions of her own library of stored thoughts, she saw him disintegrate like the pixelation of a tacky cliptrip effect. He had seemed to set some device just as the balance tipped. He fell.

Her arms almost broke from her shoulders with the force of her reflex action, stretching out in a snap that would have been rivalled only by the best transcended of martial practitioners, were it not for its over exertedness.

Reaching out in desperate motions, like the want of a baby needing to be picked up, her finger knuckles shattered as they tried to expand beyond her realm of reach.

Sensing depths of screams never heard before. Not the broken whimpering shrills of terror, nor the high-pitched alarm calls of cycling fright and fear, or even the shouts of pain cried out in reluctance when the threshold had been triggered. They were the deep instinctive reflex shutterings of a body wrenching in inexplicable agony.

She felt no action could be taken in help, lost inside of herself in a torturous observation. The claws of demons tearing at his skin and shredding his soul, contorted legs with over-proportioned muscles stomping and kicking his sagged body around amongst themselves. Nagging whisperings of hypnotic false lies being incanted to his ears.

Her own soul imploded as she echoed the experience of her witnessing. Her body vomited out tears until her skin seemed to dry out and become cracked like untended grassland turned to mud in too strong a sun.

An instant before her sight became blinded by the brightness of the darkness, she saw her shimmering tears in their whirlpool, flowing around and into the cylindrical shaft. Spiralling and rushing, draining down deep, cleansing and protecting. Washing and purifying.

There was no longer time and her formless being breathed outside of it. In the nothingness of everything, all hope of even mere existence fading with the slowing of synapse firing. Starry spots of memories burning out, with not even a candle wax left in tell to trace.

Nothing left to be, nothing left to do.

"So she sang to him"

At the end of all time,
When all light had shone,
There was nothing left,
Save my love for you.

Tears of pure pixie armour,
Wept down to shield your soul,
Reaching out into eternity,
Where I know my love resides.

In the timelessness of infinity he waited. Never doubting for an instant in his belief that she existed. Though the screams quelled not, and the wretchedness was unceasing.

She ever felt the presence of his love.

Chapter Four - Of the boy

Stamping his mind unceremoniously through a spiralling cheese-grater shaft dancing toward the decadency of oblivion, the demons raped his thoughts and kicked his sagged body husk around amongst themselves.

It had been a tough week.

Things had been getting tricky for a while. The indoctrinal banterings of various groups had been circling in his mind for a considerable time. At the start of the week he had met with his peers on the day of the moon. Parts of the discussions were the usual banter, other parts seemed strangely inappropriate, phrases he had heard before, but were somehow now being displaced into an attempt at the explanation of an unknown meaning.

"What is it? A tapeworm?"

"Break the spell."

"The good of the many and the good of the few."

"It's not black and white, it's black and white."

"Like losing control of your brain."

He had that strange awareness feeling that day, so he hadn't risked the cakes in case they were laced with an altered strain of reality suppressant. Although there was no way any right minded coder could have refused the offer of a can of fizzy pop.

Leaving and returning home, later in the day he realised he had run out of reality suppressant. There would be no powering up the rig into vr until he had restocked. Settling instead for a warm up from everybody's favourite uncle whiskey, sipping gently and reanalysing and reprocessing the day's inputs.

He felt sick. He figured he had eaten sufficiently that day, so the gurgling in his stomach was indeed somewhat curious. Without time to cross the living room and hallway, he vomited into the kitchen sink.

Focusing down into the abyss, he saw what looked like a piece of string, and there his deadlock run chase scenario began. Processing through explanations for the result of his organic equation, his message as it would be later phrased. Was it a tapeworm? Perhaps it had been hidden in a flecked ecstasy pill, to lie in wait in his stomach lining until years of water had swelled it in size like an exponentialled grain of rice.

What had he done. What must he do. Perhaps he must do good deeds to make up for his past. Piece of string. Was it a piece of a dishcloth. Would his good doings just be as dirty rags, soiled by the ego in external shows of charity. Or would he be like a cleaning cloth, which wiped away the dirt to bring forth reborn shininess, only to leave itself marked by the process until washed carefully under streams of river flow.

Whereas before his mind only might spent the odd cycle in analysis of the random unknowns, the rapidity of his Keplarisation reached a greater peak with the stimulation of the awakeness of days and nights without sleep. Thinking and attempting neuronisation in infinite pathways. In its attempt at understanding, his mind fractalled internally, searching for the truth that lay deep beneath.

The memories of his entire life hung in fluidosity in his mind. Thoughts were never forgotten, single switches of synapses floating softly in a timeless breeze. They waited there patiently and effortlessly, until the time that a processing formed a new connection to them, and instead of being isolated outside of the network they joined the wholeness of understanding. Whilst a single spark might not address much in itself, when two, then three, were ignited in communication, the waves of energy were noticed by those surrounding,   thus   inflaming   other   routeways   to comprehension.

Rapidly analysing and reindexing, cross-matching in overflowing paths of firation. The whole mass of his brain bursting in its explosions, becoming a single fusion of connectivity. Windows of thought being translaced into focus, examined, subdivided in two for closer inspection. These divisions themselves being dissected into half parts. The iterations mapping inwardly, his mind fractalling into itself, until the single cells themselves fractured like a popping bubble.

Speeding through the lightening flashes of his life in his eyes. Observing, experiencing, reliving every smile and every tear as his body reverberated from a cascading of emotions in total recall. That which he had always held dear. That which he had spent his life questing and prospecting for. An unknowable force highlighting his key moments, his triumphs and mistakes. A lifetime of miscommunication and not being understood. Searching for his points of weakness. Where his vulnerabilities lay waiting. The moments for which he blamed himself.

Spanning through the memories of girls he had loved and been loved by. Recalling how he had phoned a girl from the red telephone box, to make up for the time he hadn't in the past. Even though it wouldn't change the future, he had known that it would at least dispel that particular hold the past had over him. Spinning into failed relationships, missed opportunities, and false readings.

Spiralling backwards in linearity, then flipping and cross-comparing in a meld through the inside and outside of intermingling time. The building of a parallel processor capable of linking everything.

In the darkness of his clarity he remembered that divisive moment.

Walking through the nightclub to the left of the dancefloor. Past the tables and chairs on his left. Suddenly stopping in a larger area, seeing the girl unexpectedly. He raised his left hand like a Red Indian, as if a silent hi in truce. He couldn't remember hearing any reply. Gazing on the beauty of the girl's face and eyes, all reality and time fell forever lost in an eternal darkness. They had separated months before. In the sorrow of missing the girl he had broken the purity of their bond, sharing one night of loneliness with another. He remembered the words of a friend saying how maybe a second chance could come in the summer. He had forever broken that hope and had lost that which he had eternally sought for. He remembered both their upset from the months before. All was caused by him, it was all his fault. His self could not ever forgive him. His summer never came.

Sprinting through lifecycles of mistakes and blame. Futile attempts at self analysis and subsequent self correction. An eternal epitaph of mockery in an endless passing of equinoctial circles.

Maybe the match was never there, a remembering how sometimes the girl sneezed in his presence, joking of being allergic to him. Maybe the immune systems of their genetic bodies reacted in a way outside of their level of consciousness. But that did not lessen the blame of his self, or his sense of loss. He was always so very tired.

In the days of nights that followed his mind thought inside against itself. The meniscuses of waking and consciousness, past and present, melded into one. The incidence of coincidence exponetialling in paths of attempts at understanding and explanation.

When he saw the vidclip on the screen which he had seen some years before, his perceived unfaithfulness to the girl triggered memories of the hallucinations of scorpions. Especially as the original source was interspersed with repetitive jabs of various indoctrinal brain washing codices, to be unleased at a later date, and reinforced with a tainted batch of reality suppressant. The comm link to the clap clinic certainly manifested itself as a defcon zero, life or death situation, rising from his guilt.

In a succession of nights of dreaming whilst awake in his room, his thoughts became predictive in their firings. In the sweating of sleeplessness, his imagination became predictive, each night's thoughts echoed throughout the headings of the next day's newspaper. To try and lessen the butterfly effect of his being, his mind fought against itself, trying to think clearly and maintain a stream of goodness. Not wanting to be awake, not wanting to be asleep.

The harder that the strength of his thought swung, the harder the swing back of the echoings of oblivion. Like losing control of his thinking, losing control of the conscious thought of the brain. Everyday the paperboy brang more. The good of the many and the good of the few. Was the purpose to destroy himself so that the many may have good. $E=mc^2$. Was it the aim of the conspirators to fool him into destroying himself so that their energy would be greater by the release of his. As he walked along the muddy track, the grass either side of him seemed as green. Freedom of choice. He stepped along the path like an equilibrist.

It wasn't now so much that the reality suppressant was necessary to provide the third input to the Keplar organic transistor, but that he didn't have a reality without it. Society was a self-perpetuating illusion of society, and his reality was unsustainable. Standing at the centre of the nothingness of everything, the only way to maintain existence was to fall. So after setting the trilock, he let go, and fell into the darkness of oblivion.

It's not black and white, it's black and white. The stripes of a pedestrian crossing. A head checked by a jumbo jet. The great game of control, like some grand chess board of a masonic master. A lifetime of controlled predestination. There was no thought or action he could make to change anything. Whatever he did made no difference. The rearrangement of everything after to suit their lies. Like a rock star left dangling in a hotel room, the fabrication of false secrets of a life story paraded across the front pages of a newspaper.

As the helicopters circled in their hums, the memory to the piece of string returned. The lying deception of the centre point conspiracy. The feigning of a middle life crisis like event, to whip a generation into cramming more in, increasing their productivity. Cranking up the handle of the money machine.

The breaking free of mother's apron strings and the cutting of the umbilical cord. A progenitor conspiracy. All throughout his life he had been played as a script. The performance of the sun, moon, and stars, in the guildhall with its tiered steps when in his primary Cybertechnic. An image of a triangular pocket watch pushed into view suspended by parabolic curves. The meaning of the symbols instead of numerals as the hands of the hours ticked by. The white winged dove at the centre. The parallel flickering of an image of a white messenger pigeon cooing. The initials of the failed lovers when the pointers became level, on the towers upholding the spheres of Tesla coils. The date on the inscription of the watch. 1881. Forever lost in a fin de siècle. He was outside of time.

The conspiracy lay both in and without him, set throughout history. He never had a chance. There was nothing he could ever do, in the past, the present, or the future. All had already transpired against him. It was as it had always been, the autocompletion of reality separated from him by a transparent meniscus. Like when the primary Cybertechnic tutors separated him from the others for yapping too much after he had finished his tasks, as he was distracting them from theirs, being moved to a table in isolation, from where he couldn't communicate. The girl from kiss-chase, his eagerness to catch and kiss, their feet accidentally clipping in running, being blamed for tripping her. A continued cycle of misunderstandings. Like the girl he had loved when he was six, who moved to another country with her family when their tasks lay elsewhere. Like the girl he had been attracted to in the bank, the irony of being separated from her by a layer of bullet proof glass. As it always was. As in the incubator, no influence over external events, only a series of watching non-relevant reactions being reflected through the fish tank walls of glass. He lay there, legs crossed at the ankles, thumbs nestled between index and middle fingers. Thinking, connecting, dreaming whilst awake. The sensory overload caused his nerves to fire. Screaming and wrenching in pain.

At the Epoch Dawn where the night met the day. The sounds of Psalm like songs being sung. Something that had no proof could not be disproved by proof. Idyllic in its simplicity and yet infinite in its complexity. The point of not being able to prove the existence of God was so that it could not be faked in order to gain power and control. The true genius of God.

A church. Black and white. The models on top of a wedding cake. The ying and the yang. Part of her inside of him, and part of him inside of her. The two of them as one, the parts separated, but still maintaining the memory of each other within their selves. In the timeless infinity of the combinations of reality, the autocompletions occurred simultaneously.

Standing amidst the burning black flames of hell. Sickened, broken, breathless, in the emptiness of oblivion.

Tap, tap. The warm rain of her tears fell onto the bounds of his being. Cascading and twisting down throughout him, coating him in the love of her pixie armour. The oxygen of her phoenix blue reignited the red flames of his dragon breath with its chemiluminescence.

They stood facing each other's faces, locked in realms of matching. Their arms outstretched, palms pointing upwards. The fingers of her hands beckoning him towards her, drawing him in with the attraction of a timeless force. His arms reached out in an echoing of reply.

With the nearing of their existences, they crossed their arms at the wrist, their hands laying out centred in front of them, levelled with their hearts. Turning palms so their left palms were downward, and their right palms pointing upward.

Their open palms of no secrets met, and they delicately caressed each other's hands in a reading of understanding. Gripping in a hand-holding, and then their fingers interlacing and locking in the bonds of warm love. They kissed nine times. The connection was made.

Like the two similar halves of a peanut, separate yet keyed to another, complimentary in their twinning. An endless string tying them together through the bounds of infinity.

A few weeks later she bought a red transport. A little after that a red coat, just to be sure.

Now this is where he perhaps may have regretted watching a lifetime's worth of sci-fi and conspiracy theory films. Impaling aftershocks crunched the sketchy factor even more than the original dawn. Live comms continuing in, like the 'if they knew you knew they'd want to kill you', didn't exactly help the matter. Especially as he knew not what the they or the what were. With mind and body broken to a childlike acceptance, he lived through and experienced all of them in the months to come, evaluating and processing them, setting them on the balance and Keplaring their worth.

In their depraved taunting of him, the terrors had

whispered false bargaining lies of being able to lessen the length and extent of his torture by trading some of it to her. He would never let them anywhere near her. Their promises to make it worse for him were the only truisms in their covenants of hate.

Her pixie armour shielded him from the inside out.

How to find her. The thoughts of his last ex girlfriend floated through his mind. The irony of that comms line being near one of his suppressant stockists didn't escape him. The memory of both sparked the remembering of that feeling of being loved, but he knew neither were the truth of love that he sought.

Later he wrote the analogy in code. The Lighthouse game, light bulbs collected to energise the beacon, whilst avoiding the drains of the fanged bats.

How to find her. The obvious answer lay in his mind's life experience of training. He must hack for her.

Chapter Five – Darn shiny hackcreds

Transport parked up, neighbours avoided, perimeter secure. At last, a bit of peace and quiet. Time for her to have a bit of time for her, and she knew that this evening she would be spending that time in the rig. After slipping from her day's disguise of society clothing into her hacker slacks, she fired up the rig and got into her game.

Flying round the three-dimensional constructs as she altered her viewpoint, she toyed with the gameclip's match and reveal pipelined completion. Tapping and aligning, she used the puzzles to hone her focus back into the real of the unreal. Smiling and flitter dancing with glee as she span through the levels, her task sensations sated themselves and it was time for the true busyness of the rig's play.

Much like the gameclip, she had prepared her hack by sequencing a series of interlocking parts. She smiled mischievously to herself at the graceful styling of her configuration. The hack was a strange one really, the download was just some time-saving code. She was planning an extraction from one of the member agency freezers. She tutted at her self for the use of the freezer analogy in her thoughts, that all those jumper boys just so loved to use. That's what it was, code storage. They so loved saying that phrase of playground humour, and could endlessly repeat it along with that way of speaking while holding their noses.

Shit. She really couldn't believe she had just held her nose and repeated the phrase. What a bitch, guess it was just so damn catchy.

Anyway, a bit of refocus. The download was just time-saving code, nothing so complex that she couldn't have weaved it out herself, it was just that for some of those translation matrices which were used again and again, there wasn't much point reinventing the wheel. Or as in most

code cases, reinventing the wheel, assembling the
infrastructure to harvest all the resources required, put the
thing together, test it on a cart, in fact work out how to fix it
to the cart, and then scale the solution so that hundreds
could be spawned in an instant.

The difference with this hack then was not the download
itself, or indeed the method of gaining entry to the vault, as
it was already open to members like her. The game was to
mask her routes, so that there were no tells to trace her
identity, or indeed anything left disturbed to show that
someone had ever visited at all.

Tap, tap. She let her creations slip into the meld as
though delicately pouring champagne into a crystal glass.
Slowly, surely, letting the bubbles seep in and then pop
away into nothingness when they had performed their
retrieval. The preparation had been long in its fermentation,
and the drinking autocompleted with a gulp.

Sealing her io barriers once more, she glanced through
the pattern of the downloaded clip. It was usual for
members to leave a deliberate mistake in any code they
distributed. The error would be a trivial one, but an
understanding of the code would be needed to spot it. That
way only those who had invested the time and effort in true
learning could use the code, but if they did there were a
wealth of time-saving libraries to borrow from.

Correcting and sliding the clip in, scarcely noticeable in
its part of the enormity of her system consciousness. It was
almost nearing the end of its development, and would soon
be ready to leave the nest and take those first tentative steps
towards flight. Instantly switching her thoughts to the next
rung in her ladder, ever towards that breathtaking height
from which she could have the adrenaline rush of the slide
ride. Now to gain a host system to parse it all on.

She had made her fortunes this way and that. But there
were some things that money just couldn't buy. They

couldn't be begged, borrowed, or stolen, not even by her skill, such were their importance they were bunkered off any outside systems. For those kinds of purchases there was only one currency. Hackcreds.

*

Tommy awoke to the sharp stillness of the day. Black shadows flashed across his field of vision, and his body ached with a cold dark chill. Breathing slowing into consciousness, he deepened his intakes until his mind became relaxed. Shifting himself upright in a single motion, he stretched and flexed his body in warm up, then leapt up to the chin-up bar and began his daily hack.

After the workout, Tommy showered and fired up his rig. Although Tommy was on a martial specialism scholarship, everyone at the Cybertechnic had to learn the skills necessary for electronic survival. Ticking through the learning cliptrips, Tommy's mind echoed the databursts with a triaspect burning of knowledge into his synapses. As the quickening of neuronisation slowed, thoughts turned to more recreational pursuits.

Flipping to the gameclip, Tommy tap, tapped, as he set about his fun in galactic domination. Starting up a fresh clip, he set about the tasks of population growth and taxation to build his empire. Building to a base economy from which his planet could reach out into the unknown, contact with other planets and other players in the meld.

Jabbing through excitedly, Tommy chuckled as the charting visualisations shone in their interplay like a sound system graphic equalizer of old as the volume of his civilisation rose. Then Tommy reached that point he always reached. Having invested his time to assemble to such a point, his body almost shook with the buzz as the critical moment approached.

Bang, bang. A firework finale as ever. Tommy tapped off and paused for reflection.

Buzz, buzz. The buzz of the vidpanel entry system.

"Hey, Tommy," he said. "Tap, tap."

"Tap, tap," sighed Tommy, and tapped on the keypanel.

Tommy opened the door to the lair, and he blew in like an excited whirlwind.

"So how goes it for you, Tommy?" he said.

"Yeah, ok, I guess," said Tommy.

"What's up?" he said gently. "Been dumped again?"

"No, not at all," said Tommy. "It's far more important than that kind of thing."

"Oh?" he said. "New hack?"

"Well, it's my new gameclip," said Tommy. "It's called 'galactic megaquest'."

"Sounds explosive," he smiled.

"Yeah, erm, no," shook Tommy. "It's galactic domination, sure, but there's not many explosions."

"Oh, yes?" he said.

"Yeah," said Tommy. "Once you've got your planet up and running, it uses a complex trade system in resolution rather than combat simulation."

"I see," he laughed. "Using the financials to build greater cathedrals of trade I suppose."

"About right," nodded Tommy. "The start and midgame I can do no problem, it's the endgame that I keep getting stuck on."

"Pray tell, young Jedi," he laughed.

"Huh, huh," said Tommy. "I can sort the population growth to build the planet and increase resources, and get things all going, and get good scoring in interplanet trade. But eventually I get too big a population, not enough resources, and then my success ratings just shrapnel."

"Hmm," he breathed out slowly. A pausing moment of thought. "Maybe the way to win the game is simply to maintain your population without exceeding the demands of its resources. Get to have a longer game and you get a higher score. Sustainability rather than overflow and population-resource contention."

"Sounds plausible," said Tommy. "Maybe my population development cycle runs too smooth, and they just end up all being greedy spoilt bastards."

"Maybe you need to build in a limiting factor," he said. "Like contentment or something."

They laughed loudly.

"So," said Tommy. "You anywhere nearer finding your special girl then?"

"Oh, well, not quite," he said. "But I can sense that reality is narrowing."

"Yeah, erm," said Tommy. "Some would say the reason it's being so long is because you're a little paranoid."

"Maybe," he smiled. "But then you can never be too paranoid."

"Maybe," said Tommy, with a blankish look.

"I guess it's when you stop wondering if the girls are from an agency or not when you meet them," he said. "And you just start-off wondering *which* agency."

"Sounds like a high state of alert," laughed Tommy.

"Don't worry," he said. "I have my own gauges."

"Really," said Tommy.

"Yeah," he continued. "When I'm chipping out plaster to hide a flash ic backup, in someone *else's* house. Then, just maybe then, I might think that it's a little paranoia playtime."

"Or you really fucked up a backtrack," said Tommy.

"Yeah. There's that one," he said. "Guess context is all so important, the weighting of the scale can sometimes vary with the situation."

"I'd probably agree with you there," said Tommy.

"Anyways. Wanna have a little hack then?" he smiled.

"Thought you were doing well," said Tommy. "Almost managing a conversation for a while before retreating into the security of your hackgames."

"I'm not that bad," he said.

"Suppose not," said Tommy.

"And since that field trip got cancelled from the cybertechnic," he said. "We should really make up for the lack of vocational hacker training we would have managed in their full view."

"Ok," said Tommy. "What have you got for me this time?"

*

Not that she'd run up the tick of hackcreds with just any old story. She'd been through the brown envelope briefings at her Cybertechnic like everyone else. She knew that if you ran up too much of a tab you could end up running all sorts of shadow cracks to repay those bad gambling debts.

Mostly she just loaned from members she knew, or didn't know as the case usually was, but at least she knew what they were, if not who they were. However, for the kind of rollercoaster slide she was after, it would be necessary to loan off who some would call the bad guys, a big corp.

Sometimes it was necessary to call on the kind of processing power that one couldn't fit in a suitcase. Or a garage. Or even a street. It wasn't so easy to hide that type of system in full view, so usually it was only the big 'legit' corps who had that kind of installation up and running. Whilst there'd probably be a chance of some time on a comparable processor at some outrageous rigfest, they tended to be only once a year flings. She really wanted access to some on demand cycles, so she would get a chance to tweak some enhancements, and hopefully a few more times to experience that ride.

As the codestore clip unfolded itself in bursts like a cantilever bridgehead from Royal Engineers, forming a fortified pathway through the sea of the electric ether, she took a brief instant to examine the tag line of the download. It was signed 'J. Crypto #12'.

With the sights of her scopes secured in view, she stepped slowly around the constructs, as if shopping for a new top for a night out. Some of the tasks for hire were a bit boring for her, she had already had the high of satisfaction from completion for their kind of coding. Always best for her to have a bit more of a challenge to spur her on. Ok to throw on something from a season long gone as mere clothing, but she was in a playfully stylish mood, and fancied dressing to impress.

Hmm. That looked more interesting. It was strange that someone was looking for that kind of system. She tapped and refocused, examining in more detail. Scanning through, it looked as though some of the corps were touting for some similar things.

Ah. The reasoning became clear. The trivs were just a means to an end. What they were really looking for was a scanner. Some corps would realise they had been hacked, but there'd be nothing amiss to track, trace, or even notice. Hire a hacker to catch a hacker. Not that many hackers ever got caught these days, so it wasn't like it was fighting against your own or anything, she wasn't one for that. It was more to seal a system against them by knowing their style. The cat and mouse games between rival hackers were all just part of the fun of the overall playground.

There it was then. Gain some hackcreds to use in payment to run her ride on some high-end systems. She was to be a spotter.

Now, what to wear.

*

He was on a roll with this one. Neat idea he thought. Although not the most easiest of cracks, it wasn't like it was going to be for currency or anything, so the systems weren't going to be that strong, and there wouldn't be so many merc combat teams on standby to kill the hack if it was noticed.

That's not to say the information wasn't sensitive. So much so for some people, that one corp wasn't trusted to have all the keys to the vault at any one time. Thus the data was distributed across a grid of repositories, each holding a small part of the encrypted shield which contained the data packets within it. When a retrieval was acked by several sources, the pieces were unravelled by an adaptive decoding algorithm, which also retiered the encryption on the downloads that were received, so mere progressive scoping wasn't ever going to form even the smallest of splinters.

A difficult challenge, but not wholly impossible. Well, not if you knew someone who had contributed to the original sources, or knew someone who knew someone, who knew. Those darn shiny hackcreds.

He had narrowed things down to a solution with a reasonable amount of negotiability. It was all in the eyes, the secrets lay in retinal matching. So there it was. He continued hacking away at his tunnel into the biometrics datastore. Wait. It was Thursday. He'd better get it together. Tonight was the big night out with Tommy.

The flames of the campfire flittered in their flickerings, casting shadows of patterns through the supporting structures of the pier. Amidst the fun and the banterings, his eyes scanned their interlacing intermittently, until the projections of fading embers were replaced with the illuminating rays of the morning sunrise. Whether sourced from moonlight, firelight, or sunlight, to his mind the silhouettes all danced the same lyrics to whichever melody, his organic transistor attempting autocompletions of the three-dimensional meshed shapes.

"Been hacking too much?" asked Tommy quietly. "I know the kind of systems you like to hack tend to be a bit emotionally draining, some of those isoterics can really fuck with you."

"Probably," he laughed. "But then what does a hacker do but hack."

"Twat," laughed Tommy.

"Hmm," he sighed. "I tried the doing stuff, the not doing stuff in quiet waiting, a bit of both, and even more and so combinations. But none of it seems to be of any consequence. Just continuous keplaring."

"Like trying to get Gina to stop yapping," laughed Tommy.

"Yeah, a bit like that," he smiled. "She soon out yaps any toy given to her in distraction."

"Sure does," sighed Tommy, shrugging his shoulders.

"Guess we all have our thing," he said.

"Yup," nodded Tommy. "But fuck that, we've got a day out next week. You've gotta be excited about that."

"Of course," he said. "Should be a whole lot of fun."

"Yes," smiled Tommy. "But try not to use it as just another excuse for a trumpet hack."

"It'll be fine," he said. "As for now, I'll probably have a few days off the radar to top up some blank sheets."

Good advice from The Captain, always leave some periods of inactivity within your routine logs. Still do stuff, but do it with no trace, so that the cycles could be used to create some other history in them when a hack called for it.

He'd probably spend the time on a bit of revisional readinput. Some clips you have to read, some you have to study. It didn't hurt to have a bit of a refresh. Probably best to rest up from one fun before going to another too.

"I'm sure there'll be plenty of systems to have a ride on," he said.

"Defo," said Tommy. "The visitors centre sure does have some kit."

"Ack, ack, to that," he said. "At last, one of the cybertechnic's fieldtrips finally got arranged."

**

"So who came up with the acoustic translacing matrices then?" quizzed Gina, amidst the banterings of the group transport.

"Erm, I know this one," said Tommy. "Yeah, I know. It was Jonny. Jonny Crypto."

The back of the transport laughed at Tommy.

"For fucks sake, Tommy," tutted Gina. "We ain't never gonna get away for a break if you're in summer school."

"Cut the banterings," he said. "Just stick to the recall. Use your keplar."

"Sure," said Tommy slowly. "Ok, I know it was either steinberg or keplar. But I can never remember who did what."

"Some would say neither can they," he smiled.

"You know the codices, Tommy," said Gina. "Just spin them out like you do when we écoute et répète, you know that."

"I know that," said Tommy. "But when I get to the end, I keep forgetting which is my part and which is your part."

"We do them both, don't we," said Gina. "For if ever one of us is down in keplarisation, the other can swoop in and cover. That's why I can't be there when you run the rig scoring."

"I know," said Tommy.

"They were a swell couple," giggled Mandy. "That mister keplar and that miss steinburg."

"Sweet as," said Gina.

"They certainly got that raman effect going through

themselves together," he said.

"Ok," said Tommy. "I get it now. It was keplar who designed the translacing matrices to enable biocrypting to be rigged to audio frequency playback, and it was steinburg who improved on this and designed the modulation meshes, so that variations in the speed or volume could be used to alter the pace or the processing capability of the transaction."

"Very good," kissed Gina.

"What a star," he said.

The transport pulled up with a quiver, and the assembled rabble disembarked in a manner not exactly according to training. As their legs sped them to the entrance way, they chattered excitedly as one mass, all attempting to out hype each other with tales from the myth tags surrounding the complexity of the equipment available for free use at the visitors centre.

He was whistling and singing to himself, puffing out words or air as the whim took him. The happiness of anticipation sparking inside of him. As a red transport drove past, his mouth let out a kind of wow pop of air, and his index finger jumped involuntary in a sharp ticking motion. In the afterburn of the brief photographic moment, he saw the tick of the female driver too.

She recovered her composure. Hmm. He looked cute, and he looked. Sort of had a glow of niceness about him. Or was it just the transport he was eyeing. Bugger. Stick to the hack.

Dragged along by the bustle of the herding visitors, he felt himself warm with the memory of her innocent smile to herself. She had raised her arm in a reflex action, and rubbed the back of her neck as her head tilted slightly in shyness. Accompanied by that smile so sweet he could feel it even though she faced forward. Or was she smiling at someone else, or was she just laughing at him as he whistled along and sang like a muppet. Shit.

The memory decoupled from mind's eye view. Strolling toward the impressive doors of the complex, they shone out their sugar coated messages within their glass. Welcome to v-industries.

He had been waiting patiently in the queue for the star of the show. His turn in v-industries most valued opal, the lucid dreaming rig. It was designed to be used in the future Mars missions, the escapism afforded by the realm of space inside the constructs would be ample in compensation avoidance of space travel fever. He stepped up and into the sensorium. Encapsulated in its womb-like warmth, floating in a soft breeze.

He could sense the isoterics trying to prob into something else. His hacker instincts of paranoia clicked in, and the meshes weakened. His turn in the rig ended with a gentle fading out. It had seemed short.

He flashed Tommy, and Tommy acked.

"Be careful in that one," he said. "It's got a funny tinge to it."

"You always bring out the best in them," laughed Tommy. "It's like a gift you have."

"Some sort of analytic mapping," he said. "I'm not sure if it's just a subtle benevolent psychoanalysis trigger, or whether it's something more out of place."

"You always were fucking paranoid," said Tommy.

"You can never be too paranoid," he said. "It might be bait to reflex a hacker response."

"Not another recruitment drive," said Tommy.

"Didn't really seem that way," he said. "Felt more like a track."

"Ok," said Tommy, holding his chin. "I'll pulse the

word along."

"Play safe," he smiled.

The marketing team models came down the stair case with its white piped handrail. In a line, then a ninety-degree change of direction in a curve, down the steps onto the level of their assembled party.

Encircled like a princess and her ladies in waiting, she glowed in irrepressible brilliance. The lighthouses of their eyes shone into each other, the particles of the waves of their sight intermingling as they danced together. The beams of their gaze powered through the intensity of the rays they cast out in unison, impacting on the very lenses and refractor arrays that focused their beacons into its streams. Acking and echoing in reply, the retinal matching attempted its autocompletion, as the sense of joy brought a simultaneous smile to both their faces.

Amidst her shimmer, his sight focused in a burst into the depth of the secrets of her eyes, and all else faded from view into a smokey blur. Instinctive adrenaline rushed through his veins as his heart quickened. The infinite patternings in their eyes gleaned a match.

Passing through his sequences of iterations, the translations moved toward the bone structure of her face, nose first, all scanned in and processed like an infrared mesh defining the contours of a landscape. Cheekbones read a match too. Down to the chin. Positive correlation. The bits flipped their flags.

*

Nice smile. So who was this cheeky visitor. It was an easy match for her to glean, only a minor hack to gain the logs of the visitors. Best take a look at him, purely for professional reasons of course. Well, unprofessional

professional reasons of course, given the nature of her profession. Fuck. She was being a sketchy twat again.

Now to the true busyness once more. The spotter hack for gameclip hackcreds. Bugger. A nice team mask up job by the looks of it, there weren't any biters to the hooks in the sensoriums setup. She did tell them that it was a little too obvious, but hey, they never listen, so in the end it was always a matter of setting stuff like that up and then ignoring it.

She was a bit more mischievous than that. She had some other scopes running, so that if that type of situation occurred, she could at least try and run a trace on whoever ran on the system before the mask was put on everyone else's mind.

Unbelievable. No wonder a lot of creds were on offer. The intruder had tweaked the trail so that it was lost amongst the girders of her own concealment constructs. Time to micro the scopes. Who was this cowboy, not the original author of the struts, that Mr Crypto, it was a different style of coding. Not so much careless as carefree. Crypto's tapestries were always very neat, concise and exact.

Flabbergasting. This cheeky sod had been putting the touch on her files as well as everything else he had been concealing from the logs. How rude.

Luckily she had those all triple scoped too.

*

Back in his den he routed back in through the buddy node and continued the lock to retrieve a path to her network delivery node. Not a GPS or anything, that would be silly, someone would be bound to notice that one. Just a delivery node so a package could be sent, not many had cracked that hashing system, guess the pull of post coupled with the dual public key encryption was a safe enough bet for anything that you didn't take somewhere yourself.

May as well have a quick look at all the data on the system about her. Hmm. Something was odd. Looked like they were both using a variant of a Jonny #12, although a lot of other dabblings seemed to be going on as well. Felt like someone else had been fiddling. There were no indicators, or change in the pattern in the weave of the code. Like someone had been and gone, made some whisperings in influence, and then left again without anyone to witness. Maybe The Captain had been keeping an eye on him again, or maybe he really was just paranoid. Weird though, looked almost as if someone was hiding some of the data on her from her. Some sleep might help. He could do a retrack hack in later and check her files. He left some scopes. Tap, tap.

The next day an orchid arrived. This girl obviously had her own lookup skills. Shit. A feisty one.

**

So dinner it was. The location picked itself as it usually did. The only place to go for them was always going to be Triangles restaurant. Nervousness and smiles. Sometimes staring at each other, sometimes giving the opportunity for the other to stare in full scan, unrestrained in observation by periods of gracious looking down or away in chatter.

"Yes," she said. "So, anyway, if you were an articfical intelligence, how would you answer this question?"

She was good. Very good. Love at first hack, all bits were definitely lit.

"Hey, my *phoenix*," he smiled in a whispering.

"I love your sexy *dragon* eyes," she smiled back.

**

The coming of the tide of day at The Halfway House Inn. Playing in the love of the universe they created in themselves for one another. With his Keplarisation autocompletion end fading, a star burst from her to keep the firation going. He was the equations to her solutions. Or sometimes he was the solutions to her equations. Seemed to work that way with them, depending on who was left-handed or right-handed that day.

"It's a purple ratchet," she said. "I don't like messing with those, can you do it for me please, darling."

"Sure, babes," he smiled. "If you take down that dangling coconut for me. I know you like having a play with those kind of isoterics."

"Yippee," she laughed, dancing into her hack.

How sweet, the perfect hacker couple. As it always was with them, covering and making up for each other's faults and weaknesses, or in this case realigning and switching over so they were both having fun.

"Ok, you be the sodium and I'll be the potassium," she kissed.

"Ion on it. You're the salt of the earth my treasure," he kissed back.

"You!" she laughed.

Through kisses and more sweetheart banter, they eventually finished the morning's rigwork, and then got into their clothes for the day. Him in his white outfit, her in her black skirt and white blouse.

It was the week of the big hack.

Afterwards, The Land Rover Defender slid away quietly from the scenes of Troonhilly Downs.

"So what now then?" asked Gina.

"In my humble opinion," he said. "I think, after a nap, we should get severely wasted."

"Paarrtey!" cheered Tommy.

Chapter Six – The Captain's recap

The Captain awoke to the cold reality of his daily dawn. Sighing, then smiling, he maneuvered out of bed. He retrieved his outer gown from its draping on the wicker chair, and swung it round him.

In slow, solid steps, The Captain crossed to the curtains of the French doors and cast them back. Hacking the lock, he gently pushed the doors open, and strolled out to the glory of the morning sunshine.

Activity hung in a quiet balance of completion and new beginning. As the small birds sang their sweet song, he remembered the sadness of absent friends. Deepening his breathing, feet aligned in parallel with the nestles of his shoulders. Bending his knees and lowering himself downward, he let the parabolas of the past whip over him, until their lashings ended, and they had disappeared once more to their rightful place behind him.

Raising up again, placing his hands on the wooden railing of the veranda. Continuing his reflexed pattern of breathing, he took time to watch the minute functionings of all the wildlife in the grass, the trees, and the hedges. The Captain smiled again with the memory of the peaceful spoils of war.

Two young squirrels bounded through the swaying tops of the trees in chase, carefree in their cartwheelings of daring display. Leaping for fun, dancing through the sprigs and boughs of ash, oak and yew as though they were the veins of a leaf from a single tree.

First rubbing his hands together, and then rolling his shoulders, he stretched out and flexed the tiredness from his body. Another day, another mission.

Plans and secrets. When a plan had been running for such a long time, somehow it had a way of becoming a secret. Long in its conception of counter deception, its milestones had solidified over the patient years. Time at last for the participants to be granted their tell.

*

"You sketchy twat," she laughed.

"Look, just because my eyes aren't open, it doesn't mean that my ears aren't open," he retorted.

"Oh, ok, Mister Keplar Himself," she said in a playfully stern tone. "Then what did I just say?"

"I don't know, I wasn't listening, but that doesn't mean that I couldn't have listened if I had wanted to."

"That, my dear, is a classic example of your being a sketchy twat," she laughed.

"Ok," he muttered. "So I'm only just a little pencilled-in at the moment, but hey, good night wasn't it."

"It was," she smiled. "I'm glad you enjoyed it so, because you're going to be the one to clean up the residues."

"Erm, really," he smirked. "What did I hack this time."

"Don't worry," she smiled. "I stopped you from flagging too much. Although as usual, at one point you were showing off, dancing your thing. Still, you can remember that party piece as you're bundling out the trash."

"Shucks. Can you please get me some felt-tips to colour me in," he said. She nodded, kissed him, and left.

He thought about orange2ing Tommy and Gina, but Tommy did look a little pale when they had left, and it would be a little cheeky to get a fast response team just for a tour of litter duty. Another day, another hack.

It must be a lucky day, The Captain arrived, with that incredible sense of timing.

"I see your little celebration was as successful as ever," said The Captain. "Judging by the mess."

"Indeed," he said. "Shame you didn't make it."

"Yes," laughed The Captain. "Although I may be a little old for your baffooning around."

"Not you, Captain," he smiled.

"Hmm," smiled The Captain. "Anyway, I had some hacking to do."

"Fun or profit," he said.

"It was fun," smiled The Captain. "But it was to really pay off a hackdebt."

"Those darn shiny hackcreds," he laughed.

"Indeed," said The Captain, his smile turning to a frown. "Although in this case, it was more of a repaying something that had been stolen."

"Wow, a theft retract," he said. "Isn't like you to get caught in a brown enveloper. Although I know it gets harder and harder each day with these continued layers of abstraction."

"And so it does," sighed The Captain. "It's kind of you to empathise, but I'm not so old in the tooth as to get caught out just yet."

"Indeed," he smiled. "I am sorry."

"That's where things should be flipped," said The Captain, eyes dropping downward. "Really, it is I who should be apologising to you."

"No need for any of that from you, Sir," he said, unhappy with his choice of word to show respect.

"And no need for any of that stuff from you," said The Captain.

"Well, you've certainly helped me out and inspired me of a few run-ins, that's for sure."

"I know that," laughed The Captain. "Nice of you to sign them with a reference in deference."

"My pleasure," he smiled.

"But indeed," sighed The Captain. "The debt is all mine, and it has been long overdue in settlement. There's something I need to tell you about you and her."

"It's ok, Captain," he laughed. "We know the birds and the bees thing."

"Indeed," said The Captain. "Bees always were a speciality of yours."

"Yes," he smiled.

"Joking aside," furrowed The Captain. "There's something I am duty bound to tell you."

"It's ok," he smiled. "I have kind of been waiting for it, ever since our meeting in the royal hussar. Mister holmes would probably would have said it was a little too innocuous."

"Yes indeed," said The Captain. "It was a strange afternoon. At times I did wonder who was recruiting who."

"Things often work out to be a bit of both," he smiled.

"Very true," said The Captain. "And I guess that's where we figured you would come in."

"I see," he bluffed.

"Indeed, you did see," said The Captain. "My recordings show you figured out most of it for your self. It was always going to be your chosen path, we had nothing to do with that."

"Hmm," he huffed.

"But it is probably why you were chosen," said The Captain.

"Ok, Captain, what's the download," he said.

"As you know," sighed The Captain. "You and her have always had a rather compelling draw to each other."

"Yes," he smiled.

"It's not wholly by accident," said The Captain.

"That doesn't surprise me," he said.

"Undoubtedly," said The Captain. "There's probably more questions that you'll have, but we'll leave them for now so I can give you a quick run through."

"Ok," he said. "You always seem to know what the preferable course of action is."

"Yes," smiled The Captain. "Although sometimes the way to leadership is simply to be the least terrified of those around you."

He nodded silently.

"Well, then," said The Captain. "On with it. So we have it, you and her. You were both genetically predisposed to that thing they call love, which was going to be of paramount importance."

"Blatantly," he said.

"Hmm," smiled The Captain. "Whilst you were destined to play the role of the reluctant hero, you did seem to revel in it."

"All the fun all the fair," he smiled.

"We were glad of it," echoed The Captain in laughter. "It was always obvious even before your dawn that you had had a fair amount of extenuating circumstances. We were happy you had something to compensate."

"Thank you," he smirked.

"Indeed," smiled The Captain knowingly. "However, the downside of this was that you were only ever going to be looking for the one, that may have limited you."

"It's ok," he said. "That kind of always suited me. A longer burn in of a lifetime of future memories with her was always my preferred solution."

"Yes," smiled The Captain. "Gina would say the soppy twat factor is high with you. And probably with her too."

"To a sickly-sweet, some might say," he said.

"Yes," said The Captain. "You two were always going to be that way. Research we had done previously ensured that. In our simulations we managed to determine an exact match in your genetical compatibilities, so the specific selection of you was always going to be a success on that level."

"That's nice to know," he laughed. "I shall remind her of that when she's on a rant at me."

"Such a defence is unlikely to sway a girl of her stubborn nature," laughed The Captain. "She has some inbuilt characteristics of her own."

"Indeed she does," he smiled.

"However," sighed The Captain. "We did give nature a little guidance."

"Helping hand or a shove?" he laughed.

"Hmm," sighed The Captain. "We needed a way to ensure that you recognised each other."

"A helping hand is ok," he said. "I did have a bit of trouble finding the right match for me."

"That figures," sighed The Captain. "We may have over done it a smidge, and made sure it was the only match for you."

"Hmm," he sighed, taking his turn. "I'm guessing you're going to explain to me now why I've always determined a hit or a miss pretty much at first sight."

"We knew that it would be necessary to have someone to rescue her, so to speak," said The Captain. "And I'm afraid there was no room for error. If a side effect was that you lost out on other potential possible matches, then for that we are sorry."

"And so to the method," he said.

"Yes," said The Captain. "To the incubator. We didn't predict that you would be an incubator baby, which had its own influences as you know, probably adding to your determination. However, it was at this moment we needed to act."

"Yes, Captain, and so to the method," he said.

"The method," said The Captain reluctantly. "During the weeks in the incubator you had a visitor. Now this visitor wore contact lenses which highlighted the pattern of a retinal matching algorithm, one of our greatest successes at that time."

"Things are starting to make sense," he said.

"I knew they would," said The Captain. "Anticipatory hacking always was one of your strong points."

"Yes, the shapes are starting to fit," he said.

"Indeed," said The Captain. "Here comes the bit you may not like."

"That sounds like one of Tommy's lines when he turns up in a panic," he laughed. "It may be a bit late to justify if the end fits the means, but as I'm with her now, you probably have picked a good time to tell me. But then your timing and patience have always been impeccable."

"Some thrive on disciplined training, some on doing it their way," said The Captain, attempting a smile. "So, the crux of it being, we aided your memory of the match. We ensured the synapse burn took hold by supplementing your natural chemicals with what some might call a healthy dose of reality suppressant."

"Hmm, some would say it was a little unfair to influence things so far," he said.

"Yes, indeed," said The Captain. "Those views were aired. However, to an extent we did think of that. The wash was configured to only provoke a response in a suitable personality type. So in a way, it was what you wanted. It was designed only to trigger a reaction if you were both a true match. You see, in the analysis of nature or nurture, it does indeed turn out to be a bit of both. They are interdependent. The nurture triggers a response from the nature, so they interplay and connect as appropriate. So yes, we did kind of add to what you knew, but really, you knew it already. You were designed that way."

"I guess that figures," he said. "But I'm also thinking you really did pick a time to tell me."

"Mind you," said The Captain. "We won't go into why nature designed you that way, we haven't time now, and not that I even know. Guess you two will figure that one out between your selves."

"Nice of you to leave us with that at least," he said. "And I'm banking you're going to stick around to unleash all this on her."

"It's ok," said The Captain. "I've been having discussions with her for a while, and I brought her up to speed with the final tells this morning."

"You always get off light," he smiled. "She'll probably rib me like it was my hack."

They both took a moment to laugh at the irony in the truth.

"Yes," said The Captain. "And admittedly there were a few side effects."

"You're telling me," he said. "Some points did seem like repeatedly entering the sixteenth cavern for the first time, jarring one of the reserve clones instantly on entering till I worked out my bearings."

"No doubt," sighed The Captain. "Regrettably we didn't foresee the incubator factor. Because of your rather unfortunate experiences there, you began Keplarisation immediately. Normally this would have been triggered at a much later date, but your mind began the processing and search for her rather early."

"Patient impatience," he said.

"The process was really only meant to enable a simple pattern recognition," continued The Captain. "But your mind tried to Keplar a solution where none could be knowable, an offshoot of which was your creation of a very effective transistor network."

"Contemplation is a wonderful thing," he said.

"A possible side effect of this," said The Captain. "Was an enhanced awareness of the inability to influence external events, outside of the incubator. On top of this, you've had some strange scrapes with some strange groups. All part of your hacker training no doubt, learning to pass unnoticed through a diverse range of people."

"Of course," he smiled.

"The blade here being that you had already experienced several minor dawns prior to the epoch," sighed The Captain. "On analysis of your readouts, I detected three major defcon one indoctrination programs, and the partial matching of at least seven other defcon two's. And that's additional to what we've just talked about. All this, coupled with the additional emotional sensitivity caused in the incubator, and the tendency both you and her have to empathically Keplarise other people's problems, meant that things were pretty severe."

"Felt like it," he said.

"Thus," said The Captain. "When the moment came, you had rather too many conflicting wirings which contributed to the overall intensity of the firings."

"I accept that," he said.

"Of course," said The Captain. "You didn't make it any easier by being such a clever bastard, and setting the trilock as failsafe device. So you had to sort that out too."

"I got by with a little help from a friend," he smiled.

"Yes," chuckled The Captain. "Other friends have helped out along the years too. We did aid Jonny with the source of some of the coding that was necessary to shield her from future view."

That sure must be true. He had spent most of his residual allowances on tracing her. She spent most of her's on one of Jonny's greatest achievements, a retinal re-mark. Jonny had a near complete system ready in waiting, but the specialist parts and third-party biocrypts required to both return a new pattern and get a database tie-in were always going to be costly, and all that for a one-shot deal. Still, that was their thing, and Jonny was happy to play along with it, especially as it gave a focus to some extreme hackness.

She bounced in with some bags, full of smiling, and hugged The Captain, then kissed him.

"My darling," he smiled.

"Me that is," she smiled. "I have those felt-tips. I'm figuring you're needing them by now."

"Thank you, my treasure," he said, taking the packet of sweets from her hand in their wrapped up fruity gloriness.

"I think it could be a blackcurrant moment," he smiled. "The zap of a blackcurrant flavoured burst may indeed be necessary at this point to colour me in. So I'm guessing you know already what The Captain here is telling me."

"Of course, sweetie," she smiled. "I'm bestist, always one step ahead of your slack ass."

"You think that, that's fine," he smiled.

"Ok," she laughed. "I will. And so any creds for me for the felts then?"

"You know how it is, my darling," he said. "There's riches, and there's riches."

"Lovecreds it is then, poppet," she winked.

"All right, you two," said The Captain. "Let's press on. We've seen how the trilock externalised itself in geometry. How about using a different level of abstraction and try putting it into words."

"English."

"Yes," said The Captain plainly.

"I guess it's back to Dostoyevsky's three kinds of truth," he said. "We all have secrets, those we hide from ourselves, from others, and from God. For me the solution to the problem was to narrow the distance between those secrets. Thus the key to breaking the trilock was me, her, and God, and the moment at which the vertices of the triasm spiralled into one single, united truth."

"Really," she said. "Is that why you couldn't keep your hands off me."

"We all have genius inside of us," he continued, brushing off her sarcasm. "Some hide their genius away from themselves, to be unleashed when it is realised, others lock their minds inside of it."

"Very good, my dear," she said. "But I think your cephalic index is getting a bit high there, darling."

"I may have a big ego, my sweet," he said, pursuing the banter. "But as you know, it's my big ego, my big personality, my big imagination, my big realm of abstract conceptualisation, that gives me my skill."

"If you hadn't been such a clever bastard at your dawn it may have been easier for us all," she scolded. "Big ego, big secondary hack 'cause he was so clever and set a timeout. Maybe clever or maybe not very optimistic."

"I'd been through a lot at that point," he said. "So forgive me."

"Always, darling, always," she smiled.

"Ok," said The Captain. "You've broken the trilock in your mind with the help of each other."

"Yes," he said, and lent over and kissed her.

"So what of the data from v-industries?" asked The Captain.

"Ah, the secondary download," he said. "Yes, on the original hack for the personnel data I did come across something else in the vicinity."

"We know," said The Captain. "The blipper traffic was huge. We had to do a few in coverage just to add a little masking."

"I know," he said. "I did a couple of the disguises myself, you know."

"Neat, very neat," smiled The Captain.

"I know it might look a bit of a risky one now," he said. "And although I was rushed for time, it would have been a bit like not downing the kong beast in manic miner."

"That sucker must get it every time," agreed The Captain.

"So I pulled the levers to have a look-see what happened," he said.

"You always did prefer to learn through experience," laughed The Captain. "If there's one thing that game does teach though, it's the importance of patience and timing."

"Indeed," he said.

"As you know, I had my retrieval equipment functioning for your big hack, so maybe we should take a look," said The Captain.

"Something tells me that you already know what we're going to be looking at," he said.

"I had a feeling you might have guessed that by now," laughed The Captain. "Good for you."

"Yes," he smiled.

"I've edited it to make it a bit clearer. You don't half have some weird, dark shit in there," said The Captain.

"It ain't all mine," he smirked.

"One other thing," said The Captain. "One of the supplies of atropine you used to help soften the acceptance of the new burn. It was traced."

"Sorry hun," she kissed. "Guess we knew that might happen, we had that bad run didn't we."

"Yes, no matter," he kissed back. "Those contact lenses with the new retinal pattern worked for a while to give the burn a chance to catch, but I guess there was always the risk of a scanner picking up the hint of a match."

"Those surveillance mites are everywhere," she said.

"I hear mexico is nice this time of year," he joked.

"I reckon you've got a little lead time," said The Captain. "So no need to worry about panic stations just yet."

"Oh, ok then," she smiled. "Oh, by the way. Out shopping, I just couldn't resist this for you."

She handed The Captain the polycomposite bag.

"Ah, a new cap," smiled The Captain.

"Yes, my dear," she smiled. "It's from me and rig-burn boy here, just to show that we both have no down feelings about the ways that were took to arrive us here."

"Ok," he said hesitantly, and looked at The Captain. "But you're picking up this week's Friday tab at the beachcomber."

"Ah," smiled The Captain. "At least you didn't ask for hackcreds."

"Much of a muchness," they said together, looking and smiling at each other.

Chapter Seven – Secrets of v-industries

The transport was in action. They had picked up Tommy and Gina on the way. She was driving, him riding shotgun, The Captain sat in the front middle seat. Not really The Captain's preferred position, but it was comfortable, and at least a good view was to be had. Tommy and Gina sat in the second row seats. Tommy did look a bit pale still, green almost.

"Don't yous two ever get tired of that hack shit then?" said Gina.

"Tired of it?" he said.

"Yeah," continued Gina. "Don't you ever get fed up with hacking against all those real bad isoterics. Don't you just *hate* them?"

"If we did that," she said. "They'd feed on it. They'd notice the weakness and step it up on that focus."

"Blame them then," said Tommy.

"It's not really like that," he said.

"You almost sort of have to forgive them," she said. "Just not let anything spark any negative matchings. It's a bit like dealing with difficult people, sometimes a nasty person is just a nice person who isn't happy."

"Rather a quaint rationalisation of it, my dear," he said. "But I agreed with you, it does tend to work out ok. Live and let live becomes the modus vivendi, and the isoterics have nothing to map against to invade and destroy."

"There's many levels to it I suppose," said Gina.

"Indeed," he said. "It's not always nastiness though. Sometimes it's a bit like dancing at a nightclub."

"Or having a work out at the gym," she said.

"Bit of gaming then," said Tommy.

"Yeah," he laughed. "Some levels can be a bit shit though. And sometimes it's a bit too much like brainwork. But hey, we all have our bad hack days."

"Inevitably," said The Captain.

"Yeah, but those high-end isoterics don't half put out some low punches," said Gina.

"They were designed that way," he laughed.

"I think Gina means more the certain type of system you seem to be able to cope with," said The Captain. "Not everybody can handle progressive and reiterative dawning like you two can. There is a certain special skill involved in hacking that type of system, and hopefully you're over that self destructive fireworking of yours, so it's not like you're doing it for flagellation."

"So why do you do it?" said Tommy.

"Oh why, oh why do I do it," he said in a drunken act, and then performed his charade re-enacting a scene of throwing up after a night's alcohol. They laughed.

"You get a kick out of it, don't you!" laughed Gina.

"There is always that certain something to be had when a challenge is involved," he laughed.

"You're just a stubborn twat," she laughed. "You can't let go that 'do it my way' thing sometimes. I've seen you hack like that, as you well know, young man."

"There is that," he smiled.

"But I mean more how you do it," said Gina.

"With love and feeling, baby," she laughed.

"There's truth in that, my dearest," he said. "Sometimes it's a bit like those grey nights from titan. Having had to fight the black, they've realised that often it's more shades of grey. Sometimes there aren't two results, but a myriad of greyscales in between and encompassing. Other times the horrors of it all might have tainted them with the knowledge of the darker side."

"In the grey knights case," she continued for him. "Some of them would argue that it's valid to use the attackers methods against them."

"A bit of a contentious issue, obviously," he said.

"Of course," she said. "No point overcoming an attacker if you end up becoming like that which you are protecting against."

"Indeed," said The Captain.

"That's not to say that there's some aspects of it which aren't usable," he said. "For instance, we all have inbuilt survival instincts and aggression, which are meant to be used to defend ourselves. On lower level isoterics that can be just a bit of kung-foo fun."

"We're ok with those," said Tommy. "We can do that hacker punch and kick. It's those head-fuck systems we don't get."

"Stay away from them," he laughed. "They fuck with you. After physical attacking, the emotional attacking simulations are obviously going to come next."

"Of course," she said. "Sometimes you've got to complete that difficult level, just to get nearer to where you're trying to reach."

"Again, the lower head-fuck ones aren't so tricky," he said. "There'll just be all the usual ego reactionary shit, which is pretty easy to just let float by."

"And then to your weaknesses," she said.

"Always," he said. "Then they use any perphacking they've gleaned, either directly or from memory biasing, and try and destroy everything you hold dear."

"And so what's the codex to that one," said Gina.

"An understanding of different perspectives helps," he said.

"Yup," she said. "Back to the grey knights. Having experienced a lot of the grades on the scale, an appreciation of things is gained. Sometimes both sides are right in their viewpoints, even if they are only external validations of individualisms. Both can have relevance to the originator which is equally valid. The survival thing."

"Then," he said. "It becomes more of a test of character.

Firstly, it can be difficult not to simply justify your actions as valid as everyone else is doing that exact same thing."

"If you can't beat them," said Tommy.

"Secondly," he said. "You can become so unlike the system you are in, that you are unable to exist within its constructed realities, to the point where you are almost naturally selected out by the environment. The rules of existence in the medium become no longer applicable to you."

"Then to deciding whether you are a weed or a flower," she said.

"Cute," he said. "But maybe unfair on weeds."

"Maybe," she said. "But I like the analogy."

"In the end," he said. "It can be simply a matter of letting go really."

"That transcendence thing," she said.

"That thing indeed," he sighed. "It's having the memory of that point you reached, where everything was transcended. Material possessions, emotions, food, life, reality itself."

"Some would call that dying," said Gina.

"In a way it can be like that," he said. "Depending on the wrath of the isoterics involved."

"So how do you get yourself out of that one?" asked Tommy.

"The old kiss of life," he smiled. "We resuscitate each other."

"Now who's being flowery with their rationalisations of explanation," she said. "Although I suppose that is how it works for us."

"Having been outside of things," he said. "Outside of time itself."

"You gain a realisation," she said. "That there are things which aren't of this world, and don't have to exist inside of any medium to be."

"Love is eternal," he said. "When the isoterics wreak their havoc, we take in turns to dawn, and that attacking isoteric leaves as there's nothing to attack. Either after or before resuscitating the other with love, we exploit the rift in the system which is created by the temporary fading out of the isoteric."

"Sounds like bullshit to me," said Tommy.

They laughed.

"Some would say it is, Tommy," he smiled. "But it's our bullshit. We share that same inner hidden wiring, that logical equivalence. In the fractals of our existences we are the same, equal, equational, equivalent.

"We share it within our selves," she said. "We have that as the basis of reality that our minds exist within."

"So what happens if you both dawn at the same time?" asked Gina hesitantly.

"Then our God resuscitates us," she said. "Creates a medium in which we can sustain and exist in. Provides a link that ties us together, and breathes life into us."

"God isn't everybody's thing though is it," said Tommy.

"Indeed," he said. "Again, that is a subject isoterics can try and attack through."

"The things that sustain us, our truths of being," she said.

"Well put, my mapping," he said. "Hope, faith and love."

"How so," said Gina, providing a bit of conversational feed along, as was Gina's skill.

"When iterative fractalling begins," he said. "It's starts off with that basic sustainer, hope. Again, it's an inbuilt survival thing, hope springs eternal. When you're driven so low by the isoterics showing memories of failures, given a rest, hope refloats as all the despair has fired chemically."

"Then they do the time thing," she said. "Or they did to you. Destroying hope by making it eternally impacting over time, so additional chances and lifecycles were played out continuously to show it didn't make any difference."

"Faith next," he said.

"One other thing with the hope, darling," she said.

"Pray tell, sweetheart," he said.

"It can be coupled with sympathy," she said. "For me, hope was a little tied to sympathy, losing hope of sympathy, and empathy."

"Leads me to the next point," he said. "Lack of sympathy, like those black and white birds who didn't sing out in sympathy at the crucification. All that can't have been particularly good experience."

"So, on with the power and control of the isoterics," she said.

"Science or nature is the usual first faith attack," he said. "Maybe the evolution route, analysis to show we were evolved from reptiles or something."

"Easy," said Gina. "What were the reptiles evolved from!"

"Very," she said. "A quick download of the program containing the evolving to reptiles from something else, cells, matter, energy, outside of time, and voila, God The Creator."

"Quick clip that one," he said. "Science just really highlights God's genius for me."

"And so narrowing to your particular God," she prompted.

"Yes," he said. "By now the isoterics have narrowed the feedback reactionary mappings to which particular God you relate too. They sometimes try the multifaith crosshack first, but for me the essential issues are the same, the stuff on top of love thy neighbour can often just be the politics of religion."

"Indeed," murmured The Captain.

"With the politics and blame for distractionary wars out

the way," he continued. "It's down to the familiar anti-faith hacks. These are usually ego reactionary in nature, and often externalise themselves as an rationalisation clip of someone who has already dismissed the viewpoint. Often boils down to a refusal of being told what to do, parent moral rejection like, coupled with unacceptance of failings."

"It helps to have had a dawn with a creator like experience at this point, to spark the memory of being godlike and directly causing things, wherein it is ultimately realised that you don't want to be god anymore, and so God must be of greater being than your self. Reminds me of the time I saw graffiti saying 'god is a paranoid schizophrenic' on a transport waiting station."

"The judgmental moral thing can be a tricky one, but again, life's experience can corrupt us all, especially given our survivalist instincts, but again from different perspectives ultimately it's often clear that all sin will be forgiven. After all, it's not about guilt and punishment, but about love and forgiveness. Although that doesn't mean that one shouldn't aspire to something greater, and avoidance of justifying any action by this is best avoided. Freedom of choice and all that."

"To the proof. Or the disproof as is the case. Spanning back through history to use documentary evidence as proof against. Obviously here if you go back far enough, you can prove anything by pointing evidence towards it, especially if you want to prove the viewpoint you already have. Often the interpretation of evidence can be biased by this. A linked attack here is the use of different pronunciation and inflection, coupled with exploitation of loss in translation, like hebrew to latin or latin to english. The context is all important here, as it is often the meaning of the whole, rather than the hanging on just on a few keywords, which provides the intended meaning, rather than the ego reaction which finds your own meaning which suits your own needs and desires at the time."

"Of course, in order for the isoterics to provide evidence to back up the needs of their destructive hack, they often mistakenly use other opinions as facts. It's quite common for any published source to spawn a wealth of related stuff, whether in agreement or argument. Always common for each generation to say that the previous had got it all wrong. Back up the both and it all gets tricky. Like fox moulder would say, if you going looking for spookiness, you'll usually find it."

"So with that paradoxical round of isoteric attack, my solution was to see the obvious that God would make himself unprovable so that it couldn't be faked and used for power and control. Some could equally say that the world is proof of God's existence and love. Although that shouldn't be taken to an extreme, where your reading of the universe ends up being everything, including food wrappers on the street, twig driftwood pointing to an unknown location, and the shape of your own morning shit."

"Everything can sometimes seemed connected," said The Captain. "But it's often your self that's doing the connecting, so it would be."

"Whilst we all share the same common human experience, the collective consciousness can merely just be communicated opinion, we are all feeding from the same sources. In any system, individuality is an inbuilt mechanism to ensure ecosystem diversity. That way no single viewpoint or weakness ever destroys the whole."

"Then it comes down to a matter a faith. The basis of all being that faith is merely loving God. That's not something I find difficult."

The transport carried its way along the flat track through the cuttings of tall, straight trees. Away from it all, The Captain's lodge came into view. Nestled beside a small man-made lake, it slept dreamily in the tranquility of playful stillness. The transport eased to a gradual halt.

"Yes, then," said The Captain. "We've discussed how the v-industries defence constructs functioned, now it's time for us to take a look at the data they were shielding."

They disembarked from the transport slowly, and walked into the domain of The Captain. Amongst the comfortable sofa and armchairs, and the gentle warmness of the hearth, the secrets of v-industries became revealed.

"The successes of v-industries are no mystery," said The Captain. "We've all seen and studied how their superior systems ensured a solidified basis from which to build into a conglomeration of the finest minds and constructed codes. You've probably even worked on tweaks to the overall systems without knowing it."

"Who can remember all the codes they've written," he laughed.

"Indeed. You, given your problem hacking nature, you've probably contributed quite a few in your time. Although in your case you did often seek them out, so not so insidious as some of the missions," continued The Captain.

"Sounds ominous," she said.

"Yes, my dear," sighed The Captain. "As is often the case, good plans tend to get hijacked and used for purposes for which they were not originally intended for."

"Yeah, even I've had some of those," laughed Tommy.

"For the lures of some," said The Captain. "The new options evolved from the solutions can be too shiny."

"There can be no doubt to the genius in the piloting solutions for the future missions to that planet Mars," continued The Captain. "Having remote piloting of the settlement craft would indeed enable a far better method of control, as the crew could operate in a state of advanced Keplarisation, and then change shifts easily when the burns were too great. This obviously eliminates control problems, bar the electrical systems themselves, but that's always going to be needed, so shifting the paradigm a little wasn't too much of a conceptual leap."

"Sounds like a very tightly coupled system," he said.

"Yes," said The Captain. "And therein lay the exploitation of the solution. The piloting system necessitated a very closed system, and gaining authority to use secure constructs wasn't going to be very difficult. The end result being a highly complex, and highly secretive, system design."

"Who guards the guards," said Tommy.

"So, the first weakness," said The Captain. "Closed door design."

"My dear gentlyman," she played. "You doest spake as thoughst thine answers lay many folded."

"The veracity of your words does shine my sweet," said The Captain. "For the ratlines to the sails were many intertwined."

"Get it out," said Gina, almost impatiently.

"Yes," said The Captain. "With the weights of the project so great, v-industries effectively had a carte blanche in requisitioning whatever, or whoever, they required to achieve the successes so demanded. In order to develop the skills necessary for some of the tasks, extensive funding programs where developed for the new rise of Cybertechnics."

"That's how it all usually works," he said. "Nothing to flip my paranoia counters into red just yet."

"Indeed," said The Captain. "Funding learning networks is no blackhack in itself. In fact, the original conception was purely innocent. But we've opened up the second weakness."

They paused for drinks and thoughts. Even the odd nibble on a bit of biscuit.

"The curriculum," she said.

"It doesn't surprise me that you see that one," said The Captain. "Not only did v-industries have the design to the learning method, they also had perfectively valid reasons to influence what was taught by those methods."

"Now I'm checking my signals and thinking about Tommy's plasterboard walls," he smiled in his cheeky smile.

"The meters are ticking up with the possible tactics of a malevolent group," said Tommy.

"And rightly so," said The Captain. "Whilst thus far is as plain and innocent, it's what happened next that changed things. Once the methods were all in place, and the routes established, things were left to develop, quietly. It's the salt that was added later which considerably changed the flavour."

"Too many cooks," he said.

"Not so much that," said The Captain. "But the changing of the entire kitchen staff, once the recipes were on simmer."

"Go on," he said.

"The pattern matched response algorithms had long since been perfected," said The Captain. "In early indoctrination, it was possible to teach in a way so that it seemed the learner's own opinion. Thus by firing suggestions into target groups, a few weeks later the constructs could be retrieved with the conceptualisation of them being original ideas. The linkings were formed with a a higher validation of the truth of their own perceived opinion, even though it was merely that which they had been fed weeks before."

"Pass the salt please?" said Gina.

"The salt added," said The Captain. "Was firmware of a construct which they knew how to break, so it could be broken at a future date. Broken in a predictable and predetermined manner. Using key wirings to form a known pattern which could be interfaced into."

"For what purpose?" he prompted. She looked strangely lost in thought.

"So, to slot the pieces together," said The Captain. "An artificial layer of abstraction conceived the genesis program for the Mars settlement. By having overseer control of the piloting and environment construction programs, any information in or out of the microcosm was to be dictated. Design, journey, arrival, development, all planned out, with no opposing steering. The aim was to produce not one settlement craft, but three. All in isolation of each other, having no knowledge or existence outside of their own sources of input. Hidden even outside of the ivory realms of v-industries, in all respects viewable only as a single pioneer ship to a new colony. On landing, the three groups were to be continued to be developed individually. Once suitable growth had been achieved, the program would then turn to its perception of an aspect of nature's way. The groups would have no knowledge as to whether their competitors were from another country, planet or universe. It was to be survival of the fittest, those who adapted best to the Martian environment would survive."

"Sounds like a creepy galactic domination," said Tommy.

"I'm guessing there were no plans for contentment," he said.

"No," said The Captain. "But more so, in our assembled case, the constructs to be fought were not just out of this world."

"More masks," said Gina.

"The means to hide the three groups was in place," continued The Captain. "And so was the means to hide the method."

Everyone's drinking vessels were topped up.

"Or in other words," sighed The Captain. "The means to

hide the designs of some of the methods. The inbuilt control construct failsafes would be to socially destroy the designers. By manipulation and tamperings to such a point that they would be incapable of making a response, eventually leading to their inevitable capitulation, or in extreme cases, self-destruction. Starting off with such outward lines as reducing possible sources of creds, reaching through limiting access to certain routes of communication, making requisitioning and alterations lengthy, to eventual manipulation of surrounding associated social groups. All leading to an outward perception of just being another of life's burn-outs, so if a fall occurred, there would be plenty of other links to conceal the cause."

Drinking vessels were topped up again.

"Time for one for the road," said The Captain. "Then I must sleep some. I'm very tired."

Finishing up, Tommy and Gina left and headed an excited way to the transport, given it was going to be their turns to drive. He waited hesitantly for an instant, but read that she was hovering for a quiet moment with The Captain, and so made for the transport as well.

"Thank you," she said. "I understand now."

"I am sorry, my dear," said The Captain.

"None are due," she said. "It's all matters of the past now."

Chapter Eight – Kisses and wishes

The transport snapped away accompanied by waves to and from The Captain. Mostly silence for a while, everyone lost in their thoughts. With that occasional link of thinking into what tune was playing on the transport sound setup, as was the way of things. Human experience echoed out through the sound waves.

After the journey back to the constructed reality of society, their disparate thoughts joined into a common need.

They figured it was a nice time of day to try for it. That period past teatime and late teatime, and before the late night rush which still exhibited itself, even though these days time shifts were much more blurred. Things would be quiet, not a lot of activity about. Tommy parked up the transport silently, just around the corner from their target.

"So it's me on point again then," he said.

"Indeed, young sir, it is," she smiled.

"Go on," said Gina. "You know you love it."

"Ok," he said. "But if I get it wrong, no whinging."

"Get it right," said Tommy.

He gave her flavoured lips a gentle kiss, before changing his pace quickly and darting out the transport. On the street he changed his breathing, and slowed his pace to that of an idle wanderer. Around the corner, and the sight of the lights of the building casting their illumination out through the clear glass windows.

Empty. Good. He eased through the half open door, and faked a smile to the assistant, who pointed to one of the eight rig terminals to the right. Flashing some sterile netcreds on a stick from Jonny, he sat in and began his tap, tap.

Gina was second in. Bouncing into the rigcafé with both hair and cleavage, Gina began her dummy perphack on the assistant, alternatively giggling and blinking depending on the moment.

With the distractions in full swing, he scratched his neck beneath his jacket collar. With slow covering motions by his fingers, he drew up the string around his neck which held the hacktool container. Almost giving out a tell as his fingertips touched that beloved neoprene, that hacker texture of durability and style.

Pincering the 'prene, the fingernail sized box that was the Jonny #89 slid out. Ending his scratching with a firm rub and a slight sighing of satisfaction, his thumb slid the tool to concealment between his index and middle fingers.

Increasing his tapping on the inputboard, the vidpanel echoed back the scripting of coverage he had just entered in. With the mask of his playback hiding the true activity, he unjacked the cable from the inputboard to the rig, pushed in between the Jonny #89, and reinserted the whole as one pathway.

In the strange pattern of gloriness in the contentment of the hack, his mind cast itself back to other moments of joy. He reminded himself of how he once had to turn down developing those clips for that cubecorp mag, as that was just too tempting a way of getting an awful lot of routes into an awful lot of systems.

The Jonny #89 span out its magic. It was a code input typer variant, running at a high speed. There was also a spark to a system central update if necessary, to enable access to privileged resources if required. As public access systems tended not to allow much in and much out, the #89 solved the problem by effectively typing in a library of codes via the inputboard, straight into a keyup on the local terminal. The tie-in to the locally inputed code enabled a very tightly secured tunnel into the local ordering system.

"So," huffed Gina. "As to why I'm here. Order. Yup, that ordering I did for me to be picking up."

The idle waiting between the completion and the result

processing, and then Gina was handed the brown
polycomposite bag containing the essential supplies. He was
waiting for the flick to remove the hacktool, and set the
timer for the autocleanup routine. Gina left.

He was first in and last out. Staying momentarily behind
to tidy up by replacing the surveillance mite recordings with
blank cycles that he'd just recorded, so there was no tell of
any of them ever being there. Tasks completed, he carried
on with a little tap, tapping.

His personalcom vibrated. 'Come on hack slut' read the
display. He completed, and tapped out.

"So," he said, rejoining them in the transport. "How did
you know it wasn't just a tricky refeed to do, and that I
wasn't just playing."

They all just looked at him with that look.

"Really," said Tommy. "Ok, let's have a look, see if you
got it right then."

"Tikka starter, masala, korma, bhuna, jalfrezi," said
Gina, examining the contents of the bag. "I make you ok,
this time. And I guess we all know who the 'frezi is for, and
I'm not listening to any whining tomorrow morning."

A lot of hassle to go through for just a takeaway, but
that was their life now. The best place to hide was in full
view, passing unnoticed amongst the crowd. They had paid,
but in hidden currency, for which there was no trace.

Settling up in the bungalow for the feast, Gina and
Tommy tutted at how the pair of them had an annoying
habit of just sharing everything. Even with food, they
couldn't just order, they both had to order and then proceed
to dish out half of the meals to each other's plates. This
would result in them having an equal distribution of the
varieties each had, although finished off with a few quick
jumps of any little items that weren't wanted, or had great
personal preference. Mind you, that wasn't as bad as that

hyder-talk thing they sometimes had going on between
them. They'd both talk at the same time to each other,
apparently it worked for them, they could both listen and
speak at the same time, so they said. To anyone else it just
seemed weird, and required some extreme concentration
and an excessive amount of cycles to process any sort of
understanding from it. Luckily today they seemed less
hectic.

"Suppose the two of you will be wanting some of this
dip then," laughed Gina.

"No thank you, my dear," he said.

"Looks like green mayo, to me," she laughed.

"We like the red one though," he said.

"Probably because it looks a little like jam," said
Tommy.

"More likely because it has the most addictives,"
laughed Gina.

"Most likely," they smiled.

"So what would you have done if your dreamgirl had in
fact liked mayo then," laughed Tommy.

"Well, that could have been tricky," he winked.

"I'm sure you've got an anti-mayo universe domination
conspiracy file tucked away somewhere," laughed Gina.

"Conspiracy theories are born when there is no other
possible explanation for the proof given," he said. "Which
is ironic, since most would consider that conspiracy theories
have sketchy proof by definition, something that others
would consider a total reverse."

"So you've a fucking big file on mayo then," laughed
Gina.

"Of course," he said. "It's quite substantial."

"I bet," said Tommy, encouraging him on.

"Yeah," he said. "It's pages saying 'mayo looks like cat
sick' in really big letters."

"One per page," laughed Gina.

They ate away.

"The Captain knows we love him," she said from the silence of much munching. "Doesn't he?"

"Of course, sweets," said Gina. "We tell him often enough, don't we."

"So what of this gameclip," said Tommy, nan bread in one hand, fork full of rice in the other, as though he was piloting some sort of alien craft.

"It's not so bad," he said. "With the extra breakings of the v-industries shields, The Captain also managed to find something else which sort of, well, just sort of slipped in there."

"*hack* *slut*," she coughed.

"Hmm," he sighed. "It's a multiplayer flight simulation. Sort of space dogfighting. Get to blow each other up, and admire the detail of the planet and asteroid rendering as we space-dodgem one another into them."

"Sounds fun," said Gina.

"You had a go yet?" said Tommy.

"I had a few tussles with The Captain," he said. "The keplar incarnate whipped my ass."

"There's speed and there's instinct," smiled Tommy.

"Indeed," he said. "As a special treat for us all, both Jonny and The Captain have lent us some spare rig boxes, so if we knit them together it should be quite interesting."

"On with it then, you boys," said Gina. "Us gals are gonna bling-burn your skinny arses."

Setting up the rigs, he noticed Tommy was eyeing the partially unwrapped parcel on the edge of the table. Tommy had noticed it had international coded delivery marks.

"Chocolate, Tommy?" he smiled. "They're Belgian."

Epilogue

The events contained within the Epoch Dawn Trilogy constitute a summation of real life experiences of members throughout the world.

Justin, Anna, Tommy, Gina, Jonny, Shelia, Mandy, and especially The Captain, would like to wish you safe travels through life, and warn against depending too much on one source of information. Like reality. (That was an attempt at humour).

Diversity in the software microcosm is the key, and whilst some would say that adaptation to change is the route to survival, in reply to the question, 'how the fuck did you get through all that', the members said:

The Captain:	"For every field honour, a thousand heroes lay alone, unsung, and unremembered."
Tommy:	"I kinda winged it. Rock 'n' roll."
Gina:	"Bling, baby, bling!"
Mandy:	"It's good to talk!"
Jonny:	"Now that would be telling. It's all in the encoding you know."
Shelia:	"I owe someone hackcreds."
Anna:	"Love is all you need."
Justin:	"I did it my way."
Justin (after slap):	"Anna."

Appendix A – Glossary

555 timer: a low-cost integrated circuit, an old well-proven design, for use in timing, pulse and waveform generation applications.

backage: a hacker's backpack and baggage.

badger bait/take a badgering: see running the fox, only additionally allows self to be flagged (bitten by the hounds) in order to end trail.

brownbox (brownie): a difficult crack which only leads to useless information.

capitalisation: members only use capitalisation at the start of sentences, and when referring to each other by hacker name. The Captain is of course old school trained, so uses traditional form.

cardboarding: framed cardboard privacy using a box to conceal your pen and paper from other conference attendees, cereal packets are a favoured method of 'secure' cardboard encryption.

c'est ne pas un livre: it is not a book.

chiplasers: 'laser on a chip', can vary in size from micro light-emitting diode for display purposes, to nanoemitter for use in micro telecommunications applications.

cliptrip: a short processing trip, similar to a movie clip, in which the subconscious part of the brain is used to process information in a short burst.

conordination: concurrent co-ordination (e.g. simultaneous representation of three-dimensional co-ordinates in the brain).

debeep: unlock an electronic lock in reference to the satisfying green light and harmonious beep that is given on successful authorisation.

defcon: defined/defence condition on a scale of one to five, one being worst.

E3: a perfect match, the lines complimenting the curves, and the bonding occurring at three points.

écoute et répète: listen and repeat. The dual feedback learning algorithm used in the Cybertechnics, both for assimilation acceleration and ease of rapid playback recall.

epoch dawn: the perception of the moment in time where all possible realities fall into one.

fin de siècle: end of the century. Of or like the last years of the 19th century. An endless cycle.

fox hole/running the fox: method of tipping off hacker being tracked, by visiting all members in attempt to scatter the trail.

free software: software which is free both monetarily and intellectually.

greenbox: like a bogey, easy to pick.

hack whispers: real world geek game, in which keyphrases are let loose through gossip, and the aim is to guess/track the originator or path.

ic: integrated circuit.

init: init(), the first function call in a program, the ignition or initiation.

io: input/output.

ip (information technology definition): internet protocol.
ip (legal definition): intellectual property.

ir: infrared.

justitia ex tempore: instant justice.

Keplar: quantum physicist/computer scientist who invented the organic transistor, sometimes simply referred to as 'a Keplar'. Also used in slang, 'doing a Keplar' – performing a neat hack seemingly effortlessly.

les chevaliers d'honneur: honorary knights.

les fenêtres est fermée: windows is shut.

Matthew Smith: programming genius who created 'Manic Miner' as well as other arcade classics.

microcode: the last layer of computer program translation, microcode is finally translated into indivisible processing steps that perform functions contained in the processor instruction set. All other abstracted programming layers are above, for instance, vr representation then vrlang, c++, then machine code, then microcode, then single-step processor instructions which cannot be further divided into smaller tasks.

ML: a programming language in which everything is a function, and in which the variables are strictly typed (adhere to a specific type only, i.e. are either a number or a letter).

modus vivendi: mode of living, way of life.

natural language: human language, e.g. English, French.

node draughts: geek virtual game in which systems are captured and used as pieces in a large scale board game manner.

np: no problem.

orange2: quick flag, fast response required, but not as bad as an orange1.

perphack: the bizarre art of talking about something completely unrelated in order to extract information by ego reaction. The conversation is not repeated here to protect the innocent.

picogram: tiny fragment of picture vocabulary, composite of picture and picogram (very small weight, pun on its tiny size).

pictocabulary: pictorial vocabulary.

polymath: a person with great depth of knowledge in a variety of disciplines, especially encompassing multidisciplines such as both arts and sciences, aspiring to become 'a person who knows everything'.

pop: point of presence.

red1 (a red one): veterans only.

rf: radio frequency.

sa: software agent, a small computer program released into the network to perform a specific task, often in co-operation with other similar programs.

scoped: a system being watched.

sitch: situation check.

socket: a connection into the internetwork, as in plug and socket.

Steinberg: computer scientist/physicist. The astute amongst you will have noticed that Steinburg has a daughter, also a computer scientist/physicist.

toycheat: a software or hardware hack designed to crack something that you'd never use the device to actually crack, as that would destroy the fun of the game. Thus rendering the hack as merely a toy.

triaps: 'triangular aspect', triangular or group of three reference points.

triaos: hardware responsible for tracking triaps vectors.

unpredictive: unknowable resultant (or multiple simultaneous co-existing answer) firings in brain, as utilised by Keplar's organic transistor.

vr: virtual reality.

whitebox: good luck (with that).

xf: cross-reference.

yellowbox: the amber gambler, possible to take down but not control. ("I can't control crack this one, but I can take it out if you want. What a big lemon." - Jonny).

z: looks much better when spelt as an s, unless really necessary, as in the word buzz.

☺: smiley face. Everyone loves a smiley face. It's not difficult.

*: at the same time.

**: after some time.

***: after some more (greater length of) time.

Appendix B – User contributed notes

Epoch Dawn